The Perfume Killer is the first novel in a series of standalone murder mysteries set in Belfast and beyond.

Prologue

Lucy had felt like this before, a mixture of anticipation and excitement. Nowadays she knew what was coming and yet couldn't prevent the flutter in her stomach. The blackness all around was intense, almost smothering. So thick she felt enclosed in its steely grip. The air was hot and foetid. The only sound was the hush of almost-held breathing.

The sudden push from behind in the small of her back propelled her forward. For five seconds she held her breath too, until, with a thud, they lurched through heavy rubber doors and immediately seemed to fall headlong into space. Involuntarily she screamed, joining with her fellow passengers, glad to reach out to her companion and grasp his arm tightly, digging her nails into his bare skin and feeling the beat of his heart as she lay against his body. Then, with a splash, the boat slowed as it hit the water, and twinkling lights suddenly illuminated the scene all around. She was aware of a faintly smoky smell that was redolent of age and decay and smiled as she heard the familiar strains of reedy oriental music welcoming them to the magical world she remembered so well from her childhood.

They moved smoothly forward until a shoreline scene appeared before them. Animatronic figures – so life-like with their beady eyes seeming to follow the travellers – bickered and bartered in a market square. A snake charmer played his pipe as a cobra rose mesmerizingly out of a basket, hissing at the passers-by. Overhead a monkey swung from a branch, reaching low, laughing at the travellers, threatening to douse them with his pitcher of water. For an instant, spotlights illuminated the single figure of a drunken pirate swigging wine from a carafe. Another figure sprang into life just beside the boat, his leering grin accompanied by a loud threatening laugh. Someone nearby giggled, a nervous giggle.

The noise of clashing swords and the wild shouts of the pirates filled their ears and a young child screamed as a crocodile lurched against the boat, seemingly about to tip them all out. Lights flashed, as cannons fired and, for a moment, figures, previously hidden in the black recesses of the cavern, were brought to life. They appeared and then, just as quickly, disappeared.

Cameras clicked all around her trying to capture the scenes to be re-told to friends later. She was temporarily blinded by their flashes as she too tried to capture some memories on her camera. Eyes readjusting to the dim light, for one split second, she thought she saw blood oozing down the throat of a sleeping pirate near the edge of the water, spilling onto the front of his silk shirt. Almost instantly he disappeared into the thick darkness as the boat moved on with a jerk that snatched the camera from her hand. It fell from her grasp. At the last moment he had reached across and caught it just as it was about to hit the water.

The young woman relaxed, still clutching the camera to her, glad that she hadn't lost it. She could enjoy the ride again. How realistic that blood had seemed. A movement to the side of the boat caught her attention as they glided ever onwards. This figure was not staying within the limits of the tableau. He moved along in the same direction as the boat, darting in and out of patches of light and darkness, not with the repetitive jerky actions of the animatronic characters, but instead smoothly and swiftly almost seeming to follow them until he slipped into the total blackness of the jungle scene. She registered, in that split second, that he was not dressed in pirate garb like the others. Perhaps he was one of the maintenance crew. She was disappointed that the magic of the experience had been broken.

The boat moved on relentlessly. She had not had time, in that brief flash of light as her camera plummeted towards the murky water, to notice the sleeping pirate's head lurch forward as the slashed throat released the deep red blood, in spurts, into the air and the figure slid slowly onto its side in the sand. Nor did she read in the local newspaper the next day of the huge fire which had engulfed one of the most popular rides at the theme park destroying large parts of it. The body which had been found afterwards in the debris was not one of the park workers. The man had yet to be identified. All of this, she didn't know. She was a thousand miles away.

Chapter 1

The ache in his bones was intense — stabbing like the blade he was clutching in his hand. He could feel its cold, hard edge against his index finger, his thumb along the rough wooden handle. He felt a trickle of hot blood slip down his hand as he realised how tightly he was gripping the knife. He released his hold, only slightly, and wiped his hand down the side of his trouser leg. His eyes were already accustomed to the dimming light as twilight approached. The shadows cast by the sodium street lights on Stranmillis Road offered no threat to him. He was well hidden, invisible in the darkening gloom. He paid no heed to the scuffling and scurrying noises around his feet. Those tiny creatures didn't intrude on his thoughts. His concentration was intense — only the sound of approaching steps mattered to him. She would come. Tonight, she would come. She must come.

Chapter 2

The sun was beginning to slip lower in a late September sky. Soon it would sink behind the Belfast skyline creating silhouettes of the famous yellow cranes.

Preparations were already under way for the St George's Friday market – lorries double-parked, traders carrying white plastic trays of fish and boxes of vegetables and a cacophony of shouts mingling with loud music from within the cavernous hall. Tomorrow this street would be alive with locals, bulging shopping bags in hand, jostling with tourists searching for their guidebook's promised local colour.

Traffic was already building up. It was Belfast's version of rush hour. Gawn Girvin allowed herself an almost imperceptible smile as she faced a wall of cars and lorries moving slowly but inexorably along Oxford Street leaving no room for a quick dash across the road. The air, car fumes and all, felt good after six hours waiting around inside the Laganside Court building. Her throat was dry, probably the result of the air conditioning.

The traffic lights changed and in reaction to their nagging beep she began to walk briskly across to the multi-storey car park beside the hotel. She had often been told she was a striking-looking woman. Back ramrod straight from hours spent on the parade ground, at five feet ten inches with her love for high-heeled shoes, she often towered over her male colleagues. Today, like all working days, her long hair was held back neatly in a chignon.

On a whim, she decided to head into the hotel. No one was waiting for her at home. All that faced her was the prospect of another night spent alone with a glass of wine

4

and her music for company. She would take a few minutes, have a drink, calm down. She had worked herself up during all the waiting, her anxiety levels rising until she'd been forced to pop one of her special pills. In the courtroom, the barrister's snide comments and sarcastically clever questions hadn't helped. Once or twice, she'd had to bite her lip to prevent a tart reply that would get her into trouble with the judge. Not the sort of behaviour expected from a Detective Chief Inspector in the Police Service of Northern Ireland.

Once inside, she paused at the threshold of the bar and scanned the room. It was just beginning to get busy but there were still several free tables. The lighting was bright, too early in the evening to be dimmed yet to create a more romantic ambience. This was still the business and shopping crowd. Some dark-suited men were ensconced around a corner table enjoying a quiet drink after work. A chattering trio of middle-aged women, overdressed and over-excited, sat round a sharing platter of dips and glasses filled with colourful cocktails. She guessed they were heading to a night out and remembered passing a billboard advertising some 1980s tribute band playing in the nearby Waterfront Hall tonight. Her eyes continued to move around the room pausing as she recognised two men in the far corner as solicitors. Avoiding eye contact, she chose a seat as far away from everyone else as possible. The window table afforded her a view of the whole room and everyone coming and going. An old habit. Another symptom of her need for control.

A bar menu lay on the table. A quick glance was enough for her to decide coffee would be best. After all she was going to be driving home. She couldn't risk being caught up in the latest anti drink-driving campaign. That was all she would need. She gave her order to a hovering waiter.

Gawn closed her eyes and allowed her mind to wander. She could feel the beginnings of a headache. She massaged her temples. She sensed a movement to her right and opened her eyes to find the waiter had returned already. He held a tray complete with milk, sugar and one of those little cinnamon biscuits she liked.

'Thank you.'

She smiled and he nodded in response as he placed the items on the table in front of her.

She took a mouthful of coffee. It was strong and hot. She probably shouldn't have the biscuit. She needed to watch her waistline. It was too easy to binge on cheese and biscuits and soppy films alone in her apartment. She was sure her colleagues would never guess her secret pleasure of watching silly American rom coms. They all regarded her as a sensible, hard-headed career woman. She ate the biscuit.

She allowed herself fifteen minutes to get her thoughts under control. Her mind roamed from idea to idea flitting about, settling nowhere for long as she tried not to think about work but with little success. Even after almost a year, she was still not sure she had made the right decision coming back to Belfast. She knew she was still an outsider even though she had been born here and her father had been a sergeant in the RUC, the forerunner of the PSNI. He had been killed in service and that afforded her a certain respect but did not guarantee her being liked.

Her life in London had been wonderful but, in the end, she couldn't cope with it all. Those things that had made it so wonderful in the beginning had also made it unbearable later on... Max had been the last straw. She had needed to escape, to start over. The medics still blamed everything on PTSD. Their advice had been to take a break but instead she had jumped at the advertisement for a DCI post in Northern Ireland. Somehow, she had hoped she would feel safer, more at peace with herself and the world. And it seemed to be working. Mostly. The nightmares were less frequent now. The need for the tablets had decreased but she lived with the fear that someone would see her with one of her special pills. That would be the end of her career and without her job, she had nothing.

She checked her watch. Still enough daylight. Just. She should be able to fit in a run before heading home. The exhilaration of exercise especially with Max by her side urging her on had been not just a feature of her life but a high spot in her week. Early Sunday morning runs in Epping Forest, especially at this time of year with a carpet of leaves to kick their way through, had been a magic time for them. But now exercise was merely what her doctor had advised. Perhaps it could help stave off that headache.

She paid her bill and, as she was heading towards the exit, one of the solicitors she had noticed earlier greeted her.

'Hello there, Gawn. How are you?'

He waved. His voice was warm and friendly, his face covered with a grin. She couldn't even remember his name or ever being introduced to him yet here he was hailing her like a long-lost friend although he obviously didn't know her at all.

Before she had time to consider how it would sound, she responded, 'My name is Gawn to rhyme with Dan, not Gawn to rhyme with yawn.'

Without another word, she turned and walked away. She knew the words were unnecessarily blunt, rude even. He hadn't intended anything except to be friendly. She knew that, of course. Oh well, just add that to her prickly reputation. 'Stuck up English bitch' was what she had heard herself called on more than one occasion. She left him looking flustered and slightly embarrassed in front of his friend. No doubt the story would get round and add another chapter to her growing biography as the Ice Queen.

Back at her car, she picked up her running gear from a Nike gym bag she had flung carelessly on the back seat before setting out that morning. Just in case. She discarded her jacket and pulled a black sweatshirt over her head.

Then she wriggled into the matching tracksuit bottoms and out of her skirt before finally donning her oldest, most comfortable running shoes. Finally, she pulled her hair back sharply into a ponytail.

She drove over the bridge into east Belfast. Once this had been home. She remembered the church with the illuminated sign, gone now in the redevelopment. What had it said? 'Ye must be born again'. If only she could; could start all over again, could have lived a different life; made different choices.

A vivid childhood memory came to life before her eyes. She watched, with the same sense of wonder she had first experienced over thirty years previously, while the starlings swooped and swarmed in a choreographed murmuration over the dark waters of the Lagan as dusk approached. She could remember standing there years ago, her small hand in her father's, as they had watched hundreds of birds performing some sort of pre-designed synchronised ballet of movement before flying off to their roost.

The lower Ravenhill Road was now full of warehouses and car lots but glancing left and right down the narrow streets she could still see some of the rows of terraced houses. Now they were festooned with satellite dishes, not the flags she remembered.

She turned right and caught a brief glimpse of swings in a playground. They had been a source of so many rows with her father. She had always begged to be taken to play there but he had resisted, not wanting to hang around in the area for too long, always aware of possible danger. She didn't understand that then. She did now. She drove along the meandering embankment road past the double-storey Chinese supermarket, a symbol of a more diverse, cosmopolitan Belfast than the one of her childhood.

She parked the car and took the steep path up past the playground, alongside the University PE Centre and into the Botanic Gardens. Twilight was descending. She would have to be quick. They would be locking up soon and she didn't fancy the embarrassment of being locked in and having to climb the railings like some juvenile delinquent. She could just imagine the laughter at her expense.

There was no one about. She seemed to have the park to herself. She noticed the lights were already extinguished in the Tropical Ravine and the park was beginning to take on a slightly menacing air, the trees reaching out like creatures wanting to catch passers-by, their branches swaying with threatening intent, and there were scuffling noises in the bushes signalling that the small animals would soon take back possession of the park from its human daytime occupants. She allowed her mind to wander. Running always seemed to have a therapeutic effect for her. Her concentration was focused on the pounding of her feet on the path, mirroring the pounding in her chest as her heart rate rose and her breathing became more of an effort.

It was a shock when she came upon the woman, nearly colliding with the back of her bright yellow coat as it loomed up in front of her. She ran on but glanced back. Gawn was about to mumble some sort of apology, but the woman seemed to be in a daydream and appeared not even to have noticed her.

The main gate was in sight now. But she still had another ten minutes of running to get back to her car. She was starting to feel tired. Not as fit as I should be, she thought to herself.

She thought that was her day over. How wrong she was. It was only beginning. Soon she would be back.

Chapter 3

Suddenly he heard what he had been listening for — the tapping of high heels on the pathway. From his lair within the shrubbery, he moved his eyes to watch. It was only the very slightest of movements. His eyes were alert but his body was stilled; his breathing shallow, barely audible even to himself. He could see the approaching figure faintly illuminated in silhouette against the hundreds of twinkling lights as the windows of the palm house caught and reflected the park lighting.

He hadn't seen a girl so perfect before in his watching and waiting. He was sure. She was the one. His visits on previous nights had served him well. He felt he knew the regulars. He had watched out for the chirping office workers like multi-coloured birds, shortcutting their way through the park, eager for home. There was the occasional student, clutching a greasy takeaway to eat in his overpriced grubby bedsit, but thankfully they mostly kept to nearby Botanic Avenue, lively with its cafés and shops. The raucous schoolboys he had found the most annoying, pushing and shoving, flinging their rugby kits and heavy backpacks around in shows of machismo, sometimes coming dangerously close to his lair to retrieve them. He smiled as he thought how close to danger they came, unknowing; how with one movement he could squash their young life like the bugs below his feet if he chose to. His omniscience was absolute. He was the watcher, the lurker. This was his domain.

Then he saw her clearly for the first time as she passed under one of the lamps, her bright yellow coat standing out like a beacon in the gloom. She was new. She was different. There was a stately grace in her walk. Her gait was unhurried. Her clothes looked stylish, and he could almost taste the expensive perfume he was sure she would be wearing. He rolled his tongue across his lips savouring its imagined flavour, a drool of saliva escaping down his chin unchecked. He fingered the bottle in his pocket, enjoying its cold smoothness, its hardness. Even in the dim light, he could make out her carefully applied make-up. He almost gurgled at the thought of the blood dripping from that silken throat, spoiling the designer coat and ebbing away with the last of her breath and the lingering aroma of her perfume.

For a second, the sound of a passing car drew his attention away from the girl. But only for a second. All his focus was on her. Had he time to reach her and plunge the knife into that throat, slitting it from side to side in one smooth, swift motion before she could utter a sound? Could he risk leaving the shelter of the bushes? He had to time it just right. The park keeper would be here soon, doing his rounds, locking up. He knew what he had to do, needed to do, to assuage this longing. This urge had been building up for weeks now. He could not endure another night.

He realised he had been holding his breath. A surge of rage filled his chest as he heard other, rapid footsteps, coming from behind. Who dared to interrupt his plans? The figure was moving fast. Bloody jogger. He thought it was a woman from the shape and stride and the flash of red as her hair caught the light. As he waited for her to pass, he knew his special moment had gone. Without acknowledging each other, the jogger had moved on, while the girl was passing under a pool of light cast by one of the Victorian wrought iron lamps in the park. She was too far now for him. If he moved, she would hear him and, in the light, she would see him too. She would try to fight him off. It would be messy and he could not tolerate that. The kill must be swift and sure. Efficient. Sacred. Perfect.

Fury burned in him like a flaring pain stabbing into his loins. The rage of unassuaged desire boiled deep within him. He lurched out of the thick undergrowth mindlessly and almost collided with a tall stranger. The man had approached so quickly and so quietly that it was as if he had materialised out of nowhere. He paid the lurker no attention; offered him no word of greeting. The lurker took one step as the man passed and, in fury, plunged the knife deep into his back. There was barely a sound as the blade sliced through first cloth, then tissue and muscle until it met the resistance of bone. Years of experience had led the knife to exactly the right spot to sever the spine. *The stranger made no sound. The surprised look on his face as he tried to turn towards his assailant faded almost immediately with the light in his eyes.*

The lurker withdrew the blade. He raised the red-covered metal to his mouth and thought of the jogger's red hair. He ran the hard cold steel over his outstretched tongue. The taste of the man's hot blood brought a twisted smile of satisfaction to his face. The jogger was out of sight. But he knew he would see her again. She would be his. He would not be denied again. She would be back. He was sure. And so would he. Of that he was sure too.

Chapter 4

To an outsider the room would have looked both cosy and inviting. That is if you could have seen inside. But the heavy silk curtains had already been drawn across the floor-to-ceiling windows creating a cocoon-like atmosphere and keeping out the blackness of the night and the clanging of the rigging from the boats in the marina below. The apartment was on the first floor of a newly constructed four-storey building across from the floodlit medieval castle and overlooking the local marina.

The strings of Paul Mauriat's orchestra were playing *A Taste of Honey* softly in the background from an expensive Bose sound system evoking the spirit of the Swinging Sixties, her parents' era. The music of the Sixties was the soundtrack to Gawn's childhood and to her life. She still listened to it in preference to any other. The innocence of that time before everything had been spoiled for her forever. Sometimes, as she sat listening to Billy J Kramer or The Kinks, she could almost forget her life now and think herself back to their semi-detached house on the outskirts of east Belfast with Daddy just off shift and

Mother fussing over her brother Michael, trying to get him to sit still long enough to do his homework. The days before everything had started to go wrong in her life.

The gas fire crackled cheerfully in the hearth throwing a welcoming glow across the fireside rug, its mock flames reflected in the polished oak flooring. The lighting was subdued. A single reproduction Tiffany lamp cast a gentle light over an antique brown leather sofa. It was comfortably shabby and looked well-used but only Gawn had ever sat on it. She had never invited anyone to her home. An unopened bottle of red wine stood on a glass-topped coffee table. It should have been perfect. It could have been the setting for a romantic evening for two, but it wasn't. Only one solitary glass stood ready to welcome the wine. And now, spoiling it all, was the insistent ringing of her mobile phone, its piercing ringtone echoing around the room. Whoever was calling wasn't going to give up any time soon.

Gawn knew there was no point in trying to ignore it. Her run through the park hadn't entirely lifted her headache. She was fed-up, tired and out-of-sorts. It had been a long hard week and it was still only Thursday. She had been looking forward to a nice long soak, a couple of glasses of wine and an early night for once. That was what she had promised herself. It was nearly the weekend for God's sake. Even police were allowed a night off.

She had already begun to undress in preparation for her bath. The water was running and she had used some of her most expensive bath crystals. The suds reached almost to the rim and looked so inviting as she perched on the side of the tub dressed only in matching black underwear. She allowed the water to trickle through her fingers, humming along to the strings playing softly in the living room.

With a muttered curse, Gawn grabbed the 'sensible' pink towelling robe her great-aunt had bought as a present for her birthday. She pulled it around her, tying the belt tightly as she walked across the room. She yanked the bedroom door fully open and padded barefoot to the side table where her mobile phone lay vibrating like an angry giant insect. If only she could ignore it. But that wasn't in her nature. 'Duty first' had been her father's motto all his life and he had ingrained it in her too.

Recognising the caller ID, Gawn's answer was gruff.

'What is it, Sergeant?' Her voice was uninviting. It challenged the caller to make sure he had a good reason to interrupt her plans.

There was a moment's hesitation at the other end of the line. The use of his rank 'Sergeant' rather than his name and the note of irritation in her voice had been unmissable. Still Paul Maxwell ploughed ahead. He took a deep breath.

'Sorry to disturb you, ma'am. There's been a body found in Botanic Gardens. Looks like a stabbing.'

Possible scenarios came and went through Gawn's mind in a split second. She wasn't even supposed to be on duty tonight. Surely some Inspector could handle it. So why was Maxwell bothering her? Yet, as swiftly as these thoughts came, they disappeared again. She was already beginning to plan her quickest route to the scene. That nice hot soak and that bottle of shiraz would have to wait.

'*Think* it's a stabbing?' They better be bloody sure before she had to make the journey back to Belfast.

'Yes. I thought you'd want to know. The victim's a foreigner, ma'am,' he added, obviously hoping this would make a difference. 'We have his passport. His name is Dieter Weil. A German.'

Gawn's ears picked up, suddenly alert. Now she knew why her sergeant had called her. The heavy sense of weariness and the incipient headache were instantly forgotten to be replaced by an excited quiver in her stomach. Her reputation as a stickler for the rules and regulations and being a demanding boss, which had followed her from the Met, didn't endear her to some. Probably the only person she felt she could trust was her sergeant, and even he she didn't really know well or consider a friend, but he had her back, she knew. She knew he was ambitious too so if he was trying to rise through the ranks on her coattails, so be it. She could live with that.

This case could be a big opportunity for both of them. A foreign victim was sure to attract the press. Attacks of any kind on tourists were still relatively rare in Belfast. This would be high profile. This was a chance to make her mark.

'On my way.'

Chapter 5

He had made his escape just before the park keeper arrived. He could hear tuneless humming approaching and had crouched low behind a tree, hidden in its shadow waiting for a reaction. For a moment there was nothing. He realised he was holding his breath again. Surely, the man hadn't missed the body. Noiselessly the lurker slithered across to the outer railings keeping low to the ground and away from any pools of light. He had just reached the gap behind the uninviting public toilets when a piercing scream rang out across the park echoing off the walls of the nearby red brick university hall and bouncing back to the Tropical Ravine. So, it was one of the female park keepers. What fun! He almost clapped his hands in joy. Instilling terror was a bonus. The screaming seemed to go on forever but, by the time he had emerged into the university grounds behind the Whitla Hall, it was subsiding in intensity. Then he could hear shouts coming from all sides and the sound of running feet.

Under cover of the building's shadow, he retrieved a leather briefcase secreted earlier behind a trio of gas canisters stored there. He ripped the balaclava off his head and stripped off the black coverall he had been wearing over his shirt and trousers and the plastic covers on his shoes, pulled his jacket out of the briefcase and stuffed his lurker attire into its place. He took special care to remove his beloved hat from the bag first so that it would not be crushed.

By the time he emerged into the spot-lit area in front of the Lanyon Building and began to walk across the open space to the tall main doors of the university, he could hear the sirens of at least one emergency vehicle approaching in the distance. Probably an ambulance from the nearby hospital. Maybe the police, if they were quick off the mark. He had no fear of the police. He had fooled them before. He walked quickly but with a studied nonchalance, careful to look in a hurry to get somewhere but not like he was running away. Just a professional man, one of the academics perhaps, on his way home after a busy day. He even took time to greet the porter in his lodge with a friendly wave before making his way through the entrance hall and across the quadrangle onto University Square.

Now he had a choice to make. Common sense told him to keep going, get to his car and away from the immediate area as quickly as possible. But the chance to see the aftermath of his actions close-up was one he had never had before. Usually he was long gone before his victims' bodies were discovered. He had found the park keeper's screams particularly satisfying. They had gone some way to sating his thwarted desires. Now to have the opportunity to watch the antics of the police as they began their investigation was too powerful a temptation. To hear the speculations and watch the crowd, who would undoubtedly gather feeding their ghoulish curiosity, would add layers of pleasure to soothe his disappointment at the failure to carry out his plan.

He locked his briefcase in the boot of his car and took out a long dark-coloured overcoat and placed it and his hat on the passenger seat. He moved his car to a space nearer the university building and within sight of the front entrance to the park. Donning the coat and hat, he crossed the main road and walked at a moderate pace down the steps and across to the McClay Library. It was open late with students preparing for the new term and others meeting up with friends they hadn't seen over the summer break. Lights blazed out of the windows on each floor. The café was busy. He queued and ordered a ristretto. The blast of caffeine should help to calm his pulsing temple *and wildly beating heart. The stronger the better. That was how he liked it.*

He gulped his drink down greedily seeking that hit of caffeine; the jolt of energy it would give him. When he had finished and walked back to his car, passing the front of the park and lingering briefly to mingle with the crowd already gathering at the gates and listen to their ignorant speculation, he took his mobile out of his pocket and punched in a number. Now to get to work. He spoke briefly on the phone, a grin playing on his lips. Let the games begin.

Chapter 6

Unusually for Thursday evening, there was a free parking space on the main road directly outside a trendy bistro already busy with couples having the famous pre-theatre meal deal and directly across from the looming grey museum building. She crossed the road and headed straight for the main entrance to the gardens.

Later the old double gates with their peeling green paint would be opened to allow a mortuary vehicle through, but, for now, the only entry was the single pedestrian gate guarded by a solitary policeman, looking bored already as he stamped his feet to keep warm. The temperature had dipped noticeably from the reasonably pleasant autumn afternoon. The constable recognised the Chief Inspector as she approached, her statuesque demeanour and flaming red hair a well-known sight. He acknowledged her with a nod.

'Evening, ma'am.'

She didn't respond but, focused only on what she might find, ignored him and marched purposefully into the park. Night had descended quickly and the eerie darkness, filled with menacing shapes from the avenue of trees, was sliced in two by the arc lights rigged by the CSU team. Sergeant Paul Maxwell, standing at the flap of the forensics tent, spotted his boss and walked across to where Gawn was standing, keeping to the path, trying to take in the whole scene. He cast a long shadow behind him like an elongated Modigliani figure.

'So, what have we got so far?'

No greeting. Sometimes Maxwell wondered if her lack of social chit-chat was a shield to mask shyness or lack of self-confidence, or if she simply wasn't interested in people. Other times he admired her single-mindedness.

'Like I said on the phone, ma'am, the victim's German. We've got his passport. Don't know yet if he's a tourist. Doesn't look like it, though. No camera or anything.' He paused as a thought seemed to come to him. 'Unless it was stolen. I suppose he might be living here, maybe something to do with the university.' He nodded towards the outline of the university building just across from the park. 'But then he'd hardly be carrying his passport around, would he? So maybe he's here for business.'

He realised he was talking too much and trailed off, noting her raised eyebrow at how much they didn't know, and then hurried on before she could make any comment.

'OK. We do know for sure that he's been stabbed. In the back. The doc confirmed it. No sign of a weapon.'

'Who found him?'

'One of the park keepers. Her name's Mary McLean. She was locking up for the night. She's in a bit of a state.'

Maxwell nodded to his right and Gawn followed his line of vision to a middle-aged woman, seated beside a WPC, on one of the park benches. Even at this distance, and in only the ghostly glow from the single wrought iron lamp and the shadow cast from the crime scene lights, it was clear the woman was in a state of shock. She dabbed at her eyes with her hankie. Her body was shaking; it seemed uncontrollably. How much help she would be to them remained to be seen. Maxwell wasn't very hopeful.

She could barely tell him her name when he had first arrived on the scene.

'Have her checked over by the paramedics, Paul. Then, if they say it's OK, take her statement and get someone to take her home.'

Gawn knew Maxwell would be the best one to get the woman talking. She always said he had the empathetic touch which she lacked.

'Right.'

He moved off, glad to have something to do to get him away from other questions he didn't have the answers to yet.

Gawn donned the familiar foot covers and gloves, balancing precariously on one leg at a time and then, taking care to keep off the grass as much as possible, crossed to the crime tape and bent down under it. A constable thrust the crime scene log at her without a word and she signed it before heading towards the opening. Just at that moment, as if on cue, a figure emerged from the tent, stepping out of his forensic covering. He was carrying a medical bag but Gawn didn't need that clue to identify him although she was surprised to see him there. She had assumed one of the on-call doctors would have attended the scene to pronounce the victim dead. Instead, she was facing the State Pathologist.

'Good evening, Chief Inspector.'

With olde worlde courtesy he doffed his hat, which he had put back on as soon as he'd removed the obligatory forensic hair covering. Gawn knew, because he had once told her, that he hated wearing what he considered an old woman's hairnet but with his typical meticulous attention to detail, he would never have considered entering a crime scene without it, and all the rest of the PPE, no matter how ridiculous it made him feel. He was a stickler for formality and liked everything done just so. And he was right to be reticent of how it made him look. Many of her colleagues already regarded him as an old woman. He was not popular.

Gawn always thought his soft Scottish lilt seemed out of place in the harsh business of murder. His customary bow tie would have been more at home at a Christmas party than the cold hard reality of sudden violent death. But he had once told her he loved amateur dramatics and dressing up, and his secret wish had been to be an actor. She knew his roly poly build and the wispy hair brushed over his ever more balding pate, were often the brunt for sniggers behind his back. But his appearance and gentle speech belied his steely efficiency. God help you if you challenged his authority. There was no way he would ever be harassed or hurried into a quick judgement or rash speculation by any police officer, of any rank.

'What have you got for me, Dr Munroe?'

It was getting colder by the minute and the doctor's breath rose into the night air as he spoke. She noticed his Fair Isle waistcoat was straining across his paunch and he seemed slightly out of breath.

'I wish I could say it's nice to see you. If only we could meet in more conducive circumstances.' He smiled, showing a row of perfectly straight, white teeth which momentarily reminded Gawn of a shark. 'I'm afraid this one's a tad nasty. One thing I will say, it would have been quick and the poor chappie wouldn't have known too much about it.'

Gawn couldn't help but smile at his use of the word 'chappie'.

'Male, aged twenty to thirty. As far as I can see – but, of course, I won't know for certain until I get him on to my table – there's just one wound. In the nape of the neck. There's very little blood. Death must have been almost instantaneous.'

'Time of death?'

'From body temperature and condition, I'd suggest recent. In fact, within the last couple of hours. More specific than that I wouldn't be prepared to say at this time.'

Gawn didn't need him to be. That timing made sense. The body was just to the side of one of the main paths linking through to Stranmillis Road from the University PE Centre and the embankment. Although it was now covered by the canvas tent, uncovered, it would not have been hidden from view. Anyone passing would have seen it. It just would not have been possible for it to have lain there for any length of time without being noticed. The park was always busy during the day and the weather had been cool but dry, so there would have been plenty of people about all afternoon.

Gawn wondered when to reveal that she herself had been in the park, had passed this very spot, less than three hours previously. It had formed part of her route back to the car from her riverside run. She was sure there had been no body there then. Yes, she had been tired and a bit distracted. She had been going over in her mind her day in court and trying to imagine how good it would be to have that barrister in her interview room for a few hours. She'd make him squirm, as he'd tried to do to her. Even so, there was no way she would have missed a body. In fact, she remembered she'd passed a young woman not far from this spot, so, even if she'd missed it – which she couldn't believe she would have – the girl would have seen him. Unless she was the murderer, of course. That thought made her shiver.

'I hear there's no murder weapon. Too much to hope.' She smiled ruefully.

'Afraid not. That would make it too easy, wouldn't it, Chief Inspector?' He smiled back at her. 'But what I can tell you is that it's probably about a six-inch blade. There don't seem to be any serrations, but I won't know for sure until I can make a mould of the wound. Looks like just your common or garden kitchen knife – you can probably buy it in your local supermarket. Nothing fancy.

21

Thousands of them out there, I would expect. I probably have one myself. You probably do too.'

Gawn doubted it. She seldom cooked and her culinary equipment was rudimentary. If she had a knife like that, she wasn't aware of it. So, no special murder weapon and no fingerprints either. Great. They were off to a good start.

'Thank you, doctor. I'd appreciate your report as soon as possible. I think there'll be a bit of a push to get a quick result on this one.'

The pathologist smiled, with a smile that said he knew exactly what it would be like. He knew how it went and the politics and pressures that were involved in all big cases. Although it had happened nearly twenty years before his time, he'd heard of the case of a foreign hitchhiker murdered up the Antrim coast. The killer had never been found and the lack of closure was a raw spot on the RUC's communal memory which had been carried over to the PSNI. Momentarily he wondered if Gawn would be replaced as SIO. She was relatively young and new and they might want someone more experienced. On the other hand, he was cynical enough to think they might want a scapegoat if the killer wasn't found. A pretty young female officer might fit the bill nicely. He hoped not. He liked her and, on the few occasions he'd been around her so far, he had found her efficient and thorough with none of the arrogance or crudeness of some of her male counterparts.

'Of course. I'll schedule the PM for…' He pulled a pocket watch from his waistcoat and glanced down at it. 'Eight tomorrow morning, seeing that you're in a rush. Which will come all too soon, I'm afraid.'

Gawn appreciated him making her case a priority.

As he passed her, Munroe sniffed the air and then commented, 'I do like the perfume. New, is it?'

From anyone else Gawn might have taken offence, assuming it was a sly attempt to undermine her authority by making an oblique reference to her gender. She couldn't imagine anyone commenting on Maxwell's aftershave, if he wore some. But she knew the doctor had meant nothing by it, other than complimenting her. She took his words at face value, a slight smile on her lips, but made no comment in return, already turning away to enter the scene of crime tent.

Chapter 7

Outside the arc lights had seemed bright, cutting through the blackness of the night, but once inside Gawn had to take a minute to let her eyes get used to the even harsher glare. It was brighter than daylight, illuminating every blade of grass in glorious vivid bright green. Two SOCOs moved about filling the tent, hunching down over the ground. A camera flashed as photographs were taken from every angle. Although he was covered head to toe in his forensics suit with a mask covering his face, Gawn had no difficulty recognising Mark Ferguson, the Scenes of Crime Supervisor. She knew he would be thorough, so she merely nodded to acknowledge him and left him to get on with it.

Without moving any further into the tent, Gawn's eyes scanned the scene. She touched nothing. There had been no rain for several days so the grass was dry but that meant no helpful muddy footprints. In fact, she couldn't discern any footprints at all and hoped her fastidious team would have more success. The victim lay face down, and near his head was a flattened section of grass. It looked like the outline of a knee where someone had bent down beside the body. She presumed it had been her sergeant, or maybe the park keeper, looking for a pulse or ID. But better check. Maybe the killer had knelt there to make sure the victim was dead or to take something from the body.

'Mark, have you done anything with this?'

Ferguson showed no annoyance at the interruption.

'It was the first PC on the scene, Chief Inspector. The one down at the gate now. Paul sent him down there out of the way. I think this might have been his first dead body. He was still as white as a sheet when I got here. He says he didn't disturb anything; just knelt, checked for a pulse and called it in. He didn't even look through the pockets apparently. It was Paul who searched the body and found the wallet with the ID when he arrived.' He waited a second then added, 'Do you want us to take a mould of it?'

'No harm making sure we have everything. As soon as the park reopens, we'll lose any chance of getting anything else.'

Ferguson smiled. He would have done it anyway. He left nothing to chance.

Gawn then turned her attention to the body. She took just one step nearer and allowed her gaze to take in an overview of the supine figure. She couldn't see the victim's face but his clothes were good quality. The stonewashed jeans were designer. The corner of a well-known label protruded from the back pocket. The navy jacket looked newish and its upturned vent displayed an expensive red silk lining. The victim's hands and feet had already been bagged and his pockets had been turned inside out searching for ID and evidence no doubt. She knew anything found would already have been bagged and tagged.

Her eyes strayed up the torso towards the head and paused, only for a moment, on the neck. As she had been told, there was not much blood. What little there was had formed into a congealed mass, so little chance of blood spatter on the killer then. The blood had seeped into the collar of the man's jacket but this was no horror scene – not like some of the sights she had witnessed when called to attend paramilitary shootings or punishment beatings. On those occasions it seemed there was blood everywhere and the stench would linger in her nostrils for days after. This had been a quick kill. There was no frenzied slashing.

The victim's hair was closely cropped, not quite shaven, but very short, barely touching the top of his collar. There was almost a military look to it. She became aware of a strong scent. It must belong to the victim. She knew Al Munroe made a point about never wearing aftershave at a crime scene or in his morgue and she had insisted all her team follow that rule. It made it easier to notice any tell-tale aromas, whether pleasant or unpleasant. She was confident that Ferguson and the others would not be wearing any but cursed the fact that she had not had time to bathe and get rid of the scent of her own perfume after her day in court. She was surprised to recognize it as a Gucci fragrance she sometimes wore herself. Had he been meeting with a woman whose scent had lingered on his body? She thought again of the woman in the yellow coat.

Satisfied that she had seen all there was to see, without a word, Gawn left Ferguson to his painstaking inch-by-inch search around the body. As she exited the tent, she was already thinking ahead to what needed to be done. Botanic Gardens was a well-known and much-used area in south Belfast. She knew she would be under pressure to make sure they could get everything open to the public again as quickly as possible.

Looking around, she spotted her sergeant watching the park keeper as she was led away supported by two burly paramedics. Good timing. She beckoned to him. Using Maxwell's shoulder to steady herself as she pulled off the shoe coverings, she issued her orders.

'Right, Paul, we need to get this whole area searched quickly but thoroughly. At first light, I want as big a team as we can muster to go over the whole park, radiating out from the site of the kill. Make sure to go as far as the outside of the museum itself. A fingertip search, Paul.'

Maxwell had his notebook open and was carefully noting all she said. He didn't want to forget any detail. She would be checking in the morning that it was all done as she had ordered.

'I don't suppose there's anything to find that far away from the body but, you never know. Anyone would have had to climb over that picket fence and go through the copse to get there but get it checked anyway. And all the waste bins and that donations bin in front of the museum, in case someone "donated" the murder weapon. Once we've cleared that area, then we can allow the museum to open to visitors and that should buy us a bit more time to search the grounds. I want them gone over with the proverbial fine-tooth comb.'

Maxwell nodded to show he knew what had to be done. She could trust him to organise it.

'Make sure to have someone on every entrance into the park tomorrow morning, from before the gates are usually open. I want everyone trying to get through questioned – were they in the park today? If so, what did they see? Did anyone notice our victim or anyone suspicious-looking? You know the drill, Paul. We'll meet at ten and get everyone up to speed. Goodnight, Sergeant.'

Not waiting for a reply or giving him any opportunity to comment, Gawn turned away and started walking towards the gates. Within two steps, she saw them start to swing open, one side pushed by the constable, the other by a white-suited figure, no doubt one of the mortuary attendants. She was aware of phone camera lights blinking and a buzz of interest from the small crowd that had gathered outside on the pavement. They parted, as a black, unmarked van moved slowly through the gate. It slid past her almost silently, its electric motor maintaining the funereal atmosphere of the moment, and she took the opportunity its cover afforded her to move quickly out onto the road. She hoped she could reach her car unnoticed but, of course, she didn't make it. A phone was thrust towards her face and a friendly but insistent voice spoke.

'Gawn! Gawn! Want to make a statement, Chief Inspector? What's going on? Is it true someone's been murdered?'

Gawn recognised one of the local TV reporters. 'No comment at the minute, Nikki. The Press Office will be releasing a statement later.'

Now back at her Audi, she clicked open the door and slid in quickly before having to face any more questions. She needed that glass of shiraz even more now and some sleep before it all kicked off big time in the morning. By then, the first editions of the papers would be out and the local radio and TV channels would feature the story on their morning programmes. The morning would come quickly. Very quickly. Too quickly.

Chapter 8

The alarm buzzed at 5.59am, its loud annoying hum breaking into her dreams. She had been lying on a tropical beach with the sun beating down from a cloudless sky. Gawn reached out and switched it off. Beads of sweat sat on her forehead. At least it hadn't been the terrors of one of her recurring nightmares.

This morning her head still felt fuzzy when she sat up on the side of the bed although she had limited herself to just one small glass of wine the night before, knowing she would need to be on top form today. She crossed to the bathroom and took a long hard look at herself in the mirror as she brushed her teeth. She barely recognised the face that stared back at her – a pale, almost middle-aged woman. At least there were no signs of grey among the red hair, yet she thought ruefully. Her index finger traced the line of a scar above her right temple that she kept well hidden under a curtain of hair.

A long hot shower helped to clear her mind followed by a cup of strong black coffee on her balcony with the doors thrown wide open to let in some fresh air.

Today she chose her outfit even more carefully than usual. Her spare bedroom had never seen a guest nor was it likely to, so Gawn had re-purposed it as a dressing room. One wall was covered floor to ceiling in mirror-fronted wardrobes.

She would probably have to speak to the superintendent at some point today to brief him on the case and, who knows, she might even have to do a TV interview, so she wanted to look business-like and efficient, exuding a confidence she seldom felt. She slid open the wardrobe to reveal a row of dark skirt and trouser suits. All sombre and serious as befitted a Chief Inspector. Her formal police uniform hung beside them. Across the other side was a range of blouses, two pairs of jeans, a black dress with some diamante detail which was useful for parties or dinners – not that she went to many of those – and a bright floral dress she'd had to buy when tasked with personal protection duties at a garden party. That had been its only outing. She'd never found another occasion to wear it.

Gawn chose a grey pinstripe Italian wool trouser suit and teamed it with a white sleeveless V-neck silk blouse she had bought in one of her favourite Knightsbridge stores. She had selected it carefully ensuring that the neckline did not reveal her other scar. She didn't talk about her time in Afghanistan. That was the past and she wouldn't let it define her. She knew she was driven. She needed to achieve, needed to be able to make a difference, make her life worth something. Otherwise, why did she survive when others had died? The face of a smiling dark-haired soldier flashed into her mind. She squeezed her eyes tight shut to quench the image and shook her head as if to shake the picture away.

'Get a grip, woman. You have work to do,' she admonished herself.

She dressed quickly and examined her profile in the mirror. She was pleased with what she saw. She chose a pair of black Cuban-heeled boots and a black leather shoulder bag to match. She had already applied a light covering of make-up. No heavy eyeshadow or mascara. She didn't want to end up looking like some sad forty-something papering over the cracks of age with plastered make-up. She redistributed the contents of her bag from yesterday into the new bag and checked to make sure she had everything she needed. In particular, she checked the zipped compartment which contained her supply of fluoxetine and a small plastic bag with the remaining white pills she had picked up on her last trip to London.

With one final look in the mirror in the hallway, Gawn picked up her keys from the hall table and her coat from the chair beside it. Her car was parked in its designated space and she used her remote key to open the automatic grill. Before starting off, she turned the radio on, making sure it was tuned to Radio Ulster. She wanted to know what they were reporting about the murder. She was sure her sergeant would bring the morning papers with him so she could check those too.

Careful to keep to the 20mph speed limit outside the local primary school, she floored the accelerator when she reached the dual carriageway and headed towards Belfast, her mind buzzing with what decisions she needed to make to get the investigation off to a good start. She just hoped the search at the park had turned up something to give them a starting point. Or perhaps Munroe would find something helpful at the post-mortem. They needed a break. Who was Dieter Weil and what was he doing in Belfast that had got him killed?

Chapter 9

Harsh fluorescent overhead lights illuminated the open-plan office. Maxwell had made a detour on his way in to check how the search was progressing and to pick up some copies of the morning newspapers. He was still early but if he thought he would be there before his boss, he was wrong. The aroma of strong coffee announced that Gawn had beaten him to it. The cafetière on her desk was evidence of her presence although the DCI was nowhere to be seen. Everyone joked that you needed to keep out of her way in the morning until she'd had at least one cup of coffee and, sometimes, he stopped at the drive-thru to pick up a venti americano for her. The others mocked his efforts at trying to keep the boss sweet.

Maxwell set the bundle of newspapers to one side and took the opportunity to listen for any messages left on his phone. Nothing. Hanging his black leather jacket over the back of his chair, the detective trawled through his notebook checking everything he had arranged at the park and what was to be done this morning, ticking off his list one by one. He wanted to get all the details clear in his mind. Above all he didn't want to be surprised by some question he didn't have the answer to in front of the others. The DCI would expect him to have all the answers. He had worked with her for a while and knew she was fair, but she expected results. She didn't tolerate failure well. So far, he had enjoyed working with her, but then he'd never crossed her.

He had just picked up one of the local dailies and read the headline "Foreigner found dead in city park" when, with a thump, the door opened and in walked three of his fellow detectives, chattering noisily, clutching hot steaming cups of tea and breakfast baps from the canteen. Their bulk seemed to fill the room, immediately making it seem smaller and cramped. They spotted him and quietened their ribald remarks.

'Mornin', Sarge.'

The greeting came from the first into the room, a cherubic-looking youth. His face glowed like a freshly scrubbed schoolboy. Grant was the 'baby' of the team, only with them two months. One thing had become obvious as soon as he had joined them. He fancied himself as a catch for the ladies and regaled them on Monday mornings with details of his weekend Casanova conquests. How much was true and how much wishful thinking they had yet to discover. Maxwell had enjoyed seeing Gawn put him firmly in his place when he had tried to charm her. But he'd already proved his worth in a tight corner. His rugby conditioning training had come in useful when they'd confronted a gang of thugs wielding baseball bats and a hammer and been cornered in an old warehouse.

The two older detectives followed in Grant's wake trying not to catch the sergeant's eye. John Dee had earned the nickname 'Jack' because of the comedian. He had a sense of humour but it was a dour one. He was a hard worker who kept his head down and just got on with the job. Maxwell thought of him as a plodder. He would never make sergeant. He was happy doing what he was told but he was a good man to have beside you and he always had your back.

Billy Logan was the oldest member of the team. He was coming near retirement and the general opinion was that he was coasting his way there, doing as little as possible. Without anything being said, and with no discernible effect on his work, it was common knowledge that Logan drank too much. It had all started when his wife had run off with one of his best friends. So far, he had managed to keep it off the DCI's radar, but Maxwell thought it was only a matter of time until she found out and he expected she would expedite his desire for retirement. But Maxwell knew Logan was still a good cop with sound instincts. He could be trusted to get the job done... eventually... at his own pace. There was no urgency in anything he did, including making his way across the room to sit down at his desk.

With a coffee cup in one hand and carrying a grey folder in the other, Gawn made a less dramatic and noisy entry, but it was still head-turning. She looked as if she had stepped out of the pages of a glossy fashion magazine. Maxwell knew she would devour anyone who even whispered that any promotions might have come her way because of how she looked.

The three men parted to let her through and made their way to their desks, while she walked purposefully to the glass board across the room. The door opened again and another group entered. Maxwell was glad to see that among them was Erin McKeown, their computer go-to girl. He liked to be hands-on, out-and-about during an investigation and was glad to have someone on the team like McKeown who was happiest in the office searching online and collating all the information, making some sense of it, creating patterns, and joining the dots.

Gawn pinned a picture of Dieter Weil on the board and then swung round to face the assembled detectives. They quietened without a word from her.

For forty minutes they went over what had been learned, everyone chipping in what they had discovered so far. Gawn had called in to the mortuary on the way in and watched Munroe begin the post-mortem. Nothing had shown up there so far to help them but the pathologist had promised to let her know the results of the tests and tox screens as soon as possible. Phone calls to airlines and airports had managed to pinpoint Weil's arrival at Dublin Airport on a direct flight from Frankfurt, the previous day. From the timings, it seemed likely he had then travelled straight to Belfast. They were waiting to hear from their Garda colleagues on how he had got there.

They had caught a lucky break when they discovered where Weil was staying. Grant had been given the task the night before to find this out. It would have been a problem if Weil were visiting friends. Much more likely, he hoped, was that he was staying in a hotel. He had started with the Belfast hotels and success came first thing this morning. With tourism boosted after the end of the Troubles, there were far more hotels, guest houses and hostels than ever before for travellers to choose from, not even mentioning Airbnbs which could be a nightmare to trace. It could have been a long search but then he had tried the Titanic. He knew that its iconic position, just across from where the doomed ship had been built, attracted travellers from all over the world.

After a brief word of congratulations to the beaming constable for his quick work, Gawn issued an order for a room search and hoped something might turn up in the man's luggage to explain what he was doing in Belfast and perhaps offer some explanation as to why he had ended up dead in the park. The one possibility which she didn't want to even consider was that it was simply a random killing. A fluke. So, she wanted his room searched to see if it threw up any clues to the reason for his visit, presuming it was more than just a pleasant long weekend break. You didn't usually go on holiday like that without a companion – unless you were me, thought Gawn to herself. And you didn't rush out to some local park miles away from your hotel as night was falling without a good reason. She wanted the hotel staff questioned too. Had Weil met with anyone? Spoken to anyone? What calls had been made from his room? How had he left the hotel to get to Botanic Gardens? Was anyone with him? Did he take a taxi? Walk?

She fired the questions out barely taking a breath between each one. She was so energised that for a second

Maxwell wondered if she was on something. Her eyes were bright too. Just occasionally he was aware of something different about her. She could be secretive and he had had suspicions once or twice in the past which he always shook off. No way was she using drugs. He couldn't see it, and yet. Gawn was still issuing commands. She wanted the hotel CCTV footage sent to McKeown so she could start to put together a timeline. Grant and Jack were dispatched to the hotel straightaway.

'Erin, I want you to get on to traffic cams and then arrange to get hold of any CCTV on commercial or private premises between the Titanic and Botanic. There'll be a lot in the city centre so, if you need help going through it, use Billy.' It was fortunate she did not see the look on Logan's face when he heard that. 'We need to have a timeline of his movements. Did our victim stop along the way or meet up with anyone,' Gawn thought of the woman in the yellow coat – 'or was anyone following him or paying him any special attention?'

The girl nodded. Her fingers hovered over her computer keyboard eager to get started on her task. Logan, on the other hand, was busying himself with papers on his desk.

'In the meantime, Billy, you can get on to the phone service and get a list of Weil's calls.'

'Yes, guv.'

Gawn said nothing but everyone knew she hated being addressed as 'guv', a throwback to her time in the Met. 'Ma'am' or even 'boss', if you wanted, but not 'guv'. They all knew but every now and again someone forgot.

She then turned her attention to her sergeant.

'Any news from the park, Paul?'

'They started a fingertip search again at first light, ma'am. They've been questioning anyone who tried to walk through. They found a few people who were in the park yesterday but nobody admitted to seeing Weil or anyone behaving suspiciously.'

'Whatever that means.' The interruption came from Logan. 'There's so many junkies and weirdos hanging around there all the time, how could you tell the difference?' Having put in his comment, he immediately turned back to his desk where he was holding on the phone line.

Maxwell ignored the interruption.

'A few of the passers-by we questioned mentioned a well-dressed young woman and a jogger who were there coming up to closing time, but we haven't been able to trace either of them yet.'

Rather sheepishly Gawn confessed, 'You can forget about the jogger. That was me and I didn't see a thing apart from that other woman. I can give you a description of her.'

If the others were surprised at her admission, they were all sensible enough not to show it or to make any comment. Maxwell hurried on.

'They've finished searching the area around the museum now. Nothing of interest. In fact, they haven't found very much anywhere.' He noticed Gawn's raised eyebrow and hurried on. 'The park keepers have a thing about keeping the park tidy, ma'am. They've won all kinds of awards for anti-litter campaigns – they're really proud of it – so they patrol regularly throughout the day. Mrs McLean told me she had checked that bit of the pathway earlier. So basically, all we've got is a few chocolate bar wrappers, the odd drinks can, a perfume bottle stopper and some bits of chewing gum. But forensics will go through it all.'

'Well, if she checked it then, at least that gives us a tight timeline for the murder. What about you, Mark?'

All eyes turned to the tall SOCO waiting patiently for his turn to report. Gawn really hoped he had some good news. They needed something to give them a direction for the investigation.

The Scenes of Crime supervisor looked as if he hadn't had much sleep. In fact, he hadn't. He had worked on at the site until 4am, gone home, had a shower to wake himself up and headed straight in for the briefing.

'No footprints immediately around the body. I did have a bit more luck outside but still within the tape. I found some ground flattened in the bushes directly behind where the victim was attacked. It wasn't footprints; more like someone had been standing or sitting there for quite some time so the ground was scuffed and flattened.'

'Not footprints?'

'No, not footprints. More like disturbed ground and indentations.'

'So, what are you saying, Mark? You think someone was waiting for Weil there?'

'All I can say with certainty is that someone was in there. It might have been last night or any time, but recently. It wouldn't be somewhere many people would be hanging around in, that's for sure. It's not much of a shortcut. You'd get covered in scratches and snag your clothes if you cut through there. But I looked for any fibres on the bushes and there weren't any.'

Gawn nodded. She was sure he had been thorough. They were out of luck there then.

'Maybe it was some of the friendly local druggies shooting up or someone engaging in a spot of voyeurism with the wee schoolgirls in their short skirts,' suggested Logan with a smirk and a snigger, still holding on for a response to his phone call.

Gawn flashed him a look of displeasure which had him revolving swiftly in his chair.

Ferguson finished his report. 'They're all possible. It could even have been one of the schoolkids hiding from his friends. I couldn't speculate, Chief Inspector, whether this person was waiting for Weil, or anyone really. I do facts, not speculations.'

Ferguson, like Al Munroe, only dealt in scientific facts he could test and prove. Where speculating and hypothesising were needed, Gawn had Maxwell. They had bounced ideas off each other in the past and she was happy to leave the speculation to him.

She allocated tasks around the team. She wanted the police in Germany contacted but decided to delegate that to McKeown. She knew the girl was bright and keen and that she spoke German so she could make the initial contact and, if need be, Gawn could follow it up. They needed to find out as much as they could about Dieter Weil. Who was he? Did he have connections to Northern Ireland, either personal or professional?

'We also need to get a formal identification so see if the local police will notify the family at their end when we have a formal identification of the body here. We need to liaise with them about who can do that. They'll have to get someone over — a family member maybe.' She hesitated and then, Maxwell could almost swear she was on the verge of a smile when she added, 'Billy can make a start on the CCTV while you get onto that.'

The balding detective didn't groan but his body language revealed what he thought about it. His head sagged forward onto his chest.

Gawn turned her attention to her sergeant. She wanted to have another look around the park before they had to re-open it to the public. She really wanted to visualise her route from last night and see if she could remember anything that could help.

'With me, Paul.'

Kerri said Gawn treated him as a cross between her personal servant and a pet dog. She didn't bother with polite requests. Sometimes her tone was harsh and he thought she forgot she wasn't in the army anymore, but he didn't hesitate to follow her out the door. She was a good detective and he wanted to learn from her. If that meant being spoken to like this, so be it. He could put up with that, for a while.

Chapter 10

Gawn and Maxwell approached the park from the opposite direction this time. As soon as they rounded the sweeping bend in the road, they could see a TV van strategically placed just opposite the main museum building, almost in the spot where Gawn had parked the previous night on the call-out. A small crowd of gawpers ebbed and flowed outside the high gates, sometimes augmented by passing tourists but mainly made up of park regulars eager to find out what was happening.

Should she drive down to the gates and wait for someone to let her through? Gawn didn't fancy having to sit under the gaze of the crowd and the press, even for only the few minutes it might take for the gates to be opened. She decided it was best to avoid the front entrance. She made a right turn into one of the tiny side streets famous for student bedsits and threaded her way carefully between rows of parked cars lining both sides of the narrow roadway. They were now facing one of the other gateways into the park. With difficulty, she found a parking space in this more residential area of graceful three-storey houses, somewhat faded from their glory days in Victorian Belfast. It took a minute or two to skilfully manoeuvre her Audi into the tight space.

The policewoman on duty at the gate recognised both officers and stood aside to let them pass. Gawn was pleased to see the notice on the gate asking for anyone who had information about the murder to contact the police. They had been quick off the mark getting those distributed. Well done, Paul, she thought to herself but said nothing.

The park had taken on a totally different look in the morning light. Gone were the harsh arc lights, no longer needed in the bright autumn sun. The crime scene tape was still in place, looking a little battered, fluttering slightly in this morning's light breeze. But only a few officers remained working their way outwards, bent over like old men, scouring the ground, inch by inch, for any evidence, in the further reaches of the park. A little clique of park keepers huddled together near the entrance to the Tropical Ravine. Their interest in the new arrivals sparked a buzz of chatter. Maxwell moved off to check in with the supervising officer and get an update on what more had been found – if anything.

Gawn stood still and closed her eyes. She tried to visualise how it had been last night on her first visit to the park. No one was in sight – at least she hadn't registered seeing anyone around. She remembered how stuffy her head had been and the ache behind her eyes. Really, she had been concentrating on simply putting one foot in front of the other to get back to her car as quickly as possible. Could she have missed someone? She didn't think so; didn't want to think so. She knew she wasn't as alert to danger around her as she had been during her army days abroad. Then her life and the lives of the others under her command had often depended on watching out for any sign, no matter how small, of imminent danger. But, like any woman, she took care of her personal safety, especially at night and especially in dark areas, like a park.

She began to walk slowly, following the route she had run, gazing all around her to see if she could trigger any memory. After passing under the denuded stone pergola walkway, which in the height of summer provided a fragrant rose-filled canopy, she headed towards her sergeant, where he stood conversing intently with a uniformed officer. She was still scanning all around when she realised that she recognised one of the figures standing on the main road looking through the railings. The girl was quite a distance away, but Gawn was sure. It was the young woman from last night. The one who had not yet been found. She was still wearing the same yellow coat, bright enough to have been noticed even in the twilight when she had almost collided with her.

Gawn hurried her step as she saw the woman turn away and begin to move in the direction of the city centre. She saw the back of a tall man dressed in a long black overcoat and wearing a fedora hat walking along beside her, chatting. He had his hand on her back in a casual, protective way guiding her. But they were not trying to escape the scene. Their steps were unhurried. They had satisfied their curiosity and were now just going about their day.

Gawn didn't want to lose sight of her witness but she also didn't want the indignity of chasing after the two figures in front of a crowd including a TV crew. She wasn't dressed to go running. While she was pleased she had foregone her Jimmy Choos that morning, the shoes she had on weren't really made for speed either. She thought about calling after them to attract their attention but that would attract everyone else's attention too and she didn't want anyone to know about their potential witness. Or maybe even their potential killer?

She speeded up, without breaking into a run, but it took her until the pair were almost at the pelican crossing in front of the university before she caught them up. Maxwell had noted her hurried departure from the park and followed. They arrived alongside the couple at almost the same time.

'Just a minute, please.'

The man and woman turned puzzled looks in her direction. Gawn took her ID from her pocket and held it out for the girl to see.

'DCI Girvin. This is DS Maxwell. We'd like a word with you, please.'

Without hesitating the girl blurted out, 'Is it about the murder? I was in the park last night.' Her vivid blue eyes were sparkling with excitement. She looked at her tall companion seeming to seek his approval. He smiled back at her and nodded to her in encouragement.

'Yes. We know,' Gawn said. 'We'd like to ask you some questions about it.'

The girl didn't seem surprised that they knew she had been there. Gawn looked around suddenly aware of just how much they were in public view standing by a busy thoroughfare. The crossing lights had turned to red and traffic was halted right beside them. Pedestrians were crossing and casting interested glances in their direction as they passed by. She was aware of some of the drivers watching them too. She didn't want footage of their interview taken on anyone's mobile phone to appear on the TV news that evening.

'But not here,' she added. She was aware that some of the crowd at the gate had noticed her rushing out of the park and had turned to watch what was going on. 'It would be good to speak to you as soon as possible. Is there somewhere we could go now? A bit more private?'

The tall man took the girl's arm and said, 'You can use my room, if you like, Lucy. I don't have any tutorials this morning.' Seeing the detectives exchange glances, he explained, 'Sorry. I'm Sebastian York. I'm a friend of Lucy's and my office is just round the corner in University Square. You're very welcome to use it, if that helps.'

'Thank you, Mr York. That would be very helpful.'

'Dr York.' The emphasis on the 'doctor' was slight but perceptible.

'Dr York. Sorry. Can we go there now?' Gawn smiled ingratiatingly trying to convey how appreciative she was of his help. What a prick, *Doctor* York, was what she was actually thinking.

Chapter 11

The four had made their way in silence past the front of the university, the woman and York leading the way into University Square. They didn't hold hands, Gawn noticed, but from time to time York placed an encouraging hand in the middle of the girl's back in a gesture of intimacy and support.

Gawn and Maxwell kept their thoughts to themselves, each preparing questions they wanted to ask. Gawn had questions for the girl. Maxwell had questions for the girl and Gawn too. He was still shocked that she hadn't told him earlier about being in the park but had left him to find out with all the others at the briefing. There hadn't been a chance this morning before the meeting. But what about last night? She could have mentioned it then.

As they approached the row of four-storey terraced houses opposite the side of the main university buildings, once homes, now offices and seminar spaces for some of the university departments, York led the way across the street, past the gateless black railings and up the concrete path to a scuffed front door. Maxwell was surprised to see an obviously well-tended, but low-maintenance garden almost as if they were entering a private home. Gawn noticed a brass plate to the side of the bowed window indicating they were about to enter the School of History and Politics.

Once inside, the narrow corridor with cardboard boxes lining one side of it forced them into a single file. Light came from the fanlight above the door casting rays of weak sunlight into the gloomy space. Photographs of departmental staff lined one wall, and, out of the corner of his eye, Maxwell noticed a picture of a rather serious looking Dr York among them. Two flights of steep lino-covered stairs later, York unlocked room 6b. The first thing Maxwell noticed was the smell of fresh paint. It was all-pervasive. The whole room including the fireplace and shelves sparkled brilliantly white. The room was what Maxwell had always imagined a university professor's room would look like. Never progressing beyond three middle-of-the-road A levels before his entry to the police, Maxwell took his notions of university life from a cross between *University Challenge* with its super-smart students, where he couldn't even understand the questions never mind know any of the answers, to the version of *Educating Rita* which his wife had dragged him to at the cineplex. He had never seen so many books in one place outside of the public library. Not only did higgledy-piggledy stuffed bookshelves line three walls of the room – the other being filled by two tall windows – but stacks of books stood precariously around the room like paper stalagmites. It seemed they could be toppled by the merest touch. Almost every inch of the floor seemed to be covered, if not by books, then by piles of notes and files, making moving around hazardous.

Meanwhile York had taken off his coat, placed it on a hanger, straightened the rim of his black fedora and hung them both carefully on a lop-sided coat stand in the corner of the room. Everything was done very carefully, very consciously, Gawn thought. Maxwell examined the lecturer more closely. He was dressed in a fine blue striped collarless shirt, with sleeves rolled up to just below his elbow, a tweed waistcoat complete with pocket watch and chain and navy-blue corduroy trousers. He reminded Maxwell of a Scottish laird from one of those Sunday night TV dramas Kerri liked so much. Gawn merely dismissed him as a first-class poser. She had no time for effete men.

Maxwell's attention was drawn to a map of western Europe hanging over the painted fireplace. York cleared boxes and piles of papers off the two chairs in front of his desk and indicated with a casual wave of his hand that Lucy and Gawn should sit. The girl immediately sank down on one of them. Some of her excitement seemed to have evaporated and she was looking slightly apprehensive now at the thought of being questioned by the police. Gawn remained standing. Maxwell stationed himself by one of the windows. As surreptitiously as possible, he took his notebook out of his pocket ready to jot down anything important.

'Please excuse the mess, everyone. I've just moved into this room. I haven't had time to get my things into order yet.' York's easy smile oozed charm and seemed to imply that, of course, he would be forgiven anything, like a naughty schoolboy. Gawn thought to herself, I bet the female students just love tutorials with him. She knew his type; she had come across them before.

Lucy was waiting patiently for the questioning to begin. She still seemed to be more excited than anything else, her bright eyes moving from Maxwell to York. She studiously avoided catching Gawn's eye. Maxwell moved further back towards the window. Gawn was still on her feet wondering how she could possibly ask the university tutor to leave his own room so she could interview the girl without an audience. After all, he had offered the accommodation, so it seemed churlish to put him out of his own office, but rudeness didn't really factor into a murder enquiry.

She was just about to put her request, when York, lifting a file off the chaotic desk, said, 'I'll leave you to it then... if that's OK with you, Lucy?'

He paused and lifted his eyebrows in query. Obviously, he was prepared to demand to stay if she wanted his support. The girl, for that was what she was, Gawn realised, nodded and smiled as if to reassure him she did not need him to stay. If she was fearful, she wasn't showing it. Just nervous anticipation. She had seemed older last night. Gawn reckoned she was about twenty.

Her brown hair was like a TV ad for some shampoo. It was voluminous and shiny, neatly cut into a bob. Her eyes were sparkling and her pale pink lipstick served to emphasise her youth. Anyhow, she seemed happy enough to face them alone.

As soon as York had closed the door behind him, it was Maxwell who stepped forward and started the questioning.

'Can we have your full name, please, miss?' He smiled, an encouraging smile, to put her at ease.

'Lucy Amelia Armstrong.'

She enunciated each syllable slowly while he wrote it down. A pretty name for a pretty girl, he thought.

'And your address?'

'In term time I live in the Halls of Residence. On Stranmillis Road.' Maxwell nodded to show he knew where she meant. 'I come from Bangor but my family live abroad so it's quite nice to be near the university with all my friends. My dad's a university lecturer in Germany so I go there during vacations.'

It was as if a bolt of electricity had been fired through the two detectives. They exchanged surprised looks. It was too much of a coincidence, surely? A German victim and a witness from Germany. There had to be some connection.

'Which part of Germany?' the Chief Inspector queried, trying to keep the excitement out of her voice.

'They live in a wee village called Staufen. You won't have heard of it. It's small but it's really pretty.'

She was right. Gawn hadn't heard of it. 'Is that anywhere near Frankfurt?'

'No. Not really. It's on the edge of the Black Forest – near Switzerland. It's about a couple of hundred miles from Frankfurt, I think. My geography isn't very good.' Lucy giggled. 'Sometimes, I do fly home through Frankfurt Airport but it's quite a drive to get there. I usually fly from Strasbourg or Basel.'

'How recently have you visited your parents?' Gawn realised she was holding her breath waiting for the answer. She could feel her palms sticky as she anticipated an early breakthrough in the case.

'I came back yesterday.'

Maxwell was quicker to the follow-up question than his boss. 'Did you fly from Frankfurt yesterday?'

'No. I flew into Heathrow from Strasbourg and then on to Belfast. That's probably why I won't be able to help you much about last night,' she added apologetically. 'I wasn't long off the plane and I was feeling a bit fed up with all the travelling. It had been a long, boring day and I was a bit tired.'

Tell me about it, thought Gawn.

'I'd just been down to Botanic Avenue to pick up a couple of things from Tesco's and I was looking forward to catching up with friends later. I was sort of on a bit of autopilot, if you know what I mean, so I wasn't really paying a lot of attention to anything.'

Her smile passed from Gawn to Maxwell. Her pale blue eyes sat under perfectly framed eyebrows and she looked straight at him as if to emphasise her innocence. He noted her straight white teeth, no doubt the result of expensive childhood visits to the orthodontist.

The girl seemed perfectly open and friendly and happy to try to answer their questions. There was no hint of nervousness in her manner now, but experience had taught them both never to overlook coincidences. And the German link was a big coincidence.

'So, what did you see last night when you were in the park, Lucy?'

Maxwell noted the use of the girl's Christian name. So, the boss had decided to be 'chummy'.

'Nothing really.' She paused to show she was concentrating really hard, trying to dredge up some useful memory for them. 'I mean, there were a couple of guys hanging around on skateboards outside the library, but I didn't see anyone in the park – oh, except for a jogger who ran past me.'

'Yes, we know all about the jogger. Nothing else? No noises? You didn't think there might have been anyone in the bushes?'

The girl's expression changed instantly. Her eyes widened.

'Christ, do you think there was someone in the bushes when I was there?'

The implications of this possibility were immediately obvious to her. Her easy manner disappeared in an instant. The colour drained from her face. For a moment, Maxwell thought she was going to burst into tears or maybe even faint. Eventually she managed to speak. It was barely a whisper. 'I didn't see anyone. Sorry I can't help you.'

Even as she was still speaking, Lucy stood up and hurried towards the door. She grabbed the handle, holding on to it as if her legs wouldn't support her. Without any other acknowledgement, she flung it open, allowing it to bang against the wall and exited with a suddenness that left Gawn and Maxwell looking at each other. Maxwell was about to follow her but Gawn raised a hand to stop him.

'I think we've managed to give her something to think about. She'll not be strolling through the park by herself anytime soon.' Then, after a pause, she added, 'I wonder if we've just let our killer walk out?'

'You don't seriously think she's our murderer, do you, ma'am? You really think she was just wandering through the park with a knife in her handbag looking for someone to kill and it just happened to be a German?' He didn't even try to keep the incredulity out of his voice. 'Or maybe, she's a contract killer who was stalking Weil and waited until he was practically on her own doorstep to kill him?'

'Sarcasm does not become you, Sergeant. OK, she's probably not our killer. I grant you. I don't see her as a homicidal maniac or a contract killer either, but you need to be less susceptible to fluttering eyelashes, Paul. She looks at you with those big blue eyes and you lose perspective. I don't like coincidences and her coming from Germany yesterday is a very big coincidence as far as I'm concerned. We'll need to take a good look at her, do a bit of digging into her life and speak to her again, but we know where to find her. In the meantime, we need to find out more about Weil and see if we can dredge up any connection between them.'

Maxwell didn't like what Gawn had suggested. He thought he was as good a judge of character as she was. He moved over and put his hand on the brass handle about to open the door. Interview over, he was ready to leave but Gawn lingered to take another look around the room. She never missed the opportunity to have a pry around in people's private lives and homes during a case. At least that was how Maxwell had judged it at first, but she insisted you never knew what would pop up and she had explained to her sergeant that as far as she was concerned a cop who wasn't curious, who didn't want to find out what he could – no matter what it was or how irrelevant it might seem – was a cop who would never go far.

To Gawn's casual scrutiny, this certainly seemed like a typical academic's room – perhaps too much so. Was Dr York playing to stereotype? Did such disorganised absent-minded professor types really exist anymore? Weren't this generation of lecturers all computers and social media? York was much too self-assured for her liking and, if he was romantically involved with one of his students, which she suspected he was, then he had things to hide.

Her eye was caught by a garish postcard propped up against an expensive-looking camera on the freshly painted fireplace. It featured a girl dressed in a traditional Black Forest costume, complete with Bollenhut hat with its famous red pompoms, a cuckoo clock and a huge roller-coaster on a bright pink background. Across the bottom in crazy font and fluorescent letters was the message "Viel spass". Not caring that this was really none of her business and not likely to be linked in any way to the investigation, other than it happened to be in German, Gawn turned the card and read it. It was addressed to York at his office – did someone not know his home address? Perhaps he was married and the writer didn't want his wife to see it? Gawn's mind was racing ahead. The message read "Thank you for our fun day out. I'll always remember the Pirates of the Orient!! See you next week. Love, Lucy" and was finished with two large Xs. So, Lucy sent the professor cards with kisses, did she? Interesting.

Gawn was just setting the card back in its original position when the door swung open and thudded back against the wall. At this rate, York will need to get that wall replastered, with the battering it was taking from the door, Gawn thought to herself. The tutor entered, almost colliding with Maxwell who had been preparing to leave. He didn't seem to notice the DCI with the postcard. Instead, he turned his back to them and placed his file down with exaggerated care on the cluttered desk. Gawn recognised the show of control as a ploy to mask his anger. She had stood before enough senior army officers seething with righteous indignation or disappointed fury to recognise the signs.

He swung round. His eyes sparked with anger.

'Did you really have to terrorise the poor girl? It was bad enough when she heard there'd been a murder in the park last night after she was there without you telling her some psychopath might have been lurking in the bushes watching her. She thought that guy had been long dead.' His voice was low and controlled. He looked from one to the other, including them both in his condemnatory stare.

'We simply asked Miss Armstrong if she had noticed anyone in the bushes,' Maxwell countered innocently.

So, sweet Lucy had run immediately to the arms of the professor?

'Well, she didn't. Thank God. And now, Inspector, I do have a lecture to prepare.' His tone was dismissive and they had no reasonable cause to question him further.

'Detective *Chief* Inspector.' Two could play that game. 'By the way, just for the sake of completeness, where were you yesterday evening between say 5 and 8pm?' She might as well try to knock him off his stride with the unexpected question.

York gave no indication of surprise. It was almost as if he expected to be questioned, as if he knew how investigations worked. His response came quickly, glibly, she thought.

'I was teaching in the afternoon and then I was giving a reading.' He spoke as if naturally everyone should already know this. Seeing they had no idea what he was talking about, York continued. 'My latest book's just been published and the launch event was last night. I was giving a talk about it and signing copies. At a local bookshop on Botanic Avenue.'

'Thank you, Dr York. That's all for now.'

This time Gawn was careful to put a slight emphasis on the word 'doctor' but also on the word 'now'.

Gawn knew which bookstore he meant. She had even visited it herself to buy gifts for friends who enjoyed crime novels, its speciality. It was less than a five-minute walk from the park. The two detectives made their way back out into the street but, Gawn had already decided they needed to find out more about both the girl and about her professor. She didn't like coincidences. And she didn't like Dr Sebastian York either.

Chapter 12

The two detectives were aware of the bustle and excitement in the office as soon as they opened the door. A group of men were gathered around one desk, heads together deep in conversation. Erin McKeown was poised over her computer tapping at the keys while Grant bounced out of his seat like an excited puppy when he saw them.

'You should hear this, ma'am.'

'So, what did you find at the hotel then?' Her tone was serious.

'Not very much to be honest.' It was obvious he would have loved to be able to offer some revelation that would crack the case. Gawn was always telling him he watched too many TV cop shows; that police work was down to the boring detail, not high-speed car chases and inspired hunches that solved the case.

'We searched the room and went through his luggage. Nothing of interest...' Dee's voice trailed off.

'Unless you're into designer clothes,' Grant interrupted. 'The stuff in his suitcase must have cost a fortune.'

'Interesting but not a crime to have expensive clothes.' Gawn showed no awareness of the irony of her observation. Maxwell merely smiled to himself. 'What else did you find?' she asked. Gawn hoped their time spent at the hotel had yielded something more worthwhile than an inventory of the victim's suitcase.

'We checked with the hotel receptionist – the one who was on duty yesterday. Weil didn't make any calls on his room phone. He had a room service sandwich delivered around 3pm and left the hotel on foot just before 4pm. On his own.'

With a quick mental calculation, Gawn worked out that if he had made the journey on foot to the park he would have had to walk straight there. There would have been no time for detours. But had he met up with anyone on the way? Had they entered the park together or was he on his way to meet someone?

'Any luck with the CCTV, Billy?'

Logan swivelled in his chair and pushed a hand through his thinning hair, making what was left of it even more dishevelled than before. He had an almost permanent look of bewilderment on his face which belied his quick intelligence.

'I'm working my way through it. But there's a helluva lot, ma'am. I've got him arriving at the hotel in a taxi and checking in and then leaving on foot. I'll need to go through all the traffic cams to work out what route he might have walked. There are so many ways he could have gone. I was thinking maybe past Laganbank Court where you were, ma'am. Worst case scenario, he picked up another taxi on the way. It'll just take time to track him.'

Gawn was unjustifiably annoyed at the possibility that not only had she been in the park at the same time as the victim but now he might have passed her outside the court too. It wasn't her fault of course. Yet she couldn't shake the feeling that she should have noticed something in the park and perhaps even been able to prevent this from happening. Her commanding officer had once told her that it was impossible to try to keep everyone safe, and that she shouldn't take on the responsibility for everyone's mistakes or every disaster. But she couldn't help taking things personally.

'Keep looking. Jamie can lend you a hand. Concentrate on Botanic Avenue, the embankment and Stranmillis Road. See which gate Weil entered and if there was anyone with him or following him then. If he met someone earlier along the way we can go back later and check where, but we need to know now if anyone was with him in the park or following him when he got to the park.'

Her voice was serious as she punched out her demands. It was all too slow. Saying 'it takes time' didn't help anyone. The super would expect an update and so far, there was little to tell him.

As if to try to redeem himself for their lack of success at the hotel, Grant chirped up, 'But the Germans have come up trumps.'

Straightaway McKeown stood up, walked purposefully across the room and pointed to the murder board. A new picture of Dieter Weil was now on display alongside the original image from his passport. This time he looked younger, thinner and more thuggish with stubble on his chin which was anything but designer, and cuts and bruises on his face from having been in a fight. It was obviously a police mugshot. McKeown took a deep breath and plunged into her report. As Gawn had hoped, she had been able to turn up important information and her excitement was obvious. She was a fan of the DCI and wanted to impress her.

Pointing to the new picture she said, 'Dieter Weil AKA Bahir Saleh. Born in Sana'a, the capital of Yemen in 1994. Brought to Germany as a refugee the year after by his uncle who soon after seems to have disappeared from his life. Apparently, Weil's parents were killed by a car bomb. He was adopted by a German couple Paul and Lottie Weil, brought up in Bad Reichenhall, in Bavaria near the border with Austria. He is well known to the police there starting with low grade stuff as a kid – vandalism, bit of minor thieving. He moved to Freiburg a little over a year ago and the police there have been keeping an eye on him. He was no Mr Big but just recently he's moved up in the world. They are pretty sure he was involved with a criminal gang in Bavaria and is working for them now on the other side of the country. Minor stuff but they think he's being trusted with more important tasks recently. They suspect he was involved in transporting drugs and possibly a kidnapping in Salzburg. They haven't been able to prove anything yet, but the kidnapping ended in the death of the kidnapped girl,' – McKeown looked down at her notes before continuing – 'Inga Weissler, sixteen years old, daughter of an Austrian industrialist, so both the Germans and the Austrians were looking for him and they were putting a lot of resources into it. The guy I spoke to in Freiburg was absolutely amazed that he had turned up here. They have no idea why he would be in Belfast. As far as they are aware, the gang – the Schwarzer Adler – aren't into anything in any part of Ireland.'

All of this was music to Gawn's ears. Weil, or whatever his name was, mightn't have been that important, but the gang he was involved with sounded big-time. Could that be why he was killed? This might be something more than a single murder. In her mind, she thanked Maxwell for phoning her last night.

'There's also a possibility the gang is moving into people smuggling which will bring them into direct conflict with the Eastern Europeans who have a bit of a monopoly on that so maybe that could be why he was here.'

At this suggestion Gawn's heart sank. She didn't want to hear this. If this was linked to people smuggling, she would have to hand it over to Organised Crime. They would have all the current information and the connections to see what he was up to. DCI Maitland would jump at the case. There was no love lost between Davy Maitland and herself. He was an old school cop who resented Gawn and took every opportunity to undermine her. If you hadn't spent your whole life in Northern Ireland and didn't have PSNI running through your blood like the name in a stick of seaside rock, then you were an outsider as far as he was concerned. He would push for the Organised Crime Unit to take over and, although she didn't want to admit it, even to herself, if this was the work of some European group who were moving into Northern Ireland, they were better resourced to run that sort of investigation.

But she wasn't convinced of that yet. Until someone could prove to her this was more than a murder case, then it was hers and she would fight to keep it.

'Any suggestion of links to terrorism?' That question was in everyone's mind, but Maxwell was the one to voice it.

'As far as they know, the Germans say no. Simple criminal. This gang operates right across Germany and has fingers in all sorts of pies but no sign of a link to terrorism.'

Gawn realised the significance of all this information. She was becoming more convinced that they were not just dealing with some random killing or crime of passion. But was it related to Weil's criminal activities or was it personal? A German turns up dead in Belfast within hours of arriving. With his background and contacts, it would be too ironic if he was the victim of some deranged junkie who just happened upon him by chance in the park. She wanted the opportunity to stay with the investigation. But to do that she would need to convince Superintendent McDowell and probably the Chief Super too that she had it under control and was making good progress.

'We need to find out more about this gang. See if we can work out what Weil was doing in Belfast. I'll get on to the Germans myself. Do you have a contact name and number, Erin?'

'Yes. I spoke to the police in Bad Reichenhall first and they agreed to arrange the notification to Weil's adoptive parents once we have a positive identification here. The police in Freiburg, where Weil was living, gave me the details of who to contact from there. His name is Hauptkommissar Norbert Schneider. He's been monitoring the Schwarzer Adler group and he knows Weil so he could identify the body for us. Apparently, he's on leave at the minute but he's their main man so they think he would be the best one to deal with. They've given me his mobile number. He's been told to expect a follow-up call from us.'

'Good work.'

Gawn took the proffered slip of paper and gave McKeown an encouraging smile and then moved on.

'What about Weil's mobile phone? Have we got the details of his calls yet, Billy?'

'We're waiting for the service provider to get back to us.'

'Chase them up, man. Keep at them. We need to know who he was talking to and we need to know today, not tomorrow.' Irritation sounded in her voice.

Maxwell followed Gawn into her inner office. Through the glass he could see the others already busying themselves, re-energised by the information they had just heard and the DCI's obvious irritation at the lack of progress.

'What do you want me to do?'

She had already lifted the handset and was about to punch in a number.

'I'll have to update McDowell though God knows I don't have much to tell him. I need you to go and see Al Munroe. See if the PM has turned up anything useful. He did it early this morning so his preliminary report should be ready.'

She didn't wait for his reply. He heard her speaking to someone on the other end of the line as he closed the door behind him.

'This is DCI Girvin. I need to see Superintendent McDowell sometime today, please. When can he fit me in?'

Chapter 13

The traffic was already building up on the Westlink. Maxwell cursed himself for having chosen to take a route through the city centre to reach the mortuary. He had wanted to avoid the bottleneck that is Boucher Road coming up to Friday evening's early rush hour but had ended up instead crawling along in heavy traffic hemmed in by high walls of exhaust-blackened stone and occasionally intimidated by lorries forcing their way into the line of traffic from the slip roads. He was glad when the white-framed sculpture at Broadway roundabout came into view signalling that the hospital wasn't far. To locals, this metal framework had various nicknames. With typical Belfast humour, it had become known as Balls of the Falls, rather less uplifting than its official name of Rise. His view was that public money being spent on a piece of roadside sculpture was a load of balls so for him the nickname suited well.

Maxwell took the turn off the roundabout signposted to the RVH and waited to enter the hospital complex. When the way ahead was clear he followed an ambulance into the site. It continued straight ahead towards the main hospital building while Maxwell followed a sign to the Northern Ireland Regional Forensic Mortuary hidden away in a nondescript single-storey red brick building. Hundreds of people must pass the building every day without realising what it was. It was not his favourite place to visit. He disliked the sterile atmosphere and disinfectant smells, and he was intimidated by the pathologists, especially Munroe. They were all so stiff and full of themselves and he found their sense of humour macabre.

Parking at the hospital was notoriously difficult but at that time of day – between afternoon and evening visiting times – there was ample space directly outside the double glass doors. They swished open as he came within range of the automatic sensor, and he identified himself to a bored-looking receptionist seated behind a desk in the foyer. She flicked her platinum blonde hair out of her eyes and looked up at him. He flashed his ID.

'I've come to see Dr Munroe. My name's Maxwell.'

'He's in his office – just at the end of that corridor. Last door on the left.'

Maxwell was delighted that Munroe wasn't still in the autopsy suite with its overwhelmingly sickening smell of formalin and all those hard steel surfaces.

'Thanks.' He threw her a smile. It never hurt to be friendly.

He had never been in Munroe's office before and found himself wondering what it would be like. He could imagine no clutter, everything in its designated place, lots of framed diplomas recognising the pathologist's qualifications and a cold atmosphere rather like the cold persona which Munroe projected. On the other hand, thinking of his infamous knitted cardigans, perhaps it was all tartan cushions and photos of his mother. Maxwell smiled at the image that conjured up.

He made his way down the hallway. As he moved further away from the reception area it became increasingly gloomy. There were no windows, no natural light. The overhead lights were not switched on yet. He could imagine this could be quite a spooky place late at night. The corridor was long. He was backlit from the foyer. He could just picture the scene in some Jack Nicholson movie about a maniac on the loose. All it would take were some flickering fluorescent lights to set the scene. He wouldn't like to be spending time here by himself after dark. Best not to let his imagination get the better of him.

Munroe's name was on a brass nameplate on the last door before the corridor came to a dead end. Maxwell knocked respectfully and waited.

'Come in.'

No mistaking the sing-songy Scottish lilt. Munroe sounded in a good mood. Well, it was Friday afternoon. Even pathologists might have plans for the weekend.

'Ah, good evening, Sergeant. No Chief Inspector today?' Munroe was jovial but he seemed genuinely disappointed that Gawn had not come herself.

'No. She's up to her eyes at the minute. She asked me to get your report… if it's ready.'

He had hesitated before the final three words as he watched the pathologist's hooded eyes take on a colder gleam. Reports could take a while, he knew. All the pathologists were sticky about releasing any information until they had everything ready. But he was hoping that this time Munroe might provide an interim report to help them out.

'I'm afraid my report's not ready yet, Sergeant. It will take a day or two but, of course, I will get it emailed to the Chief Inspector as soon as I can.' The doctor finished with a smile which did not extend beyond his teeth and mouth.

'I think Chief Inspector Girvin was hoping that you might have some preliminary thoughts you could share with her. It would really help her out.'

He had been going to say help us out but realised he would have more chance of success using Gawn as a sweetener. At the mention of her name, like the wave of a magic wand and an incantation of abracadabra, Munroe's geniality returned. It seemed he would be happy to help her.

'Of course, of course.'

Munroe walked to his desk, sat down and entered a password on his computer. While he searched his files and pulled up the information, Maxwell scanned the room. As Gawn had taught him, using your eyes and doing a bit of snooping could sometimes prove useful. No information gleaned was ever a loss. He was not so sure about that, but he was interested to get an idea of what Munroe was like and seeing the man in his private domain was an opportunity to learn more about him. Although he had been working with the PSNI for years, no one seemed to really know him well. He kept to himself. Didn't socialise with anyone. There were rumours and speculation about his private life. The main one was that he was a homosexual but watching his reaction to Gawn, Maxwell wasn't convinced of that. He came, did his job, and went. He was a bit of an enigma.

The office was not exactly what Maxwell had expected either. It was cosier, with some personal photographs on the wall including one of a teenage boy who he guessed was Munroe himself with a man he assumed was his father on some moor. The older man was proudly displaying a dead deer and clutching a rifle while the boy held a huge knife. There was the expected range of heavy tomes, reference books of various kinds but also some beautiful pieces of glass in a lighted display case. Maxwell thought they were antique medicine bottles perhaps.

Munroe glanced up from the screen.

'I see you are admiring my glass. I collect pieces of antique glass, mostly perfume bottles. That one at the end was the first I ever obtained in Murano.'

Munroe's eyes had gone back to the screen and were scanning his notes.

'Let me see… yes. Mr Weil was in good physical condition. Well nourished. No overt signs of alcohol or drug abuse but I'm running tox screens. Results will take a couple of days. His only distinguishing marks were a tattoo of an eagle on his left forearm and a scar from an old knife wound on his upper left thigh. The fatal knife trauma however was to the nucha.' He looked up and, seeing Maxwell's quizzical look, added, 'The nape. The blow almost severed the spinal column. Death would have been more or less instantaneous.'

'Would you say that would require medical knowledge, to hit the right spot, doctor?'

'It could indicate some element of medical knowledge or it could just have been a lucky strike. What I would say is there was a degree of force used.'

'So, a male killer then?'

'Or a strong woman.'

Munroe seemed to be determined to leave all options open, not to commit himself to anything.

'But a tall one for sure. The blow came from slightly above Weil and from the right.'

'OK. A right-handed killer. Height?'

'Weil was five foot eight so perhaps somewhere around the six-feet mark. Unusual for a woman but there are some around – especially in their heels.'

This was obviously Munroe's attempt at humour and a reference to the DCI.

'Anything else to help, doctor?'

'Not really. The knife is a common kitchen type. The blade is 5 inches long and slightly serrated. Very common, I would say. I think it is normally called a utility knife. I have one myself at home. I use it for cutting vegetables when I'm cooking.'

This seemed to be all Munroe was prepared to give him, so, with a brief word of thanks, Maxwell left the office. Once outside the building he realised he had been almost holding his breath without being aware of it. He was glad to be able to suck in a few deep breaths of the fresh night air. He felt his head had been almost starting to swim from all the chemical smells which he had probably mostly imagined. Munroe would be used to it. Maxwell was just glad he didn't have to be.

Chapter 14

Maxwell found the journey back to HQ much quicker. Rush-hour traffic was already beginning to thin. He had promised Kerri he would be home early tonight to help with the kids. He had let her down once too often and knew she was becoming irate at how he seemed to be at Gawn's 'beck and call'. She had called him Gawn's poodle in one of their arguments and that had stung. He was no pushover but to be fair to Kerri, Gawn could be quite demanding. She expected everyone else to be as committed as she was. Kerri had suggested getting her together with some of his unmarried friends and seeing how a bit of romance changed her. Or to be more exact, she had said see how a 'good seeing to' might change her perspective. He had first been shocked at the suggestion and then they both had dissolved into fits of laughter.

As he approached the office, he was aware of how quiet it was. Surely everyone hadn't gone home already. OK, it was Friday night. He knew some of his colleagues would have plans. Grant had already shared details about his hot date. But he had expected at least some of them would still be around finishing off.

Maxwell opened the door and realised straightaway that nearly everyone was still there listening in silence as Gawn filled them in on the state of the case. Because he was beginning to know her so well, he could read the mixture of relief and zeal on her face. Her visit to the superintendent had been successful enough to keep Special Branch and Serious Crime off their back... for now. The superintendent had stressed that all three units needed to work together and make sure to share intel. It was not a competition. This drew some weak smiles in reaction from the team. Gawn was to remain as SIO – at least for now. She didn't add 'at least for now' but Maxwell added that for himself under his breath. He knew they would be under heavy scrutiny. The bosses would expect results and quickly.

This was as much of a pep talk as she felt they could take on a Friday evening. Grant was practically bouncing in his seat as if his trousers were on fire. Some of the others just looked tired and Gawn knew she was tired too and needed a break. Even Maxwell who had just slipped in at the back of the room was looking as if he could do with an early night. She knew there was little that could be done until their German liaison, Hauptkommissar Schneider, arrived on Monday morning. The forensics people were going over everything that had been found in the park. They might have turned something up by then too. McKeown was already started on a background check of Lucy and Dr York and hopefully that might discover something to link it all together. She had already decided they would interview Lucy again after Schneider had identified the body and given them more information on Weil. Till then the best thing for all of them was a break and a fresh start first thing on Monday morning.

With a mock serious command to go home and relax ready to get going again on Monday morning, Gawn dismissed them and headed into her inner office. Maxwell followed, pausing at the threshold and knocking before walking in.

'Did Organised Crimes want the case?'

'You joking? Of course they bloody did.'

Her smile was forced and her voice betrayed her tiredness. She ran a hand over her forehead sweeping the hair out of her eyes as she flopped down into her chair. He could see she had had to put up quite a fight to keep the case.

'We'll really be under the spotlight, boss, won't we? Maitland will be waiting to see us trip up. The press'll be breathing down our necks and the brass will be all over it.'

Gawn nodded. She didn't need him to tell her all that. She was only too aware of it.

'Go home, Paul. Enjoy a night with Kerri and the kids. There's not much we can do until our German colleague arrives on Monday. By the way, can you pick him up, please? He's arriving at 8am from Heathrow.'

Maxwell was careful not to sigh out loud although maybe his expression would have given him away if Gawn had been looking at him. That would mean another early start on Monday morning to get to the airport and probably more complaints from Kerri.

Almost as an afterthought she added, 'How did it go with the PM? Was Munroe able to come up with anything new?'

'Nothing much new and nothing much to help us. Tall, strong murderer but could be male or female. Right-handed. Really cuts down our suspects... if we had any.'

'I've been thinking about that. We need to take another look at our friend Lucy. She's just about tall enough and appearances can be deceptive. She could be stronger than she looks. Is she just a witness who essentially saw nothing or could she have been the killer?'

Maxwell's voice was incredulous. 'Lucy!' He pictured the slight girl who had turned pale at the suggestion that someone might have been lurking in the bushes. He couldn't see her as a killer.

'OK. OK. We don't get many murders like this committed by women. Domestic stabbings, yes, but not strangers in public places. If he was a stranger.' She emphasised the word 'if'. 'We need to find something that links them. Monday, we start over and you and I will have another go at the lovely Lucy.'

Chapter 15

He hadn't really registered her properly at the park. He had seen her, of course. Cursed her for even being there but he hadn't recognised who she was then. His focus had been only on the girl; the one he had been waiting for. The jogger had been a distraction which had cost him his prey. It was only later that he had realised who she was. He had watched as she arrived at the park, taking charge, issuing orders, every inch the boss. Later he watched her on television, on the news report, as she left the park refusing to answer questions. She looked different by then, of course. The tracksuit was gone, replaced with a stylish business suit, her hair no longer tied back carelessly in a ponytail which had swung rhythmically from side to side as she ran. Her clothes were every bit as fashionable as the girl's and her perfume… he could only luxuriate in the idea of being close enough to her so that he could take deep breaths of its fragrance. Sometimes he had to be so careful walking through department stores as he passed the perfume counters. He knew the smells could trigger his almost insatiable desires, a visceral response which threatened to overwhelm him.

Now he imagined her scent and what it would be like to run his fingers through her burnished hair. He imagined caressing her porcelain-like neck, running his long cold fingers down her smooth skin even colder, like the perfume bottles. He felt a rush of blood to every part of his body suffusing him with a sense of superhuman power as he imagined the taste as he would lick her face and kiss her unresponsive dead lips. Gawn. He loved her name, so unusual, like her, and he rolled it around on his tongue, repeating it over and over, enjoying the sound and the sensation as his tongue hit the back of his teeth and slid down to his lips. Saliva escaped from the side of his mouth and he wiped it away with the back of his sleeve.

Watching her would be difficult but that only made it more of a challenge and heightened his sense of the hunt, just as he had experienced when stalking animals in the wild. He had learned those skills as a child from his father. He had found out where she lived easily enough. The simple expediency of following her home had worked perfectly. She seemed not to have realised that she was being followed.

He had watched as she pulled into an apartment building, waited as she parked her red Audi in the underground car park and then an almost interminable wait until lights came on in a first-floor apartment overlooking the marina.

That much had all been easy. A hotel stood across from the apartment building and between them was an open car park. He didn't park there for fear of security cameras. Instead, he chose a space in the main car park beside a motorhome charging point. When the amorous couples and noisy twenty-somethings had discarded their fast-food wrappers and roared off for the night, there were still a couple of empty cars and the motorhome so he reckoned he would not attract attention. He had sat in the car until his feet were so chilled, he lost feeling in them. Just to know he was so close was a thrill. He barely slept, savouring her nearness and allowing the ecstasy of anticipation to bring him to a climax and slowly quench his longings.

In the morning, as he drove back to the city, his mind explored how he could maintain his vigil without being discovered. There was no lush shrubbery here to hide in. He needed to find somewhere he could use as his lair. He considered an abandoned control tower at the end of the pier, but the floor was rotten and full of gaps. The view from the tower would be perfect but it was just too dangerous; a potential trap for him. Then it came to him — the marina. He was sure it would be easy to break into one of the yachts moored in front of her building. The weather was so changeable, holidays were over and apart from the odd weekend the boats probably sat unattended. He would have to check out the position of any security cameras and work out where he could park his car — near enough to be quickly available but not too near so that it would be noticed by any nosey neighbours. If he went on board late at night and left early in the morning he should be safe enough from discovery. Anyhow it was worth taking the chance to be so close to her; to be able to watch her all night.

Most of Friday passed in an ecstasy of anticipation. He spent time researching the marina and the boats in their moorings. It was amazing what he could find out without even making a phone call. Thank God for the internet. Tonight would be his first night of watching her. He had selected a medium-size yacht, the *Luscious Lady*, as his base. What an appropriate name, he thought. Its owner had posted a message on the internet that it was for sale, but he would be out of the country until the end of the month if anyone wanted to arrange to view it. It was moored tight up to the walkway directly across from her balcony. Perfect.

As twilight was beginning to fall, he went on board carrying his supplies, making sure to avoid direct line of sight of the security cameras. Experience had taught him that he should merely walk on board as if he owned the yacht, not try to slip in furtively which might only arouse suspicion. His most precious cargo, his newly purchased high-powered night-sight binoculars, were safely stashed within his bag of groceries. With them he would have a perfect view of Gawn's apartment, day or night. Please God she did not draw her curtains.

Just before dawn on Saturday morning, as he lay naked on the bunk watching through the narrow window, all his unspoken prayers were answered. He saw the light turn on in her apartment. She threw the curtains fully open with, as she thought, no one to see in from the darkness of the lough outside her window. She leant against her balcony railing enjoying the peaceful start to her day. She was covered only in a skimpy towel, hair wet and tousled from the shower, beads of water glistening on her face. He imagined their naked bodies intertwined, skin against skin. He felt the pain of his arousal and moaned aloud unable to control his response. It was the first time he had realised how little different he was from the tiny insects he had dissected at school – all primitive beings. Those insects he could so easily have obliterated under foot in the park.

The lurker was not sure how long he could sustain this ecstasy of just watching; of simply imagining. Soon it would be like it had been with all the others. Soon, soon he would need to touch, to caress, to *possess that body and that spirit. Soon, Gawn. Soon. I promise, soon.*

Chapter 16

The weekend had gone by as weekends always do. Gawn had made plans to do all kinds of things – a visit to the local library, maybe coffee out at a local café, some housework although she had a cleaning lady who would be there on Tuesday as usual to restore everything to its freshly-polished best. What she had not intended to do was think about the Weil case. At all. But, of course, she did. Her mind was awash with possibilities, some of them, like having the case taken over by Maitland and Organised Crime, very unwelcome.

She speculated about the German officer who was arriving on Monday morning. She wondered what Schneider would look like. He had sounded a little brusque on the phone but having to converse in a foreign language often did that to people. Gawn was glad his English was so good. Her German, after a deployment there, was fair. She could hold a conversation but she was glad not to have to dredge it up now. Schneider's English was, as she had found with many Germans, tinged with a slight American accent from the number of American troops in the country and the influence of American TV shows.

Having risen at her usual early hour, even though it was Saturday, by 10am, feeling the need to be doing something, anything, Gawn decided to indulge her interest in art. She had been watching a local auction site online. It would take her mind off the case to go along and watch the bidding in person. She might even put in a bid or two herself. She changed into a casual outfit of designer jeans, a tight-fitting cashmere jumper and white leather trainers. It was still mild enough not to need a heavy coat, so she picked up a navy tweed jacket, draped her favourite Gucci scarf around her shoulders and headed to her car. Belfast was busy but there were spaces in the multi-storey car park near City Hall and more importantly near the auction room which was her destination.

The unmistakable smell of musty old furniture mixed with polish assailed her nostrils as soon as she walked in from the street, through the double doors and across the familiar checkerboard hallway. A flight of wooden stairs, with dips worn by years of feet making this upward pilgrimage, led to an outer office. It was busy and Gawn had to wait her turn to register so that she could bid if she saw something she fancied. She was already known to the staff having bought several pieces of art and some antique furniture in the past, so the process was smooth and speedy.

The auction room was quite full with some people sitting and others choosing to stand to get a good position where they could be easily spotted by the auctioneer. Men and women of various ages lounged against the walls either consulting their catalogues or chatting quietly, waiting for the auction to begin. There was a buzz of anticipation, pages turning, and people readying themselves to place their bids hoping for a bargain.

Gawn managed to find a seat at the back of the room near the high windows and glanced through her catalogue as she waited for the proceedings to begin. She quickly identified the two items she was interested in. They were not coming up until later. One was a nineteenth-century watercolour of a County Antrim countryside scene. The other was a piece of more modern art by a new local up-and-coming painter, Jonty Boal. She had met him a few months back at a gallery opening she had attended in the Cathedral Quarter.

The gallery was just down the street from The John Hewitt bar where she enjoyed the occasional glass of gin and listening to local musicians. That was where she had first heard of Boal's exhibition and, on a whim, had gone along. He had been there in person and they had chatted for a while. He was easy to talk to. He seemed like a fascinating character, older than she had anticipated. He was taller than she had expected too and his fashion sense reflected his artistic bent with a garish floral shirt teamed with mauve and black striped trousers. He had been wearing his trademark pork pie hat which he used as part of his signature on all his paintings. His work was bright and a bit garish too, not her usual style of painting but there was something vibrant and appealing about it. She didn't really have anything else like it and was unsure whether it would suit the décor in her home or if she could live with it. The piece for sale today was called *Perfume bottle with flower* and featured a blue elongated scent bottle with a red rose lying by its side and a streak of red flowing from it. It was number five in a series of 10 paintings featuring perfume bottles.

The auctioneer, complete with pink carnation in his lapel and a flamboyant matching pink silk tie, took his place on the podium. Gawn let her mind wander as the first few items went under the hammer. They didn't interest her. The auctioneer's patter faded to the edges of her consciousness as she gazed out of the high window beside her. All she could see was a patch of grey sky and the tip of the spire on nearby St Malachy's Church. As she moved her head to check her catalogue, her eye was caught by a tall man at the other side of the room half hidden by a pillar. She could only see his back, but it was the fedora he was wearing that made her take notice. The one person she knew who wore one was Dr York. Could it be him? That would be some coincidence. She decided to move position to where she would be able to see the man's face clearly.

She stood up and moved up the room staying close to the side wall.

Before she reached her target, the auctioneer announced item 208. That was the perfume bottle painting. He went on to say that they were pleased to have the artist himself with them. She noticed Boal dressed today in an ordinary suit but with his famous hat perched on his head standing near the door looking embarrassed at having been singled out. She realised that he was rather a nondescript looking man without his outlandish clothes. He could blend into any crowd. The painting had a reserve price of £1,000 and that was quickly reached. There seemed to be two people in the room bidding although she wasn't quick enough to identify who they were. Gawn waited, not wanting to tip her hand too soon. Eventually the bidding reached £1300. She had decided that her limit would be £1500. She would put in a bid. She raised her catalogue and no one in the room responded to it. It looked like she was going to get it.

'We have an internet bid of £2000.'

Gawn was disappointed to hear the auctioneer's words.

'I'm looking for £2100.' Pause. Gawn liked it, but not that much. 'Then 2000 going once… going twice… sold to our internet bidder for £2000.'

'Ah well, you win some, you lose some, eh, Chief Inspector?'

Gawn jumped; she was surprised to see Al Munroe materialise beside her. He touched the rim of his hat to her in an old-fashioned gesture of respect. He had obviously been standing somewhere at the back of the room, somewhere behind her. She hadn't noticed him and was slightly thrown that he could have been watching her for some time. To bump into one acquaintance at the auction was not particularly surprising given that Belfast was small and the kind of people who frequented art auctions would further limit the pool of possible attendees but to come across two was quite a coincidence. It made her wary. *If* the other man was York, of course.

'I didn't know you were interested in art, Al.'

'Just a wee hobby.'

At that point, she noticed that the tall man she had spotted earlier walked out from behind the pillar and turn to make his way outside. It *was* York. She could see his face clearly now. What were the chances of him turning up here today?

Munroe had noticed her interest in the exiting figure.

'I think that was one of the people bidding against you. Well, I'll not hold you up. Places to go; things to do. Bad luck about the painting. Good day, Chief Inspector.'

With a nod and another tip of his hat, Munroe was gone, following York out of the room. Gawn found herself wondering what to do next. Unlike Munroe, she had no places to go and things to do. She had decided she would forego the watercolour painting. She had enough of them already. She wasn't going to start following York around and she didn't fancy shopping. Anyway, there was nothing she wanted to buy. It was still only mid-afternoon. Maybe a lazy end to the day would be the thing. Next week was probably going to be even busier than this one had been. She was determined to put in whatever hours were necessary to get this case resolved. A night spent relaxing, watching a movie on TV and then early to bed could be a plan.

Outside, Gawn headed straight back to the car park taking care crossing the busy street, oblivious to the fact that she was being watched... again.

Chapter 17

Sunday was the laziest day Gawn had spent for as long as she could remember. She was always an early riser, a habit from her army days, but because her day was clear – nothing planned – she could spend the free time all on herself. An unusual luxury but also a bit of a challenge. What would she do to fill her day? A shower to bring her fully awake and then a jog along the coastal path right to the edge of Belfast. Not that jogging was a particular pleasure anymore. It was a necessary evil. She needed to keep fit. She needed to keep ahead of her team. If they ever got into a tight spot she didn't want to be the one lagging behind, holding people up. In her army days she had always led from the front and she wanted to keep it that way.

As she dressed in a sombre plain black tracksuit with white edging and her comfiest running shoes, her mind wandered over other occasions when she had enjoyed the lure of exercise and clean fresh air. But it wasn't the exercise and it wasn't even the scenery which at times could be spectacular, that had been the attraction. Most of all she had enjoyed the company of Max as they ran together early on a Sunday morning. The cold invigorating air, the morning sunshine flickering through the branches of the trees, those same trees shedding their leaves to form a lush carpet under their feet. Their laughter as they shared some silly joke or the touch of Max's hand as they negotiated some obstacle in their path. But she didn't want to think about Max or about what had happened. That invisible scar was deeper than any physical scar on her body. It would always be there just like the scars on her forehead and abdomen. They might fade over the years, but they would never go away. There would always be a trace of them shaping who she was and how she thought.

The lough was glassy calm this morning as she ran along the uneven path dodging the odd cyclist whizzing by. She paralleled a huge cruise liner, its lights blazing even in the daylight as it moved majestically up to Belfast port. This was becoming a familiar sight, a bonus after the Troubles. She imagined the tourists sitting in the restaurant having breakfast and looking forward to a day spent sightseeing, full of anticipation and excitement. What would they do first? Head up the coast to the Giant's Causeway and join the others snapping their keepsake photos at the Dark Hedges? Few would head into Belfast until later when shops would begin to open. Had Weil arrived in Belfast full of anticipation with plans to visit the tourist sites? Somehow, she doubted it. His record suggested he would be here for a different purpose. But whatever it was, he certainly didn't anticipate being slaughtered in a park.

At first, there had been few other people around on her route but by the time she was on her way back towards Carrickfergus she met up with a gaggle of park runners and groups of power walkers.

As she reached her apartment block, the bells of the local Norman church were ringing calling the faithful as she had heard the muezzin's call to prayer.

Lunch on the balcony followed – the weather was mild enough for it so might as well. Winter would be long. She liked to enjoy whatever sunshine there was, no matter how weak. Some cheese and that delicious artisan bread her cleaning lady always collected for her on Friday from the local bakery. She washed it down with a bottle of Pellegrino. No alcohol just in case something came up and she had to drive. Then a full cafetière of her favourite Ethiopian coffee and an afternoon spent reading. She preferred non-fiction to fiction and avoided crime novels at all costs. Those clever detectives, who solved complex mysteries with their stunning intuition, annoyed her most. Instead, she happily lost herself in a biography of the last Russian Tzar.

She phoned the local pizza delivery and ordered a pepperoni pizza and curly fries for her evening meal. She washed it down with some of the shiraz from Friday. She felt she could risk the wine now. She didn't expect anything to break in the case before the morning with the arrival of the German.

Gawn expected to spend the rest of the evening plonked in front of the television, but Sunday night TV listings weren't very exciting so, almost against her will, she found herself ruminating about Dieter Weil and his untimely death. She switched on her computer and called up an interactive map of Germany. Bad Reichenhall was easy enough to find. It was close to the Austrian border just as McKeown had told them.

She then turned her attention to finding Staufen, where Lucy had said her parents lived. It took several minutes. It must be quite a small place. She was disappointed when she realised that it was right across in the western extremes of the country near the border with Switzerland and France. It seemed highly unlikely that in a country that size Lucy's path would ever have crossed with Weil's but then she remembered that although the dead man was from Bavaria, his passport had been issued in Freiburg and indicated that it was his place of residence. And Freiburg was only a short distance from Staufen. Fifty miles, maybe less.

She tucked that information away in the back of her mind and was on the verge of shutting the program down when a pop-up offered a special rate for visiting what it claimed was Germany's premier magical theme park ride – the Pirates of the Orient. The postcard from York's room immediately came into her mind. Her hand had been hovering over the computer mouse and she had been so close to missing it. Clicking on the link, she was taken to a video of a ride in a theme park.

She watched as a boat full of tourists of all ages was conveyed through a vast dark water ride with animatronic figures dressed as pirates. They glided past scenes portraying the pirates drinking, fighting, carousing. A mystical temple seemed to be their goal and the storyline told of searching for a magical dagger. Smiles were etched on the faces of all the tourists as they listened to the recorded story. The children especially were squealing with delight. It was your typical tourist fodder.

So, Lucy likes theme parks and so does Dr York. Not unusual; nor a crime. She closed the video content and glanced down the list of other links on the page. The one which referred to a huge fire jumped out at her. She clicked on it and read with increasing interest a news report of a fire at the theme park. It had happened only a week ago. Hundreds of firefighters had battled the blaze which had started in a storeroom at the Pirates of the Orient ride. Her eyes widened in excitement as she read how, in the aftermath, a body had been discovered. The dead man had not yet been identified.

Gawn trawled the internet to find a more up-to-date report where the deceased was named but couldn't find one. Perhaps he had still not been identified. She would be able to ask Schneider about this in the morning. Another coincidence? Was Lucy just unfortunate that death followed her around? Or was she a black widow type who precipitated murder and mayhem wherever she went? Of course, she didn't know if Lucy had even been there at that specific time. She was jumping to conclusions, using intuition like those fictional detectives she despised so much. But? Just another reason to have a further chat with that young woman.

Gawn shut the computer down. Her mind was whirling with ideas and questions. She wondered if she would be able to sleep. As it turned out she fell into a deep sleep almost as soon as her head touched the pillow. Outside the lurker was still wide awake. He had watched the light in her window being extinguished.

'Good night, my dear Gawn. Sleep well,' he whispered, imagining his lips close to her ear as he would lie beside her... *soon*.

Chapter 18

The Monday morning traffic heading out of Belfast to the international airport wasn't as heavy as Maxwell had anticipated. He had left home aiming to reach his destination just as the plane was arriving so he would not have to hang around too long. And it looked like it had worked. An orange Fat Albert plane was just circling overhead as he pulled into the short stay parking area. By the time he had found a space in the surprisingly busy car park, walked across to the terminal building and queued to get through the security check, he was pleased to see that the arrivals board was showing that the plane from London had already landed. He made his way to the arrivals hall and stood across from the luggage carousel to get a good view of the passengers as they came to collect their belongings. He wondered how easy it would be to recognise the German. Perhaps he should have made a notice with his name on it to identify himself and attract Schneider's attention.

The first travellers had already emerged through the automatic doors from the plane and were loitering around. Some, obviously businessmen, didn't wait to collect suitcases but headed straight to the exit. One or two couples and a small family group hovered around the carousel keen to find their belongings and get away.

Maxwell hoped he hadn't missed the German. The plane had only landed a couple of minutes ago.

Maxwell noticed a tall, dark-haired man walk up to the moving conveyor belt. What made him stand out was his black leather jacket, sunglasses perched on top of his head and designer stubble. Sunglasses in Belfast in October was a little unusual but so was the unshaven appearance for a senior police officer. It wouldn't pass in the PSNI for sure. Then he remembered Schneider had been on holiday so perhaps this was his off-duty look. Just as he was about to walk forward and greet his German colleague, he was intercepted by one of the dark-suited businessmen.

'Sergeant Maxwell?' His voice was deep and confident but there was a slight accent and a foreign intonation to his words. He seemed a little breathless. Perhaps he was asthmatic, Maxwell thought.

'Yes. Sorry. I didn't see you come through, Hauptkommissar,' the sergeant said sheepishly extending his hand. They shook and Maxwell found his hand held in a steely grip. All the while, Schneider's eyes were locked on him. He noticed their deep blue, a cold blue.

It was not exactly a good start. The man before him looked more like his idea of a banker than a policeman. The formal dark blue suit and the leather briefcase Schneider was carrying presented a very different image from the individual he had identified wrongly as a German policeman. His blond hair was slicked back not attempting to hide a receding hairline. He was taller than Maxwell and more sturdily built. His jawline was square like some comic book superhero and covered with a fine layer of designer stubble.

Still sounding slightly flustered, Maxwell introduced himself and welcomed the man to Belfast.

'Thank you, Paul. I hope that my trip will prove useful to both of us.' As he spoke, Schneider lifted a leather bag from the ground at his feet. A dark peacoat and a navy-blue mariner's cap were draped on top. Schneider donned both. The coat and hat totally changed the German's appearance. Now he could be a tourist or a local.

'Ready. Shall we go? I am keen to meet your inspector in person and get brought up to speed with your investigation.'

Maxwell wondered if he should offer to carry the man's bag but before he had a chance Schneider was already striding off towards the exit bag in hand. He walked briskly but his eyes scanned the various tourist posters lining the walkway as he passed.

'Ah, the Giant's Causeway!' he declared as he identified a huge photograph of the world-famous sight. 'I have not been to your country before, but I hear it is very beautiful. With many beauty spots to visit.' He smiled and nodded.

Bloody hell, thought Maxwell, I hope he isn't going to expect a tour guide, I'm right out of local stories and funny anecdotes. But Schneider was already hurrying on. It was obvious that he felt he had done his duty in complimenting his host's country and could now concentrate on work. He was not looking to chat anymore. As soon as they reached the car and he had placed his bag in the boot, he took out a thick file which he had extracted from his briefcase and sat perusing it in silence as Maxwell drove back towards Belfast.

As they headed down the sweeping M2 with a view of Belfast Lough and the city laid out before them like a child's Lego set complete with cranes, Schneider commented, by way of explanation, 'Sorry, Sergeant. I am just reminding myself of Weil's record. Your inspector sounded as if she is very – what is the word I am looking for – demanding? I want to make sure I have all the answers for her she expects.'

This man seemed to have summed Gawn up very quickly if he had deduced that from one short telephone conversation.

'Chief Inspector Girvin expects results, sir.' Maxwell felt defensive about his boss. He wasn't sure exactly why.

'I am not criticising her, Paul. Please don't think that. I too am a demanding boss. I get results. I would guess Chief Inspector Girvin does too.'

Maxwell didn't respond, simply nodded. He didn't know why he felt uneasy about this man. He had taken an instant dislike to him, rather as Gawn had to Dr York. Maybe it was just the fact he had been wrong-footed when he had almost missed him at the airport and had felt at a disadvantage ever since. Just stick to the facts, don't let it get personal, he had to tell himself. He's here for a day or two. That's all. He'll give us the information we want, identify the body and leave. Simple as that.

They both lapsed back into silence. The sergeant concentrated on his driving, Schneider on the file. He had just reached the final page when Maxwell swung under the rising barrier and pulled into a parking space near the doorway into the building.

'Here we are, sir.'

'Perfect timing. A very pleasant drive, Sergeant.'

Schneider let himself out of the car.

'We have you booked into a hotel about ten minutes from here, sir, but I thought you'd like to meet the Chief Inspector first. You can leave your bag in the car for now.'

'Perfect. Thank you.'

Fifteen minutes later, all formalities completed, Maxwell led the German through the office aware, as he was sure Schneider was too, of the glances in their direction, and the judgements being made about the visitor. The females seemed especially interested in the new arrival.

Just before they reached Gawn's inner office, the door opened. She had obviously seen them coming. She was smiling – a welcoming smile which extended to her eyes. She was pleased to have the opportunity to liaise with the German authorities and hopeful they would get some useful information which would lead them to their killer.

They had little else to go on at the minute. She held out her hand in greeting.

'Willkommen, Hauptkommissar. We're delighted to have you here.'

Rather than shaking hands, Schneider took her hand in his and held it. Maxwell would not have been surprised if the German had clicked his heels together and bowed his head slightly as he had seen German officers do in war films. Instead, he simply enveloped Gawn's long fingers within his strong grip, his tanned skin making her pale skin seem almost translucent in comparison.

'It is my pleasure to be here, Chief Inspector.'

Maxwell thought he held on to Gawn's hand just a fraction of a second too long, but she didn't seem to register it. Or if she did, she made no attempt to withdraw her hand. It was Schneider who released his grip first.

'Please, come into my office and we can talk in private.' She stepped aside to let him walk through. 'Paul, can you organise some coffee, please?'

Maxwell knew this wasn't the time to react or show how he felt about being ordered to get coffee. He wasn't used to being treated like an office junior. Normally, it was the two of them who went over cases in her office. Now he was being shut out in favour of the foreigner. If he hadn't liked Schneider before, he liked him even less now.

'Please, have a seat, Hauptkommissar.'

'Do we have to be so formal? Call me Norbert. After all, we are going to be working closely together.'

He flashed a warm smile as he took off his coat and jacket and placed them with meticulous care over a chair in the corner of her office. He picked an invisible speck of dust off his shirt cuff before sitting down. Then he crossed his legs in one languid movement, supremely at ease. He had the confidence of a man who knows he is attractive to women. Gawn found herself slightly flustered. It was an unexpected feeling for her. She could feel his eyes boring into her, seeming to be able to read into her soul. It was unnerving.

'Norbert. Yes. Then you'd better call me Gawn.'

With a slightly quizzical look the German responded, 'I don't think I've heard that name before. Is it Irish?'

'No. It's a family name. But perhaps we should get down to business.'

She was uncomfortable getting so personal with someone she had only just met and especially with a colleague who she was going to be working alongside. It was not her style. She preferred a more impersonal approach to her job, but she had to admit to herself that he was certainly attractive, perhaps she would even concede, many women would find him sexy. He was tall, over six feet. His shoulders were broad and his body looked as if he worked out regularly. She could see bulging biceps beneath the sleeves of his crisp white shirt. His smile was hard to resist. She could not help but notice his eyes which were a soft blue reminding her of the shimmering water off the coast of Santorini. They lit up his whole face when he smiled which he did often. His blond hair was slicked back but fell across his eyes from time to time meaning he had to push it aside in a gesture of impatience that it would not stay perfectly in place. Gawn suspected he always expected everything around him to be perfect. She noticed his hands. She had felt their strength when he had taken her hand in his in the outer office but now she noticed the long artistic fingers tapering to perfectly manicured nails. And she was sure women would find his accent appealing and endearing too.

Gawn shuffled together a pile of papers which had lain scattered over her desk to give herself time to gather her thoughts. She glanced at the top one.

'I'm interested in a fire at a theme park in Baden-Württemberg.'

Schneider's surprise was obvious. He had expected to be questioned about Weil and had all the details ready for her. This query left him momentarily speechless.

'Sorry. I should explain myself.'

Now it was her turn to offer a charming smile, this time in apology for springing the question on him. Just as she was about to launch into an explanation about the unidentified corpse and a possible link to Lucy, Maxwell knocked on the door and walked in carrying two mugs of coffee on a tray.

'Two black coffees, as ordered.'

He made his voice sound cheery but there was an underlying slightly sarcastic tone and an almost imperceptible emphasis on the word 'ordered'. 'I can bring milk if you need it.' This latter was directed to Schneider.

'This is perfect. Thank you. I do not take milk.'

The older man reached out and took the proffered coffee with a nod of thanks.

'Thanks, Paul. Join us. We were just about to discuss Lucy and the fire at the theme park.'

Maxwell was partially pacified to be invited to stay and participate in the discussion, but his expression never changed. His annoyance was still bubbling and he couldn't hide his surprise at mention of a fire. He perched on the window ledge slightly behind Schneider, hands thrust deeply into his pockets, clenching and unclenching his fists to curb the tension he was feeling. He caught Gawn glancing at him. She knew he wasn't happy but didn't realise why.

'Our star witness, who admittedly says she didn't see anything, so is not much of a witness, is a young woman called Lucy Armstrong. She must have just passed the point in the park where Weil was killed seconds before it happened. Weil arrived in Belfast on Thursday afternoon and the funny thing is she had just returned on the same day from visiting her family in Germany, in a small town near Freiburg. That is just too much of a coincidence for me.'

Schneider said nothing but nodded his head thoughtfully in seeming agreement.

'We have nothing to link them other than that.' Maxwell felt he had to defend Lucy. She was the one who might have ended up as a victim. He distrusted coincidences just as much as Gawn but he wasn't going to jump to conclusions. 'They didn't travel on the same plane or fly from the same airport,' he added to support his opinion.

'And the theme park, where does it come in?'

'Well, from our investigations we know Lucy had visited it some time recently, but we don't know exactly when yet. We also know there was a fire, and a dead body was found in the debris, and I wondered if there could be any link with Weil. We couldn't find anything on the internet about the body being identified or anyone charged if it was arson, but I thought you might be able to find out some more for us.'

Schneider set his coffee mug down on the desk and stood up purposefully.

'I have heard about the fire of course. It made the front pages in our local papers, but I am not involved in the investigation. If you can point me to a desk and a phone, I'll contact my colleague who is in charge of the case and see what I can find out.'

'Use my office. I have to catch up with my team anyway. We'll leave you in peace. Just dial five for an outside line.'

Gawn headed towards the door signalling for Maxwell to join her. Schneider had already moved around the desk and seated himself in Gawn's chair. Making himself at home, Maxwell thought to himself. He was lifting the phone before they had closed the door behind them.

Chapter 19

'What's this about a fire?' Maxwell demanded, in a harsher tone than he had intended.

'Sorry, Paul, I only read about it myself last night when I was doing a bit of surfing on the internet. You were picking Schneider up at the airport so I didn't get a chance to tell you.' Her voice was contrite. She knew Maxwell could be sensitive. 'It was at the theme park just last week on that ride that Lucy and York were on, the Pirates of the Orient. I just thought it was another coincidence and worth finding out more about.'

'Aren't we rather jumping to conclusions, ma'am?' The question was out of his mouth before he had thought about how it would sound to her. Was he criticising her? Well, yes, maybe he was, but he didn't think he was wrong and he was annoyed enough not to care if she didn't like it.

She chose to ignore his tone.

'I'm just covering all the bases, Paul. We have Schneider here. We might as well make use of him. If he turns up something interesting, then we can follow it up when we speak to Lucy this afternoon. She's coming in for an interview at two. In the meantime, check and see if Billy and Jamie have turned up anything yet to help us on the CCTV footage. They were still going through it last time I asked.'

Maxwell knew there was no point in arguing with her and, of course, she was right. They couldn't ignore the coincidences. They needed to be investigated and Schneider could help them. He walked across to where the older detective was hunched over his computer. Grant was lounging by his side, legs outstretched, hands behind his head in a relaxed attitude. He didn't see the sergeant approaching from behind and jumped, straightening up when Maxwell suddenly spoke from just behind his shoulder.

'Well, what have you found?'

Flustered, his face took on a scarlet tinge. He had obviously been daydreaming. It was Billy Logan who responded.

'We've got Weil arriving in the park on a camera at the corner of the main university building. He had come from the Botanic Avenue direction.'

'Same as Lucy then. She told us she was shopping in the local supermarket.'

'Yes. We've got her too. She was about ten seconds or so ahead of him.'

'What about anyone following him?'

'No sign of anyone, sarge,' Grant responded. 'Nobody came in by that entrance or any of the other entrances at that time – except the boss of course.'

'And there are no cameras anywhere inside the park itself?'

'No. You would think there would be to catch out the druggies and pervs that hang about it, but no.' Logan's opinion was clear. He swivelled round in his seat to face Maxwell as he continued. 'We couldn't find anything useful. There's one at the entrance to the museum but we checked it and there's nothing on it. We're going to check if any of the premises on the main road have security cameras but they were closed over the weekend so we're planning on going over this afternoon to chase that up.'

'Yeah, and we're going to check with private houses in case they have home security cameras. We've already watched the traffic cams below the gate and there's nothing there.

'OK. What are you waiting for then? Get over there and see what other footage you can find.' Maxwell's tone

86

suggested that they move quickly which they did, even Logan.

Gawn meanwhile had been talking to Erin McKeown. Having started the trawl through the footage to get a timeline for Weil, Gawn had asked her to pass that on to Logan and instead contact forensics and see if they had come up with anything. Unfortunately, the answer seemed to be no. As Maxwell had reported, the items found were ordinary, mostly food wrappings — chocolate bar wrappers, chewing gum, the normal detritus of human occupancy. They had reported that it might be possible to get DNA from the discarded chewing gum but as they didn't have a suspect there would be no one to match it to. It was just too expensive to go on a fishing trip testing everything for DNA on the off chance it would match someone in their database. The superintendent would never agree. Budgets were too tight. The only other find was the stopper from a perfume bottle. It might be unexpected but not particularly suspicious and they couldn't see how it fitted in with the murder.

'It seems a bit of a strange find when they didn't turn up an empty perfume bottle to go with it but it's not really suspicious as such, ma'am. Maybe it just got lost or left behind when someone sprayed some perfume. It could maybe have been lost in a struggle except there were no signs of a struggle.'

Gawn was about to leave it at that when she turned back and asked, 'Do we know what kind of perfume it was? Just in case it belongs to Lucy Armstrong.'

'Well, actually I do, ma'am. I recognised the bottle. It's quite unusual but I read about it in a magazine. It's French and expensive. The bottles are in the shape of a cat and the stopper is the cat's head complete with ears.'

'Well done, Erin!' Gawn's smile was only eclipsed by the smile on the younger woman's face. 'Now we have something unusual to work with. See if you can trace if and where it's sold here.'

'Yes, ma'am.'

As Gawn turned to face her office door, it swung open and Schneider beckoned to her across the room. She had expected him to take a long time getting any information. Was it a good sign or a bad one that he was finished so soon? He held the door open for her until she had walked past him and was about to close it behind her when Maxwell followed her through.

'I was in luck. I have been able to find out about the case for you. My colleague in charge of it was in the office today, so I was able to speak to him straightaway.'

Schneider sat back down in Gawn's chair behind her desk leaving her no option but to sit in the armchair across from him. Maxwell was outraged that he was making himself so much at home but he tried to keep his face as neutral as possible. Instead, he chose to stand behind Gawn in an almost defensive pose. The German seemed totally unaware that his behaviour was inappropriate. He was concentrating on a notepad covered in scrawling handwriting on the desk in front of him and was oblivious to the effect he was having on Maxwell.

'According to my colleague the fire at first seemed to be accidental. The Feuerwehr, sorry, the Fire Brigade, thought it was caused by an electrical fault, but they have just amended that to "suspicious". They now believe it is possible that the electrics were tampered with. That of course means they are suspecting that the fire was an attempt to hide the body found afterwards.'

'Has the dead man been identified yet?' Maxwell queried.

'Yes. Fortunately, although the fire was quite…' – he struggled to find the correct word – 'extensive and destroyed large sections of the building, the body itself was reasonably untouched. There was a lot of water in the ride as you would expect and that prevented the fire spreading to some areas. So, we have his name. He was Klaus Wörndl and, you will find this interesting,' – he nodded to

Gawn – 'he was an associate of the Schwarzer Adler group. Like Weil. In fact, the two were known to each other.'

Both detectives reacted. Gawn sat up straighter in her chair; Maxwell took his hands out of his pockets where he had been feigning nonchalance since Schneider had started speaking.

'Was he killed by the fire?'

'No. Our people say he was dead before the fire broke out. There was no smoke in his lungs. Cause of death was – what is the word? – ah yes, exsanguination.' He pronounced the word slowly, carefully, enunciating every syllable. 'He bled to death very quickly. His throat had been cut from ear to ear.'

'What else can you tell us about Wörndl?' asked Maxwell, eager, in spite of his feelings, to hear more.

'He was not a major figure in the gang. He was more of a messenger boy than anything else. It is possible he was involved in a kidnapping in Salzburg that went wrong. The ransom drop was botched and the kidnap victim ended up dead. My colleague believes his death could be the gang clearing up their mess and getting rid of anything or anyone that could link them to the kidnapping. But that of course is just speculation, Gawn.'

Although Maxwell had asked the question, Schneider had directed his answer to the DCI, putting the junior officer in his place. Maxwell was shocked to hear the German using her first name. He was certainly making himself right at home.

'But it does give us a possible motive for Weil's killing if he was involved too.'

Gawn spoke thoughtfully, almost to herself. In one sense she didn't want this gang involved because then the Organised Crime branch would want to take over. But why was he in Belfast and why did they follow him here, if that was what had happened?

'I have kept the best for last, as they say. Weil was one of the people they were looking for in connection with Wörndl's killing and the fire. They suspect he was there but haven't been able to prove it yet. Like your men, they are trawling through CCTV footage but, as you can imagine, with a huge amusement park there are many, many cameras and many hours to go through but his name kept coming up in the investigation.'

Things seemed to be coming together. If Weil killed Wörndl did that mean he was trying to hide out in Belfast and someone had come to kill him? Gawn's mind was full of possibilities.

'I think we need to get the identification of the body over with. That will move us one step on. After all, that's why you're here.'

At least they could get that out of the way. And get rid of Schneider, Maxwell added to himself.

Gawn stood up and lifted her jacket.

'I'll drive. Paul, can you get on to the Guards and check if there were any other interesting travellers on Weil's flight? Anyone that could have been following him. And phone the mortuary and let them know we are on our way. I don't want to be held up over there. Then keep on top of Billy and Jamie to get any CCTV footage. We'll be back by two for the interview with Lucy.'

Gawn led Schneider out of the office and down the corridor. She didn't speak until they were waiting at the lift.

'How well did you know Weil?'

'I've known of him for about a year, ever since he came to Freiburg from Bavaria. We came across him for minor stuff – like Wörndl. He was questioned a few times but nothing ever stuck. I would never have thought of him as violent. He was more of a talker; would try to talk himself out of any trouble but I guess if he was trying to run with the big boys he had to do what they wanted.'

The lift arrived at the third floor and the doors slid open noiselessly. Two men were already inside so Gawn and Schneider waited until they were out of the building and in her car to continue their conversation.

As Gawn drove, Schneider looked out of the car window and commented on some of the places they passed. He was especially interested to see some of the famous Belfast murals.

'Perhaps when I have finished my work here you could show me around Belfast?'

The question was posed casually, as if he had just thought of it. Perhaps it was just an idea he had come up with to spend a few days of his holiday in Belfast but there was something in the tone of his voice which suggested he might well have more in mind. Gawn didn't want to appear ungracious, but she had no intention of acting as an unpaid tour guide or getting personally involved with any officer on the case. As far as she was concerned, once Schneider had identified Weil's body and passed on any other bits of information he had for them, he could safely be returned to the airport to fly home.

'I think I'll be very busy with this investigation for some time, Norbert.'

Her tone was friendly but firm. She hoped he could take a hint and back off. It seemed to have worked because he said no more about it. In fact, he didn't speak at all again until they reached the mortuary building.

* * *

The receptionist was looking at something on her desk and didn't look up immediately when she heard the door open. Gawn started to speak to explain why they were there. Once the girl looked up and saw that Gawn was not alone, her manner changed. She smiled at the German as she explained that Dr Munroe was waiting for them in his office. Gawn might just as well not have been there. The girl had eyes only for the German. If she had known him better, Gawn might possibly have teased Schneider about his effect on the ladies.

Gawn had expected they would be directed to one of the viewing rooms where an assistant would take them through the formalities and they would be in and out in a matter of a few minutes. Instead, she now found herself being pointed to the room at the end of the corridor where Maxwell had met with Munroe. She too had never been in his office before but unlike her sergeant she wasted no time speculating about what it would be like. Before she could knock the door, however, it opened. The doctor had obviously been listening out for them.

'Ah, Chief Inspector, how lovely to see you again.'

His words sounded more like a welcome to an old friend's home for afternoon tea, than a business meeting between a pathologist and a senior police officer. Schneider seemed surprised at the tone of Munroe's greeting to her. Munroe's eyes slid past Gawn and came to rest on the tall man behind her.

'Dr Munroe, this is Hauptkommissar Schneider from Freiburg. He's going to identify the body for us.'

'We are all ready for you, Chief Inspector.'

He started to walk towards the door to lead them out when Schneider spoke.

'What a lovely collection of glass.' He indicated the illuminated cabinet with the display of bottles of various sizes, shapes and colours. 'May I?'

Before Munroe could respond, Schneider reached out and lifted a heavy blue bottle from the bottom shelf. It was obvious that the pathologist wasn't happy to have his precious glass touched. He was almost squirming in dismay.

'Please, Hauptkommissar, it is very delicate and very expensive.' He took the bottle gently out of the man's hand and replaced it in its original position. 'I have spent a great deal of time and money putting my collection together and I'm afraid I'm a little protective of it.'

The words were said with a smile but it was obvious that Munroe was displeased. He then almost chivvied them out the door in his desire to get them away from his collection. Gawn thought it all rather strange. She collected art so she could understand someone having a collection of something that appealed to them. What did surprise her was Munroe keeping it here in his office rather than having it at home and his reaction when someone touched it.

The rest of the formalities were gone through quickly. The pathologist seemed keen to get it over with as soon as possible and get them out of the building. Schneider had no difficulty in identifying Weil's body and the paperwork was completed efficiently so that it was only a matter of a few minutes before Munroe was waving them off from the front door of the building.

'I have often found pathologists are a somewhat weird type,' observed Schneider as Gawn pulled the car out of its parking space and headed towards the main road.

'Al Munroe is brilliant at his job.' Gawn defended him. She wasn't going to agree with the German although she too had thought his behaviour rather strange.

'I have no doubt of it. Where to now, Gawn?'

'Now, it's back to the office. I'll get someone to drop you to your hotel and we'll arrange your flight home for tomorrow.'

'That won't be necessary. I have been on leave, as you know.'

'Yes. We appreciated you breaking into it to help us out.' She glanced across at him and flashed a quick smile to indicate her thanks.

'I have decided to spend the rest of my holiday here in Northern Ireland.' Seeing a frown pass across her face, Schneider quickly added, 'At my own expense of course. I would not expect the PSNI to pay my bill. I will find a hotel for myself and re-arrange my flight. There is, however, one thing I would ask.'

Gawn wondered what was coming next. Was it going to be another request to take him sightseeing?

'I would very much like to watch your interview with this witness, Lucy, is it? I may be able to offer some ideas about her connection with Germany.'

It was on the tip of her tongue to refuse the request. Then she realised it wasn't such a bad idea. If Lucy gave them some useful information about Germany or the fire, Schneider might be able to help. There was no way she would let him get involved in the interview but it couldn't hurt to let him watch.

'Yes. That's fine,' she agreed.

Chapter 20

This time Lucy appeared less confident. In fact, she seemed rather subdued when Gawn and Maxwell entered the room. So different from the young woman whose eyes had sparkled with a sense of adventure and excitement when they'd first met her. Erin McKeown had been the one dispatched to reception to bring her up to the interview room, Gawn hoping that a young woman of around her own age would be less threatening. The detective had chatted to her about all sorts of mundane things as they walked along but had avoided any talk of the murder and the park. She had fetched Lucy a cup of milky coffee and then left her to wait for the senior officers to arrive.

The room was bare, just a table and four chairs, a tape recorder and a couple of posters. If they were there to brighten the place up, they weren't successful. The walls needed repainting, and the posters replacing. One of them – about car crime – was peeling at the edges, threatening to slowly wend its way down the wall. There were bars on the window and a long fluorescent light hung on chains casting a glare into every corner. The girl looked tiny and forlorn and very alone without her protector, York, as she perched uncomfortably on the edge of her seat, cradling the coffee cup in her two hands. She had the chair tipped forward so she rocked slightly backwards and forwards in it, her feet hooked around its front legs. She glanced at her watch from time to time even though there was a clock on the wall behind her.

Lucy looked up as the door opened and Gawn walked in, Maxwell behind.

'Good afternoon, Miss Armstrong.'

Not 'Lucy' this time. This was a more formal interview, but Lucy was not a suspect – yet – and she had not been cautioned. The interview was being recorded so Maxwell introduced the three for the tape while Gawn took time to collate the papers in her folder, all the while never taking her eyes from the girl's face, trying to judge what she was thinking. Lucy merely smiled weakly, looking at Maxwell, and fixed her hair hooking it around her ears. She had only glanced at Gawn sensing the older woman's more suspicious attitude. Gawn noticed her nervous habit of picking at a rag nail on her left thumb.

'As you know, I'm Chief Inspector Girvin and this is Sergeant Maxwell.'

Nodding, Lucy spoke but it was barely above a whisper.

'Yes. I remember you, of course.' Then, more confidently, she lifted her head and said, 'Yes. I remember you both.'

'You've been given the opportunity to have a solicitor present but as we explained on the phone this is just to get some more information from you as a witness.'

Maxwell decided to take over. It was obvious that the girl was a bundle of nerves which he knew from experience didn't mean that she had done anything wrong or had anything to hide. Often, people who had never had any dealings with the police were nervous when it came to being questioned in an interview room, while others who were as guilty as hell could appear calm and confident. It could be an intimidating experience. It was meant to be. The only ones not intimidated were the ones who were so cocksure of themselves they thought they could never be caught.

'Lucy... You don't mind me calling you Lucy?' He leaned forward towards her and smiled encouragingly.

'No. That's fine.'

She seemed relieved that it was the sergeant speaking now and half turned in her chair to face him and away from Gawn's direct stare.

'We're really hoping that you may have had time to think over Thursday night and maybe you've remembered something else that could help us.' Maxwell allowed his intonation to rise slightly at the end of his statement turning it into a question.

The girl paused before shaking her head decisively.

'I just didn't see or hear anything. I'm really sorry. I'd like to help but I'm glad I didn't see anything. I've been having nightmares about it all as it is. I keep imagining what would have happened if I'd seen him. The murderer, I mean. I don't know what I would be like if I'd really seen something. Seb says I might need some counselling.'

So, Lucy had been talking about the case with Dr York. Not surprising. The two seemed very close. Both officers had anticipated Lucy's response. She had seemed definite when they had spoken to her on Friday morning. If she was going to remember something from Thursday evening it would most likely have been then. It was just so infuriating to know she must have been within feet if not inches of the killer and could offer no help at all.

Gawn opened the folder lying on the table in front of her and extracted a photo of Weil.

'Have you ever seen this man before?'

She slid the glossy black and white photo across to Lucy and the young woman reached out to touch it but withdrew her hand just as it reached the picture, as if it was contaminated.

'Is this who you think committed the murder?' Her eyes were wide and her voice was shaky.

'No. It's the victim. His name is Dieter Weil.'

'Oh, yes. I heard his name on the news.'

'Have you ever seen him, Lucy?'

The girl took her time and, picking the photo up, she studied it carefully. With a disappointed look on her face, she set it back down and pushed it over towards the detectives as if she didn't want it near her.

'I don't think I've ever seen him before. Did he live in Belfast?'

'No. He comes from Freiburg in Breisgau.'

Gawn's statement was made in a matter-of-fact voice but she waited for a reaction. She didn't have to wait long.

'Gosh.' Lucy's eyes widened. 'Then I might even have walked past him in the street. My dad teaches at the University of Freiburg.'

The two detectives exchanged glances. Was she really so innocent, so naive? Didn't she realise there must be some connection between herself and Weil?

'Take a look at the photo again, Lucy. Think if you can associate him with Freiburg or the university,' Maxwell said encouragingly, pushing the photograph back across the table.

Ten seconds, then almost twenty seconds passed. Maxwell was aware of the movement of the second hand on the wall clock above Lucy's head. There was no audible ticking of the clock but the sense of time passing was palpable. The girl bit her lip as she concentrated on the picture.

'No.' She shook her head. 'Definitely not. I'm sure. At least, I mean, he's very ordinary-looking, isn't he? I could have seen him, maybe, but I don't remember. Sorry.'

Changing tack, Gawn asked, 'Did you lose part of a perfume bottle in the park, Lucy?'

The girl looked at her as if she was crazy. 'No. Definitely not.' At least she was sure about that.

The next question surprised her too.

'Did you visit a theme park when you were in Germany?'

The girl was clearly puzzled at this sudden change of direction. It seemed to throw her for a minute. Her brow furrowed.

'How did you know?' She laughed, a nervous giggle. 'I love theme parks. I try to get to Phantasia every time I visit Mum and Dad.'

'Was this before or after the fire?'

The surprise on Lucy's face was clear to see. Her reaction seemed genuine. Her brow crumpled in a frown.

'What fire?'

She pulled at the rag nail again and this time blood oozed out from the tear. She took a paper hankie from her pocket and wiped her thumb. Maxwell explained about the fire on the Pirates of the Orient ride and the destruction. He didn't mention anything about a dead body being found.

'No, that would have been the day after I was there, I think. Everything was fine the day we went.'

'We?'

'Seb and I. Seb spent a couple of days with my parents on his way back from a conference in Austria. He went with me to the park just like old times.'

'Is Dr York a family friend then?' Maxwell asked.

'Yes. My dad taught him and they've stayed in touch. Seb's like a sort of big brother. I've known him for years.'

Maxwell looked across at his boss. So much romance then, his glance seemed to say.

'Did you ride on the Pirates of the Orient?'

'Yeah. Of course. It's my favourite ride. I love it. I hope they rebuild it.'

There was something almost childish about her reaction. She was, after all, quite young and caught up in a murder investigation. It must have seemed almost as make-believe as the theme park ride.

'Was Dr York on the ride with you?'

'Yes. Thank goodness.'

'Thank goodness?' Maxwell was puzzled. 'Is it so very scary then?'

'No. It's not really scary at all. Even little kids can go on it. No. I said "thank goodness" because he managed to rescue my camera when I nearly dropped it into the water.' She paused and then went on to explain. 'I'd been shooting some film and it slipped out of my hand. It's very expensive. I could never have afforded it, but my parents gave it to me as a birthday present and I need it for my course – I'm doing film studies – so it was great his reactions were so quick. It just touched the water but we weren't sure if it had been damaged so Seb brought it back to Belfast with him to get it checked out. I must get it back from him, now I remember.'

Gawn recalled the camera she had noticed sitting on the mantelpiece in York's office. So, it was Lucy's. And it could have film footage from the theme park around the day of the fire, if Lucy remembered correctly. It would be worth getting a look at that.

'Lucy, we're going to be having another word with Dr York. Would it be alright if we get the camera from him and look at your film? We're only interested in anything taken at the theme park and of course we'll make sure you get the camera back safely.'

Gawn was at her charming best. Reassured by the inspector's smile and friendly attitude, Lucy readily agreed. As she was about to leave, Lucy threw out a casual remark which made the two detectives look up.

'I'm not having much luck, am I? First, I nearly lost my camera. Then you tell me there was a fire and then my parents' apartment was burgled and worst of all I was near a murder!' Her voice rose in intensity as she spoke.

'When did the burglary happen, Lucy?'

'The night before I left. Mum and Dad took me out for a meal. I won't be seeing them again until Christmas so we went out for a treat.'

'What was taken?'

'Nothing much. Some cash Dad had in his desk. The local police suspected it might be one of the refugees. There are refugees living nearby, you see. But I don't think the police were too bothered. It was less than a hundred euros. But my mum was really upset to think someone had been in the house and gone through everything.'

Gawn nodded in what she hoped was a sympathetic manner as she led the girl to the door.

'Thank you for all your help today, Lucy.'

Erin McKeown was waiting outside and escorted her out of the building leaving Maxwell and Gawn alone in the interview room.

Maxwell's first comment when the girl had left the room showed his disappointment.

'I don't think that got us too much further forward.'

'Don't you?'

Before she could continue, a knock on the door was quickly followed by Schneider's head appearing round the side.

'Very interesting. I hope I am going to be able to see this film.'

The German had been allowed to watch the interview from the control suite, an arrangement which Gawn now regretted. Now there was no reason for him to leave and every reason for him to want to hang around.

Chapter 21

They had phoned ahead to make sure York was free to see them. He had seemed surprised that they wanted to question him but agreed to meet with them. He had lectures until five o'clock, he said, but could meet them in his office after that. Schneider had been very keen to come with them, had pleaded to ride along and promised to stay silent. His pleas had fallen on deaf ears. Gawn had been adamant that he couldn't come but she had promised to share anything interesting which York might tell them that related to the fire in Germany and the murder there.

They left the German in the office trying to disguise his displeasure as disappointment. It was a minor victory for Maxwell that he was with Gawn while Schneider wasn't. Childish, maybe, but he enjoyed the feeling all the same. He didn't like the man and couldn't really say why. He wouldn't admit even to himself that he might be a little jealous about how Gawn was behaving around the German and how he treated her.

The main university building was illuminated by the low afternoon sun beaming down like a spotlight onto its imposing façade and reflecting off the tall windows. At this time of evening most classes were finished and the students back in their flats and halls of residence, so it was relatively easy to get parked near the law library and across from their destination. They were slightly early and Gawn was tempted to detour to the nearby Starbucks but decided against it. She didn't want to give York any excuse to complain about them being late and keeping him waiting.

They were outside the door of York's office at five o'clock sharp but, when she knocked, there was no reply.

Before Gawn could begin to vent her annoyance that he was not there as he'd arranged, they heard footsteps coming at a run up the stairs behind them and the lecturer appeared carrying a packed briefcase and a pile of folders.

'Sorry. I did say the lecture was till five. I had to walk over from the main building.'

Was there a hint of annoyance or rebuke in his tone if not his words even though he was full of smiles and apologies for not being there when they arrived? Maxwell noted he was not even out of breath though he had obviously been hurrying. It was the first time he had taken the opportunity to look closely at York. Truth be told, he had spent more time looking at Lucy during their previous meeting to notice much about the lecturer. His dirty fair hair was swept back from his high forehead and his rimless glasses added to the impression of a stereotypical scholar. He was tall, taller than both Gawn and Maxwell, so well over six feet but his lean build emphasised his height even more. Broad-chested, presumably with the obligatory six-pack – Maxwell couldn't be sure under the loose overcoat he was wearing – but he was obviously fit. He suddenly realised who York reminded him of – that actor in the film that was on every Christmas. Hugh somebody. He could imagine York's lectures and tutorials were popular with all the female students.

York juggled the files he was carrying while extracting a keyring from his jacket pocket and with difficulty selected a Yale key from the bunch. He opened the heavy wooden door and swung it wide open. At least this time it didn't bang back against the wall, Gawn thought to herself.

'Excuse me walking in ahead of you, Chief Inspector, but I'm in danger of dropping all this stuff if I don't get it set down soon.'

He flashed that smile again as he walked in front of them into the room. He crossed to the desk, now tidy and organised, and deposited the papers in a neat pile in the centre. Gawn and Maxwell followed him in. Expecting to see the same state of chaos as on their previous visit, the two were surprised to be greeted by a clear floor and neatly arranged bookshelves. There were no random piles and stacks of books and papers. The chairs were clear of any obstructions and a vase of bright yellow roses on the window ledge lent a touch of homeliness and colour to the room. Two filing cabinets had been added to the furnishings, no doubt to take all the extra paperwork, but it was what had also been added that brought Gawn to a halt, mouth slightly open in surprise. Over the empty fireplace, where previously a map of Europe had been hung, was the painting of the perfume bottle Gawn had been bidding for at the auction. York noticed her reaction.

'Rather interesting piece of art, don't you think?' He smiled, seeming to dare her to contradict him. He stood in front of it, looking up, admiring it, with a proprietorial look on his face.

'Yes. Indeed.'

She didn't know what else to say. It wasn't often she was lost for words and Maxwell was surprised at her obvious confusion. Of course, he didn't know about the auction.

'I was only just moving into this room last week when you were here, so it's taken me a few days to get it organised to my taste. I thought it needed brightening up a bit, so I bought some flowers and the painting. Do you like it?'

The latter question was directed to Maxwell.

Gawn wasn't sure if he was playing with her, taunting her, or was completely oblivious of her attendance at the auction and her attempt to buy the painting. Had he seen her there? Had he known she was bidding against him? The auctioneer had said it was an internet bid that had been the highest. In that case, how did it end up in York's office?

'It's not really my taste.' Maxwell offered his opinion as much to cover the slightly awkward silence that he didn't really understand as anything else.

'Please sit down.' York motioned to the two worn armchairs spaced evenly across the desk from the lecturer's own chair. It was obvious he felt himself very much in charge of this situation. It was his room. He was used to being the one in control here. Gawn determined to change that. They would play by her rules, not his.

Still on her feet, Gawn asked, 'Do you know this man, Dr York?'

No polite conversational foreplay. She held out the photograph of Weil she had previously shown to Lucy and placed it on the surface of the desk directly in front of him. She had the immediate feeling York was not surprised by this tactic, in fact he had been expecting to be shown the picture which only proved in her mind that Lucy had already told him all about her interview even though it had only taken place a couple of hours before and he supposedly had been busy teaching all afternoon and hadn't been able to see them until now.

He didn't reach out to take hold of the picture, merely glanced in its direction.

'I'm afraid I've never seen this man before.'

York managed to inject the correct amount of disappointment into his voice – not too much but enough to signify he really wanted to be of help but couldn't. That was how Gawn interpreted it.

'His name is Dieter Weil.'

'As I said, I've never seen him. Should I have? Is he a student here?'

The disingenuous question riled both detectives. Weil's name had been on the news. His photograph had been in the local paper and on TV. Surely, he was playing with them? Was that even a slight smirk on his lips?

'This is the murder victim as I would have thought you would have known, Dr York. He was killed inches away from your girlfriend and he comes from the same part of Germany that she had just returned from the same day.'

Gawn's angry reaction surprised Maxwell. He was used to her being so calm and in control when questioning suspects. Her annoyance had made her betray more information than she had intended.

York rose, a look of indignation on his face. His voice, when he spoke, was controlled and calm. Maxwell had heard of people speaking between clenched teeth but never actually witnessed it for himself before.

'By girlfriend, I assume you're referring to Lucy Armstrong. She is a girl and she's my friend, but we are not and never have been in a romantic or sexual relationship, if that is what you're implying, Chief Inspector. Furthermore, I resent the suggestion that we are, and that Lucy is somehow involved in this murder, and I presume you're suggesting I must be too.'

If the righteous indignation was an act, York was worthy of an Oscar nomination. But was the anger just a tactic to divert any suspicion or distract them? After all, Lucy was an attractive younger woman. Would it be so awful if she and York were an item, Maxwell wondered?

York's face had taken on a reddish blush. Maxwell noticed a vein pulsing in his neck. He lent forward over the desk, and bowed his head, so they couldn't see his face. His knuckles were white from the pressure he was applying to the desk. He straightened and bunched his hands into fists. Maxwell tensed preparing for York to spring into action. He was obviously fighting for control of his anger. He looked up, clenched his jaw and stared directly at Gawn. Their eyes locked, both determined not to be the first to look away like the game of staring each other out played by schoolchildren in the playground. He expected a reaction from her.

And he got one. Gawn was the first to waver. She turned away. She decided that the best thing to do was try to placate him. There was absolutely no evidence against him at all. He had freely agreed to assist them. A few coincidences were all they had. And her personal dislike of the man which she couldn't explain even to herself. If they were going to get his cooperation, she would need to diffuse this situation and convince him he was not under suspicion. She turned back and smiled in what she hoped was a disarming way. She didn't usually play games. She preferred to be direct.

'I had no intention of suggesting you're involved in any way, Dr York. If I gave that impression, I must apologise.'

It hurt Gawn to say the words but she needed to get more information from him about the day at the theme park. Getting him annoyed wouldn't help at all. He would just shut down, perhaps ask them to leave or refuse to speak to them without a solicitor present and that would get them exactly nowhere. He might even put in an official complaint which she didn't need.

'And Lucy?' He wasn't going to give in easily.

'Of course, Miss Armstrong is a witness. That's all. There's no suggestion that she was involved in the murder at all.'

York relaxed. The tension went out of his body, his arms lost their rigidity and he sat down heavily on his chair. He ran his hand through his hair pushing it back from his eyes and moistened his lips with his tongue, sighing loudly.

'You have to understand, Chief Inspector. It would be a serious matter for a lecturer to be involved with a student – even someone from another department. You must know how it is. No smoke without fire and all the rumours and innuendos. It could be the end of a career.'

Gawn nodded. She knew only too well of the problems work romances could cause and especially relationships with junior officers. She wondered if York had come across this problem before and made a mental note to have McKeown check out his time at Berkeley and Maynooth for any hint of scandal.

'Yes. I understand, of course. You're old family friends. I used the word "girlfriend" incorrectly. I apologise.'

York even managed a weak smile before asking, 'Was there anything else you wanted to ask me? I do want to help, you know.'

'Look, Dr York, I think we got off on the wrong foot. We really do appreciate your cooperation.'

Maxwell had hung back all this time acting as a mere spectator in this little drama. He wasn't sure exactly what was going on between these two but there was something more than a few questions at the core of their encounter. He watched fascinated.

Gawn stepped forward and sat down in the chair beside Maxwell. She leant back and crossed her legs trying to look relaxed although she felt anything but it. For no reason he could explain, an image of Sharon Stone in *Basic Instinct* which he and Kerri had watched on TV at the weekend came into Maxwell's head. He glanced at York and caught a look on his face which left him wondering if somehow, he had shared the same thought.

'Dr York, I'd like to ask you about the trip you took to Phantasia Theme Park with Miss Armstrong.'

Gawn got the impression he had been expecting this topic to come up. Lucy again, she thought. York said nothing but held her stare as he waited for a question to follow.

'She told us that the two of you went on the Pirates of the Orient ride.'

York smiled at the memory. 'She's loved that ride for as long as I can remember. No way was she going to miss it even though we had to queue for nearly an hour.' A warmth came into his voice as he remembered their trip. He visibly relaxed.

'Did you happen to notice anything out of the ordinary on the ride?'

York's face crumpled into a frown as if he seemed to be concentrating, trying his best to recall something to help them.

'I think, it was pretty much just as normal. They might have put in one or two new figures into the sets but nothing out of the ordinary happened as far as I was aware.'

Maxwell leaned forward in his chair so that he was almost touching the desk in his eagerness.

'Can you describe the new figures, doctor?'

'I said they might, Sergeant. It's a couple of years since I've been there. I just had the impression there were more figures than I remembered being there before. I'm not sure but if you pushed me, I'd say there was a snake charmer that I can't remember ever having seen before and maybe a drunken pirate in the market scene but they might have just moved them around a bit.' He smiled like a little boy who expects a reward for getting the correct answer. 'Oh, and of course, I got a bit distracted when Lucy dropped her camera.'

'Yes. Miss Armstrong told us about your catch. I believe you still have the camera, Dr York.'

'Yes. I got it checked over in town just to make sure it was OK. They said it was fine and the SD card hadn't been damaged so she shouldn't have lost anything.'

As he spoke, he rose and walked across to the fireplace. He moved the postcard Gawn had read on her previous visit and lifted the camera which had been propping it up. Gawn walked over to him and held out her hand. For a split second, York seemed to hesitate.

'Miss Armstrong has said we can take the camera and look at what she filmed.'

'Of course.' He handed it over. She took the camera and immediately passed it to Maxwell.

'I think that's all for now, doctor. If we need to speak to you again, we know where to find you.'

It was said in a friendly tone, but the words held just a hint of something more. Not threat, not menace, but something. York felt it and Maxwell did too.

Chapter 22

It was obvious Schneider had been prowling the corridor outside the office watching out for them. He must have spotted them getting out of the car and crossing the car park. As soon as Gawn and Maxwell stepped out of the lift, he was there, striding over to them.

'Well, how did it go?' His voice betrayed his impatience and his eyes shone with anticipation.

Gawn had already told her sergeant on the way over from the interview with York that she intended looking at the footage herself with McKeown before letting anyone else see it. She wasn't about to turn what could be a crucial piece of evidence in the case into a home movie night. She would brief everyone in the morning. The rest of the team would have gone home already so there would be no difficulty getting some peace and quiet to take as long as necessary looking through it.

'We got the camera and I'll have a look at what's on it tonight. Then I'll update the team in the morning.'

It was a statement of fact and did not invite negotiation, but Schneider didn't take the hint.

'Two pairs of eyes are better than one. I'd be glad to help. I have nothing better to do than sit in my hotel room anyway.' He smiled but the smile lacked warmth.

Our German friend doesn't have Dr York's charm to get what he wants, thought Maxwell, enjoying the fact that Gawn was going to close him out of the investigation. He would have liked to stay with her himself and share the viewing but Kerri was expecting him home. Anyway, it was a price worth paying if it meant Schneider didn't get to see it.

'Can I give you a lift to your hotel, Hauptkommissar? It's on my way home.'

It wasn't of course, but Gawn had asked him to make the offer and make sure Schneider had no excuse for hanging around.

'That is most kind, Paul. Thank you. Perhaps you can also pick me up in the morning, so I am on time for the briefing?'

Bloody hell, he was being turned into a taxi service between the two of them. That would mean leaving home earlier in the morning to collect the German. Great. Kerri would be pleased. Gawn smiled at him with just the slightest nod of her head as if to say 'thank you'.

'I'm sure Paul would be glad to do that. Now get home and don't keep Kerri waiting.'

Schneider had no choice but to say goodnight and walk with Paul towards the lift. Gawn watched them until the doors closed blocking them from sight. She breathed a sigh of relief. She needed time to think and inside she was as excited as Schneider had seemed to be at the prospect of finding something useful on the film.

Pushing open the office door, Gawn was surprised to see an empty chair at McKeown's desk. She had phoned ahead and asked the girl to wait, that she had something special for her to do. She was sure the young officer had seemed delighted to be asked to take on something extra so where was she? Just at that moment, the door squeaked open behind her and the detective constable walked through clutching a plastic carrier bag. The aroma of fish and chips immediately filled the room.

Hesitating she said, 'Sorry, ma'am. I didn't have time to get anything to eat and I thought you probably didn't either, so I got us something from the local chippy. I hope you don't mind.'

Gawn could have hugged her. With everything that had been going on she had had nothing to eat since breakfast. A tasty meal of fish and chips, smothered in salt and vinegar of course, would be just the thing.

The two women settled down to the food, sitting in Gawn's office at her desk, eating out of the white wrapping paper. McKeown had offered to fetch plates from the canteen but Gawn had insisted it would taste so much better out of the wrapper. She was glad too of the opportunity to have a casual chat with the younger officer. She had already marked McKeown out as someone who would go far. She was intelligent, ambitious and could follow her instincts. Along with that she was hard-working, always prepared to put in the extra hours when needed. In many ways she reminded Gawn of herself, a younger more naive self, of course.

They chatted as they ate, studiously avoiding anything to do with the murder. Gawn heard all about McKeown's family. If she was aware that all the confidences had been one way and she had learned nothing new about her boss, she didn't mind. It had been a pleasant interlude for them and Gawn realised how long it had been since she'd had a normal conversation with anyone that wasn't about work. They gathered up the chip wrappers and empty cans and McKeown took them to a bin outside the building. Gawn opened the office windows to let in a blast of cold night air. She didn't want comments about the smell of the food from the others in the morning.

Her stomach was starting to flutter. It was a sensation she recognised from working on other cases and from those minutes of waiting just before setting out on important missions. This could be the big break. She could sense it. Gawn settled herself at McKeown's desk. The girl clicked the arrow to start the film.

It started off with lots of silly touristy stuff with Lucy and York.

'I take it that's Dr York.'

Gawn had forgotten the detective constable had never seen the lecturer. She determined to get hold of a photograph of him for the board. They should be able to download one from the university website.

A smiling Sebastian York, dressed so differently from any time she had seen him, filled the screen. His garish shirt wouldn't have looked out of place on a Caribbean beach. It was unbuttoned almost to the waist and his bronzed hairless chest was on full view. It had obviously been a very hot day because beads of sweat were sitting on his skin. His bermuda shorts revealed his tanned legs. Designer sunglasses – what else? she thought to herself – perched on top of his head, he was smiling into the lens. He looked relaxed. He was obviously having fun.

'Yes. That's him,' Gawn confirmed.

The two featured on various rides. They were eating ice cream, sitting on the grass chatting, sharing a huge hot dog, Lucy almost falling over laughing at something York said.

'Can you get us to the Pirates of the Orient ride?'

McKeown clicked the mouse once more. Without being aware of it, Gawn had edged closer to the girl's shoulder to get a better view. The two women watched intently as Lucy and York fooled around, pulling faces at each other and at the camera, queuing for the ride. It was a very different Sebastian York she was seeing. They were like a pair of kids just having fun. They could certainly be mistaken for a couple and Gawn wondered if York had been lying about their relationship; if there was something more between them. Then she watched as the two sat waiting in semi-darkness. The screen went totally blank and, for a moment, Gawn thought this must be a fault in the camera from being dropped in the water or for some reason Lucy had stopped filming. But the sudden sound of screams followed by a splash showed the film was still running. The screen came alive again with movement and noise and light. Oriental music was playing and Gawn recognised some of the sets she had seen in the promotional video on the internet.

'All pretty normal so far, ma'am.' McKeown's voice displayed the disappointment Gawn was feeling.

'Hey! Watch out!' A man's voice – Gawn recognised it as York's – made them both sit up.

The picture shook and went in and out of focus. The water came within inches until, at the last minute, the camera appeared to be swept up in the air.

'There!'

Gawn had noticed nothing but McKeown was pointing at the screen. She rewound and then froze the frame so that they were looking at a fuzzy image of a man crouching down beside a figure on the shore. She rewound and then started the last sequence again and the light caught and reflected off something metallic in his hand. A spurt of red was visible for a second before the camera was swept up and switched off.

'It's very fuzzy. I'm not sure exactly what we were looking at.'

'I think the tech boys should be able to do something with it. Maybe make it a bit clearer.'

'Can you print off a copy of that frame?'

'Yes, of course.'

McKeown hit a few keys and then rose and walked across to the printer. She lifted a single sheet of paper and walked back across the room holding the printout in her outstretched hand. Gawn scrutinised it closely.

'It's a man. Maybe it could be Weil,' she added, not totally convinced. 'But someone up to no good. Anyhow, get it over to the experts and we'll see if they can work some magic on it.'

McKeown nodded. It was clear she wanted to ask something.

'Yes, Erin?'

'I just wondered... Hauptkommissar Schneider was asking to see the film whenever we got hold of it. I wondered if it was alright to let him see it tomorrow.'

Gawn didn't respond right away. She considered before she answered.

'I don't suppose it can do any harm. Make a copy and let him see it all. He might spot something in the earlier section, people we don't know. But sit with him while he's watching and make sure to note anything he finds interesting. Goodness, look at the time!'

Gawn had glanced at the clock on the wall and was genuinely surprised at how long they had taken over their task. She placed her hand on the younger woman's arm.

'You'd better get going. I'm sorry to have kept you so long. Thank you for your help, Erin. I really appreciate it. And I enjoyed the chips!'

Gawn smiled to back up what she was saying. It had been a good night. She felt maybe they were getting somewhere at last. But more than that. She had enjoyed the girl's company and had felt normal for the first time in a long time. She had enjoyed the fish and chips – not just the food but the casual companionship. It was something she had not allowed herself to experience for a long time. Her life was essentially solitary eased only by her personal extravagances and her driving ambition. They didn't fill the empty spaces or lessen the loneliness of the nights. Gawn was smiling to herself as she left the building and began her journey home.

Chapter 23

It was crazy, of course. He knew that and he didn't care. A sort of overwhelming flash of desire, an uncontrollable itch drove him to it. He had never done anything like this before. But, of course, the other women had been strangers. He had not got to meet them, to talk to them, to get to know them as he had with her. He had fulfilled his fantasies and desires and left them covered in their own blood and his perfume, the empty bottle beside them. He had discarded them as of no further use, like an empty perfume bottle. Useless. Expended.

He still had the perfume bottle from the night in the park. It had been in his pocket ever since, never leaving his side. How the stopper had fallen out, he didn't know. But the bottle was still there just a touch away. He could finger its smooth coolness when he became agitated. He had even been able to enjoy its rigid promise of what was to come when he had been talking to her. He could sniff the remnants of the aroma of the Gucci perfume he had filled it with. It was his talisman to show he would complete what he had started. Now he would complete it with her.

From watching he had learned the entry code for her apartment block. His high-powered binoculars made that so easy. Now he had to decide when and how to leave his little gift to her. There was the little matter of security cameras. He had noticed one at the main door into the foyer. That would be difficult to get past. He could try to disguise himself, but he knew enough about forensics and technology to know what marvellous things they could do to manipulate pictures and determine height and weight, and people had even been identified from the way they walked. The car park entry seemed like the best bet for getting in unobtrusively.

From overheard conversations, he had learned that maintenance work on the building had been going on for some time and he noted a large white van with a painter's logo coming early on Saturday morning and leaving just before five. He thought it would be easy to walk in alongside the van without being seen and when the time came it worked perfectly. He waited until she had left. He would have to be quick. It was still dark as he knew it would be. She would always leave early; be the first in the office. He knew her character. He waited for the van, made his way in, hid behind a pillar until the men had entered the elevator and then used the code to get to the stairs.

He was careful to check for cameras as he opened the stairwell door and entered her corridor. There were none. He knew which door was hers. It was absolutely silent in the corridor. He was ready to run if anyone appeared but no one did. His plan worked like a dream. He was able to position his precious little gift dead centre in front of her door just touching it and no more. She couldn't miss it. His only worry was that someone else would spot it and he would miss the pleasure of seeing her reaction. He had also placed a micro camera on the door frame of the apartment directly opposite hers so he could see what was happening. He took a photograph of the package on his phone as a keepsake.

Making his way out was simple. He lifted one of the waste bins in the basement and walked out. If they checked the security camera, they would only be able to see his back and would assume he was one of the decorators. The nearby public toilets at the castle car park gave him somewhere to change and he dumped his overalls in a bin at Hazelbank Park, a small park overlooking the lough, far enough away that it wouldn't form part of any search.

Now, as he drove along, he could allow himself to savour what he had done. He was singing with joy. Stopped at a set of traffic lights, he noticed people in the car beside him glancing across and looking at him strangely. He would have to be careful. Don't get overexcited. That time will come but not now. He parked the car but before he got out, he checked the remote feed on his phone. There was the package sitting, waiting.

'I hope you enjoy my little gift, my dear Gawn. You will get the rest of what I have for you, really soon. I promise.'

Chapter 24

She was in a better mood than she could remember for a long time. It had been a more than satisfactory day. She felt that at last they were beginning to get somewhere. She had a few theories about Weil's death she wanted to discuss with Maxwell in the morning.

The drive home was pleasant. She enjoyed driving especially on a night like tonight when the full moon was low in the sky. She was aware of its silver reflection on the waters of Belfast Lough and the twinkling lights of the County Down coastline were almost magical. Soon the floodlights illuminating the medieval castle signalled she was nearing home and she let out a sigh of relief that her day was nearly over. She hoped she would be able to sleep tonight. She approached the roundabout and registered the colourful floral display which the local council workers must have just renewed. She smiled. Life was good.

She used her remote key to open the iron grill to the car park as she approached at slow speed and placed her car dead centre with mathematical precision in her allocated parking space. She lifted her bag from the passenger seat, locked the car and headed to the elevator. She was tired. She would forgo the stairs. The lift arrived almost instantly when she pressed the keypad and the doors swished open. The journey to her first-floor apartment was smooth and speedy. Stepping out, her eye was immediately drawn to a small package on the floor outside her door. She stopped abruptly, backing away into the elevator again. She could feel her stomach do a somersault. She had a postal locker in the foyer. All the occupants did. The postman and delivery men left the mail and parcels there. No one ever came up to her door. No one. Ever. It should not be possible for anyone to get through to the apartment entrances from the foyer without the security code or someone buzzing them up. So where had this come from and what was it?

She had just started to walk across to it to get a better look when she glanced down and saw that her hands had started shaking and she could feel her legs turning to jelly. She felt they would no longer hold her. She found herself, without conscious thought, backed away and crouched in the corner of the corridor. She put her hands over her ears but even then she could still hear the sound of gunfire and shouting. Screaming. Grown men calling out for their mothers. She could feel the heat on her face. For a moment she was transported far away to a time and a place she didn't ever want to think about. It was more real in that instant than the pale grey walls of the apartment building she was leaning against and the deep carpet beneath her feet.

Minutes passed. How long, she wasn't sure. As some of the overwhelming sense of panic started to slowly subside, she slid up the wall until she was in a standing position pressed tightly into the brickwork, its solid coldness giving her some sense of comfort. Her hands were wet and sticky, her mouth dry. With an act of will which strained every ounce of her determination, she approached a little closer to her front door. Not too close. Letter bombs and attacks on PSNI officers were rare but they still happened and from time to time memos came round reminding everyone to take care about their personal safety. She couldn't remember the last time she had received a warning. Her mind was working overtime just trying to concentrate and still her swirling brain.

There would have been a time when she would have simply walked over and lifted it up, carried it inside and opened it. But she had seen the aftereffects of too many bombings. She knew the destruction and carnage even a small bomb could cause. She didn't need to be reminded of the broken bodies, the distorted limbs. She could almost feel the gap in her abdomen and the hot sticky blood oozing out of it.

She had moved away from the door back into the stairwell to make the phone call in a voice shaking so much she could barely recognise it. Then she knocked on the door of the other apartment on her floor. It was occupied by a retired teacher and his wife. In their late sixties they were unobtrusive neighbours. They had exchanged the occasional good morning in passing and they had invited her in for a glass of sherry at Christmas, but she knew little about them other than their names. They were remarkably calm when faced with her news. Having lived through the Troubles in Belfast, they knew all about bomb scares. They grabbed their coats and left immediately to stay at their daughter's house until they got the all-clear. Then the Bomb Squad arrived and it was all out of her hands. She was just a spectator like everyone else. She was escorted out of the building right away. She explained to the officer in charge who she was and what she had seen. He told her that it would take some time for them to do their work and advised her to go to the hotel just across from the apartments.

She took his advice. The bar restaurant was busy. Cheery music was playing but not so loudly that it stifled conversation. Customers were enjoying their drinks and chatting with friends. Diners were finishing off their meals in the restaurant section. Everywhere was bustling. They all seemed oblivious to what was happening just a few feet away. At first, she went to the bar area and ordered herself a gin and lemonade. She was surprised to see how much her hand was still shaking as she lifted the glass to carry it over to a table. She chose one at the window where she could watch the comings and goings across at the apartment block and sat over the drink, barely sipping it; just letting the liquid moisten her lips. She delved into her bag and lifted out one of her tablets and swallowed it down with a chug of gin which took her breath away.

Other occupants were starting to arrive, refugees from the apartments like herself. She recognised a few of the faces but didn't know any names. They didn't acknowledge her, probably didn't realise who she was and that was just fine with her. She didn't want to have to face questions about what was going on or, even worse, face hostile reactions from people displaced from their homes on a chilly night because of her.

Gradually the customers finished their meals and drinks and took their leave shouting thanks and cheerios to the bar staff. The normal noise and bustle of the restaurant lessened and eventually only the apartment dwellers were left, waiting. The manager had announced that she would keep open for them as long as needed. But when it got to midnight Gawn decided to check in to the hotel. She couldn't just sit there all night although some of her neighbours seemed to be quite happy just drinking and chatting. It was an interruption, a disruption but also a bit of excitement for them. They expected it to be a false alarm, a hoax and something to tell their friends and co-workers in the morning.

Gawn was allocated room 24 and walked outside to let the PSNI officer on the perimeter know where she could be contacted. She was surprised at how cold it now was and found herself shivering as she headed back into the hotel. Once in the room, she did not press the light switch but walked across and looked out the window. She was pleased to see that she had a view of the apartment building from her window, even of her own balcony. She watched for a few minutes. Her eyes drifted over to the marina and she registered that the hotel, like her apartment, must have triple glazing as the tinkling of the rigging on the boats could not be heard although the wind had strengthened and the little boats were bobbing up and down in the water. There was little to see at the building except for the flashing lights on the police cars. All the activity was going on inside, out of view.

Tiredness was beginning to catch up with her. She drew the curtains and turned on the light. She flopped down onto the bed and slung off her shoes letting them drop to the floor and then began massaging her toes. Her shoes were her pride and joy but wearing them since seven o'clock this morning – no, make that yesterday morning – was a bit much and they had started to pinch. Then, suddenly, unexpectedly, a wave of tears just flooded over her. She had held it together for so long but now, try as she might, she was unable to stop the torrent overwhelming her. Loud sobs emanated from deep within her body. She was shaking uncontrollably as she lay fully clothed on top of the bed gripping the bed cover. She drew her knees up close to her chest and hugged them to herself. The room was warm and the pillow was soft and fluffy. Her head sank into it. She didn't expect to fall asleep, hadn't intended to but that is exactly what happened.

She was disorientated when she heard knocking on the door. For a few seconds she couldn't think where she was. Or what time it was. The bright central room light was beating down on her. It wasn't her bedroom; she knew that much right away but then she remembered what had happened. She propped herself up on an elbow and looked at her watch. Three thirty. Making her way groggily across to the door, she caught a glimpse of herself in the mirror to the side of the door frame and was shocked to see the tear streaks down her face and her hair falling crazily over her shoulders where it had escaped the barrette holding it in place. She wiped her hand across her eyes and patted her hair to try to tame it into some sort of shape. Only then did she put her hand on the door handle. She was careful to look through the peephole before opening it. She recognised the officer in charge.

'That's it. All clear, Chief Inspector.'

He smiled. Another job done for him. His night over.

'What was it?' Her voice sounded strange. It was huskier than usual. Probably the result of her crying.

'It was just some sort of hoax. Maybe someone with a grudge?' he suggested. 'We were able to X-ray it and see it was OK, so we have the package intact. I'll get it to the lab first thing in the morning.'

'I'll take it.' She held out her hand. He didn't react immediately.

'What about the chain of custody, ma'am?'

'I'll take responsibility for it.'

Reluctantly he handed over the small cardboard box, the lid open. 'I hope it means something to you for I can't think why someone would want to leave you a gift-wrapped empty perfume bottle. Maybe it was some kind of joke?' A quizzical look accompanied his words. Gawn's blood ran cold. Her mind was razor clear.

'Was there a stopper in the bottle?'

'No. No stopper. Does that mean something?'

She shivered. Whatever it was, it was no joke. She didn't know exactly what it meant and what sort of game the killer was playing but it seemed he now wanted to play it with her. This was now personal for him it seemed, and for her. Gawn didn't like games, but one thing was certain, she was going to have to play this one to win.

Chapter 25

All evening, as he waited, his anticipation had been growing making it impossible to concentrate on anything else. Then, when he had almost exploded with rage that she was so late, he had seen her car driving into the underground car park. He wondered how long it would take her to reach her apartment. As the seconds passed, he became aware of his heightened arousal, watching the screen on his phone intently. The package sat just as he had left it right in front of her door. He waited and waited. Just when the waiting was becoming unbearable, he caught a glimpse of the lift doors sliding open and Gawn appeared. She took only one step before she noticed his gift.

The look on her face gave him instant gratification, as long and satisfying as any he had ever experienced. He laughed out loud as she backed away horror-struck and collapsed into the corner of the corridor, her hands over her ears. The ecstasy of her suffering flowed through his body. He had never known such pleasure other than at an actual kill. He never realised inflicting psychological torture and pain could be so satisfying.

How long could he hold off making her his? How long could he derive his pleasure from her pain? Maybe a few days. No more. He needed that ultimate fulfilment. He needed to see the light fade from her beautiful eyes. He needed to feel the heat dissipate from her body. He needed to feel the blood flow from her neck and taste her skin as the perfume flowed over it. He had already chosen which perfume he would use. Gucci, this time. Like her scarf.

He needed Gawn.

Chapter 26

The package lay open on the car seat beside her as she drove into the yard at the PSNI Forensics Lab in the old factory complex at Seapark only a few minutes' drive away from her home. She had not touched the contents wanting to deliver it exactly as it was when the bomb disposal officer had handed it over to her.

She had watched as the police vans and cars pulled out of the roadway and a group of her neighbours, looking even more now like the refugees she saw nightly on the news, had straggled back from the hotel. Gawn had set the open box on her kitchen countertop and sat watching it as if it might still explode or offer some other threat. She knew she was exhausted and needed to sleep but only managed a few minutes of fitful slumber in between vivid dreams of explosions and giant knives and perfume bottles. Now all her nightmares were merging. The noise of helicopters filled the air and shouts and gunfire rang out. She could feel the desert heat and the sweat running down her face. It felt like perfume had been poured over her head. She had awoken with a start, a yell on her lips and the fragrance of perfume still in her nostrils. Her mind was in overdrive. He had been outside her apartment. He knew where she lived. She had never had a case become so personal; never had a criminal invade her private life like this. She had reached for her bag and dropped her tablets before she could take one, her hand was shaking so much. She had to get down on her hands and knees and gather them up off the floor.

She took a long shower allowing the steam to build up, obliterating her image in the mirror. Standing there, naked, she pressed her forehead against the shower screen and felt her tears merge with the streams of hot water. She hated this feeling of being out of control, being weak, being vulnerable. Girvins were never weak. Her father had been strong and had expected it of his wife and children. Weakness of any kind was not tolerated. Her brother's homosexuality had been a weakness to her father. In the face of terrorists Sergeant Girvin had never shown weakness until the day the bomb had detonated under his car and he couldn't be strong any longer.

Gawn chose to dress in a conservative dark green suit and paisley-pattern top. It looked sombre, fitting her mood and contrasting with the lightness of her skin, making her look even paler if that was possible. She hadn't eaten any breakfast, simply brushed her hair, dressed and applied her make-up all in full view of the box. She didn't want to let it out of her sight as if some shred of evidence might be lost if she couldn't protect it.

Carrying the box with care, as if it was dangerous of itself, she entered the Forensics building. She was greeted at reception by Joe Lester. She had worked with him on a domestic murder case when a wife had struck back at her abusive spouse, battering his head with a hammer to a bloody pulp.

'Good morning, Chief Inspector. I heard about the excitement last night. Is this the culprit?'

He reached out a gloved hand to take the box although it had already been fingerprinted the previous night by the bomb squad.

'I want everything you can find out about this, Joe. Fingerprints, DNA, anything and everything.'

'You'll get our express superior service. Don't worry.'

'How soon—'

Before she could finish her question, Lester cut in, 'As soon as we know anything, you'll know.' He smiled reassuringly. 'Don't worry.'

Much as Gawn appreciated his attempts at encouragement, she would rather he could give her something to help her find this bastard.

* * *

By the time she arrived at the door of the office, news of the previous night's events had already reached her team. Maxwell was the first to refer to it.

'OK, ma'am?'

'Fine, Paul.' Then speaking a little more loudly so everyone could hear, she said, 'It was a hoax. I'm getting it checked out so let's just forget about it and get on with this case. We have work to do.'

They didn't know the details and probably thought it was a terrorist-related bomb hoax — or someone with a grudge against the police. No need to let them know about the perfume bottle. She would share that snippet of information with Maxwell later when they were alone. The words were hardly out of her mouth when Schneider walked in. He strode across to her. If he had enclosed her in a hug, Maxwell would not have been surprised.

'The sergeant downstairs just told me what happened last night. Are you OK, Gawn?'

He took a step back from her as if he was suddenly aware he was in full view of everyone in the office.

'Fine. I'll say it again and then I don't want to hear anything more about it. I am fine. Let's get to work, people.'

Her tone, as much as the words, made it clear that that was an end to the subject. First to speak up was McKeown.

'I checked that perfume bottle you asked me to, ma'am.'

Gawn had almost forgotten that she had asked her to chase up any stores that sold the perfume.

'I'm afraid it's very high-end stuff. It's been out of production for a couple of years and nowhere this side of the border ever sold it. A few of the big stores in Dublin did but no luck tracing anyone who bought it. Sorry.'

A dead end.

'Our killer must have kept it for some time.'

Something about old perfume bottles clicked in Maxwell's brain.

'Perhaps we could ask Dr Munroe for his expert opinion seeing he collects old perfume bottles.'

'I'll leave that to you, Paul.' Then she turned to Schneider and said, 'Erin will take you through the film we got from York yesterday. Perhaps you'll see someone you recognise. We think we might have spotted Weil, but the tech boys are trying to enhance the image for us.'

Schneider followed McKeown out of the room. Gawn turned on her heel and walked into her office closing the door firmly behind her. That was something she seldom did, preferring to be available to the team; not putting up physical barriers between them and her although, God knows, she put up plenty of psychological ones. But this morning she just needed a bit of time and space. Finding the package had hit her hard. She wouldn't admit it to anyone, but she knew it herself. Making sure she had her back to the general office, she slipped a tablet out of her handbag and gulped it down with some water. Now she just needed a little time until it started to work its magic. But that was what she didn't get. Maxwell knocked and walked in. It was on the tip of her tongue to yell at him and tell him to get out. She clenched her fists instead, digging her nails deep into the palms of her hands as a distraction.

'Look, I know you don't want it mentioned but this has obviously rattled you. What do the anti-terrorist boys say?'

'It has nothing to do with terrorists.'

His face puckered in a frown.

'It was a perfume bottle.' Her voice was low, monotone.

'Christ, Gawn. A perfume bottle?'

He realised as soon as he had spoken that he had used her Christian name. Either she didn't notice, or didn't mind. She shook her head. Gawn could feel tears welling up and she didn't want him to see. It would be unprofessional. She couldn't be weak.

'It's OK. *I'm* OK. And now we know for sure we have a weirdo out there.'

'Who's decided to target you.'

'Well, yes, but it means he has come out in the open. Now we know to look for him. It wasn't some foreign assassin who killed Weil and headed straight out of the country. He's still around so that means we can catch him. I'm going to get the CCTV footage from my building and Jack can go through it. I want you to follow up on the perfume bottle.'

She managed a smile to go with the words.

Maxwell felt an almost overwhelming desire to rush round the desk and hug her. He realised how stupid and immature he was being. It was just a fantasy. Gawn wasn't interested in him. He knew that. He was her colleague, her sergeant. Nothing more. If she even suspected he had any feelings for her she would have him out of the team in a heartbeat. But none of that meant he was not going to protect her, not going to find this scumbag and make him very, very sorry he had ever approached her.

Chapter 27

Maxwell sat at his desk. He was reluctant to approach Munroe for help. He couldn't help thinking him a little, well, weird. The way he dressed, the way he talked, his whole demeanour. Anyone who spent all day every day working around dead bodies couldn't be quite normal, could they? That's what he thought anyway. Instead, he decided to do a bit of web surfing and see what he could come up with. This was more McKeown's forte and he had thought of asking for her help, but he knew she had other work to do and anyway he wanted to do something for Gawn himself.

There would be no point searching 'perfume bottles'. There would be hundreds, if not thousands of sites trying to sell him perfume. He decided to try 'perfume bottles plus murder'. It was a long shot, but it was all he could think of.

First up was a story about a nerve toxin used to try to kill someone in England. It had been kept in a perfume bottle. Then he discovered that there was a film called *Perfume: The Story of a Murderer*. Maxwell read the synopsis. The next heading down caught his attention: "Swansea perfume bottle murderer's sentence upheld". He sat up a bit straighter in his chair but then his shoulders slumped again, disappointed when he read that the bottle had been used to stab someone to death, not exactly what he was looking for.

He could find no crimes with a similar MO anywhere in the UK. What if they were not looking for someone just in the British Isles? Their victim was a German. What if the killer was from further afield, say even Germany? He regretted he had no access to the Europol Information System but that was way above his pay grade. He decided to try the National Database. And that was when it all appeared before him. His eyes widened as he read down the page. Not one or even two or three but four murders where the victim had been stabbed, drenched in perfume and an empty bottle discarded at the scene. The victims were all women, which didn't tie in with Weil, but then he had one of those intuitive flashes which Gawn so often derided. What if Lucy was the intended target and somehow Weil had got in the way? Someone could have been following her and got disturbed by Weil, taking his revenge by killing the German and dropping the stopper in the process.

Maxwell started noting down the dates and places of the murders, getting more and more excited as he read. The first was in 2010 in Venice. The victim was a twenty-six-year-old dentistry student who was there on holiday. The second followed two years later in London. He noted that this killing had also taken place during the summer months. A thirty-year-old mother of two, Monica Lacrois, was killed while out running early in the morning on Clapham Common. Her throat had been slit from ear to ear and she was found reeking of perfume. Then there was a gap of four years with the next killing in Berlin. This victim was younger. Just eighteen. She was found naked in the Tiergarten. A perfume bottle had been found beside her but, as they estimated her body had lain undiscovered for five days, there were no traces of perfume evident on the body until her skin was swabbed at post-mortem. Then just last year, twenty-five-year-old Ingrid Sorenson, a Swedish languages student, had been murdered in Amsterdam. Same MO. Clean, a swift slice with a knife across the throat and perfume at the scene. It had happened in early September.

Four murders. Same MO except three of the murders had taken place in the summer months, while the Berlin victim had been killed in late November. But even so some Berlin cop had made the connection and flagged it on the system. He had happened to be on holiday in London when the Lacrois murder had taken place and had remembered reading about it at the time. Then, when the PM turned up perfume on the Berlin victim he had joined the dots. Clever boy, thought Maxwell to himself. And now they had another case and he was the one who had turned up the connection. He couldn't help but feel a little excited that the case had taken this turn. Now they seemed to be looking for a pan-European serial killer. This would make the national papers… and his career.

Should he tell Gawn about what he had found? He decided no. He wanted to do a bit more digging first; come to her with more information; see her pleased expression that he had shown initiative. He would go and see Al Munroe after all.

* * *

'An unexpected pleasure, Sergeant.'

Maxwell had taken a chance and driven to the mortuary without phoning ahead. He was relieved to be told that Munroe was free and could see him straightaway. So, he had found himself lingering outside the pathologist's office once again, preparing to knock, when the door had opened and the white-coated Scot had greeted him.

'Thank you for seeing me, doctor.'

Munroe smiled as he moved back into the room and positioned himself behind his desk.

'I don't know what more I can tell you, Sergeant. I've already sent the PM report through to your boss along with the results of all the tests.'

'It's not actually about the PM, sir.'

'Then, how can I help you? Oh, excuse my manners. Please take a seat.' He beckoned to an easy chair facing him. Maxwell didn't sit. Instead, he walked over to the cabinet and pointed to the doctor's collection of glass bottles.

'It's about your collection, sir.'

Munroe first frowned, surprised at this unexpected turn of the conversation and then smiled, the smile of a fervent collector with the chance to talk about his passion.

'What do you want to know, Paul?' This was the first time the doctor had ever addressed him by name.

'How did you get started collecting?'

'Very simply, really. My mother always loved perfume and my late father used to buy her a bottle each year for her birthday. I loved to sit in my mother's bedroom and watch the light catch the bottles. They sent rainbows of colour around the room. They were magical to me as a young boy. Unfortunately, they were all thrown away after my father died but then, a few years ago, I was on holiday and decided to buy my mother some perfume as a present. I kept the bottle afterwards because it was so beautiful and that was the start of my own collection.'

The policeman listened carefully. He noted the tender tone of voice that Munroe used when speaking of his experience; the almost reverential way he referred to the bottles.

'Is it here?' Maxwell pointed to the illuminated cabinet.

'Yes, indeed.'

Munroe crossed to the wall display and lifted down a blue bottle from the lower shelf. Even to his usually undiscerning eye, it was a stunning shade of blue, graduated from almost clear glass at its wide base to the deepest of blue as it tapered and then finished in a circular collar. A stopper fitted neatly in the top and Maxwell could see no flaw in the glass. It reflected and diffused the rays of colour and reminded him of the deep azure of the Mediterranean Sea.

'The glass is called Sommerso and is from Murano, near where I was holidaying in Venice. It's in the Art Deco style.'

He didn't offer to let Maxwell hold the bottle but rather held it tenderly – there was no other word for it – in his hands, and the word 'caressed' came into Maxwell's head too.

'And the others?'

The pathologist placed the bottle back on the shelf, adjusting its position so that it was exactly in the spot to catch the light.

'These all remind me of somewhere I have been or of someone who is important to me. A few, of course, I bought simply because they are stunningly beautiful or as an investment.' He smirked. 'I wonder if you have any idea, Sergeant, how much a vintage perfume bottle can cost. This one for example.' He pointed to a tall unusually shaped bottle. 'It is over 100 years old. Bohemian Clear Crystal. Cranberry in colour as you can see and engraved with a galloping stag. I paid over £500 for it.'

'Blimey.'

He seemed pleased at Maxwell's reaction.

'If I was interested in finding out more about perfume bottles is there somewhere I could do some research?'

'There are lots of websites, Paul. I would recommend auction sites which specialise in glassware. You'll be able to get an idea of what's available, what they are selling for now and who's buying and selling.'

This latter was exactly what Maxwell wanted to know. The killer must be getting his bottles somewhere, if he didn't already have them. Just at that moment the telephone interrupted their conversation.

'Can't it wait? Alright. I'll come and sign it now.' Munroe replaced the phone. 'Excuse me, Paul. I'll only be a moment.'

It was on the tip of Maxwell's tongue to say he had got enough information already, but it was clear that the Scot was enjoying showing off his collection. Once the doctor had closed the door behind him Maxwell took the opportunity to look more closely at the bottles. There were twelve, six on each shelf. He found himself thinking, Gawn must be rubbing off on me, as he took out his phone and snapped close-up photographs of each of the bottles. It seemed like something she would do. His phone was safely back in his pocket and he was sitting innocently in the armchair when Munroe arrived back.

'Sorry about that interruption, Paul.'

'Quite alright, sir. You're a busy man and I've taken up enough of your time already. Thank you so much.'

Before Munroe had a chance to argue Maxwell had already made his way to the door. He had the impression the doctor would have liked to have the opportunity to show off more about his hobby. With his hand on the handle, he turned and said, 'Thanks again, sir.'

He was struck by the expression on the other man's face. He wasn't sure whether it was disappointment or relief or, could it be, fear?

Chapter 28

Seb was approaching Albert Mooney's Bar and Restaurant. He could see the glossy black façade with gold lettering picking out the name and when he turned the corner to the entrance, a group of smokers standing huddled around a table outside came into view. At least that was one vice he had never acquired. Ah well, good thing for them it wasn't so very cold this evening or raining yet either, although the TV weather girl had foretold of its imminent arrival.

Mooney's was one of the older establishments in the area and still very popular. He had been here many times before. He supposed it was his local although he didn't make a habit of spending the night at the pub. A glass of wine and a good book or, if he wanted company, a pretty girl to impress were his preferences. His friend Jonah had chosen this venue for their meeting.

Inside, the long bar counter was lined with customers waiting to order their drinks. There was the buzz of people enjoying a night out, lots of noise and laughter. The brown leather armchairs and squishy sofas in the raised area which fronted the main road were already all taken and Seb was glad they had had the forethought to book a table in the restaurant at the back. At least they would have somewhere to sit and the chatter all around them would mean they could talk freely without fear of being overheard. He walked through the bar and made for the restaurant area.

'Do you have a booking, sir?'

Before answering the waiter, Seb looked around. Most of the tables were already filled and it took a moment for him to spot Jonah in the far corner.

'My friend's just over there.'

Seb strode across the room picking his way between the tightly packed tables, excusing himself as he brushed past a middle-aged lady almost tripping over her handbag.

'You made it safely then, mate.'

Jonah Lunn's eyes sparkled and his lip curled with amusement. He looked at his friend with a critical eye – hair fashionably long, sitting on the back of his collar, falling forward over his eyes, trendy metal spectacles lending an air of gravity to the professor persona, heavy black jacket over a trendy collarless shirt and designer jeans, and finally black brogue lace-up shoes. Perfectly dressed. How else? He expected nothing less. He liked Seb but considered him a bit of a Walter Mitty character. Jonah knew all about Seb's background and was impressed that he had overcome so much to do so well and get to where he was but sometimes he found him almost overbearingly pretentious. That meant at times he just could not resist the urge to bring him down to earth. He knew how much Seb hated being addressed as 'mate' so took every opportunity to use the title.

Seb sat down opposite him on a red velvet-covered chair which clashed with his carefully chosen pink shirt and returned the smile. Jonah had known him for years but still enjoyed it when his friend was not perfect in every way. He was so used to Seb being the perfect scholar, the perfect tennis player, the perfect man about town, even the perfect boyfriend for his sister Anne but not the perfect husband. Jonah had never regarded Seb as husband material and thankfully his sister had realised that too before it was too late. He was glad when they had split up and Anne was now happily married with two kids, something he thought she would never have been with Seb.

The two men had kept in touch, off and on, since school. Their paths had diverged when Seb went off to Oxford and Jonah had stayed in Northern Ireland getting his English degree at the local university. When Seb had eventually returned to Ireland with a first-class degree, a year's experience travelling around Europe on a rail pass, a PhD and three years in California teaching at Berkeley, it was Jonah who was on the other side of the world with an internship at the Washington Post. Now they were both back in Belfast and it suited them to meet up from time to time. They would invariably start by reminiscing about their days at their alma mater, but then would pick each other's brains for whatever information they wanted. Jonah was now Northern Editor of an Irish paper and he had proved a useful source of information for Seb when he was working on background for his novels.

'I take it you haven't ordered yet?'

'Waited for you, mate.' It added extra fun for Jonah to use the epithet as often as possible. 'What do you fancy on the menu, mate?'

'If you call me "mate" one more time, *you'll* be on the bloody menu!'

It was said in fun and Jonah felt he had made his point and could leave it at that. He didn't want to push it. He knew his friend was generally even-tempered, but he had seen him lose it once or twice during their days at school and he was sure Seb would still be a handy boxer if he had to be. He had had a fierce right cross which had floored a lad two classes and three inches above him one time over some comment or other he had made about Seb's family, a touchy subject which all his friends knew to keep well clear of.

They spent a few minutes in silence perusing the menu. When the waiter approached, they were both ready to order.

'Shall I choose the wine, Jonah?'

Jonah nodded. He had expected that. He knew Seb fancied himself as a bit of a wine connoisseur and was happy to play along. His palette was not so discerning. So long as it didn't taste like vinegar, he would be happy. Truth be told, he'd have preferred a beer but let Seb have his little pretentions.

'I guess it better be white.' Seb scanned the wine list settling on a South African chenin blanc.

Once the hovering waiter had left their side, Seb asked, 'Well, what did you find out for me?'

Jonah realised his old friend must be really keen to get his information. There was no semblance of trying to play it cool. For whatever reason, Seb was obviously eager to find out about Gawn Girvin.

'What exactly is it with you and the lovely Chief Inspector, JS?' Jonah couldn't help but ask even though he could see that Seb was almost literally on the edge of his seat waiting for information. His friend must have a good reason for asking about this woman but Jonah couldn't work out what it might be.

'Just some research. You know me,' Seb said, hoping to distract his friend by adding, 'mate.'

'Yes, I do know you and you've never asked me to check in to a cop before. Have you heard some whispers about her? Is it something that I should know about? Come on, JS, spill the beans.'

Seb was horrified. Jonah was a successful investigative reporter. There had been cases of police corruption and all sorts of rumours about collusion and now he had put Gawn on Jonah's radar.

'No. It's nothing like that. Nothing like that at all.' He wondered if he sounded too vehement, as if he was trying to hide something.

'Then what is it? Tell all.'

Seb hadn't intended to be forthcoming about his interest in the policewoman but Jonah was leaving him no alternative. He was just about to launch into an explanation when the waiter arrived at his elbow carrying their starters. He waited until he was safely out of earshot and Jonah had taken his first bite. It all looked delicious but Seb was starting to lose his appetite. This meeting was not turning out as he had hoped. Best to come clean.

'Look, I don't want the info for work. This is purely personal. I ran across the chief inspector a couple of days ago and I was just interested in finding out a bit more about her. That's all. I think she's quite attractive and I might ask her out.'

He held his arms out in a gesture of openness and put on what he hoped was an innocent expression.

'OK. I believe you.'

Jonah chewed another mouthful of his food before continuing. So, Seb was smitten. Well, well, well. He certainly hadn't expected that. The great Seb York, lothario of his year group, used to girls swooning over him, now the one doing the chasing and chasing a cop at that. Jonah smiled. Perhaps his friend was finally growing up, interested in a real woman for once, not some pretty blonde he would discard after a week or two.

'I have actually met your chief inspector a couple of times. She's a bit of a prickly one, isn't she? Word is, she's a tough cookie.'

'That, I can certainly believe. What do you know about her background?'

'She's from Belfast originally.'

'Is she now? I thought I detected a bit of a Belfast accent.'

'Her father was in the RUC. He was killed in a bombing in 1995. That left her, her mother and a brother. I think the brother was older. Anyway, from what I've heard she was bright at school, headed over to England as soon as she was old enough and ended up at Sandhurst.'

Seb whistled.

'Sandhurst, eh? No wonder she's a bit of a martinet. What rank… no, let me guess. Captain.'

He sat back in his chair and waited for Jonah to confirm his prediction.

'Nearly right. Major Girvin of the Royal Military Police. Did two tours of duty in Afghanistan as well as a deployment to Germany. As far as I could find out she was wounded in Afghanistan but she's very private. It's hard to find anything out. She never talks about her army days. I could try to get some more info on that if you really want?' He paused and took another bite of his food. Seb nodded to show he wasn't asking him to do that. 'OK. When she recovered or when she left the army, she went back into civvy street, joined the Met and was in the Personal Protection Unit. She's a first class shot by all accounts. So better watch yourself, JS old boy. Try anything on with her and you could end up being shot.' He laughed at his own joke.

Further chat was left until they had worked their way through their main courses. A couple of glasses of wine loosened Jonah's lips a bit more and he offered some juicy tidbits he had heard.

'I can't verify this, OK? But I have heard she had some kind of a breakdown. An ex-boyfriend or fiancée or something was killed in Afghanistan after she had left the army and was in the Met and she took it badly. Had to get treatment. Was off work for a while. Then turned up here.'

'Is her family still in Belfast?'

'I don't think so. Don't know actually.' Jonah looked at his watch, stuffed the last of his food into his mouth and stood up. 'I didn't realise the time. I'm gonna have to run. I'm supposed to be picking the kids up from their judo club. Thanks for the meal, buddy. I enjoyed it. I enjoyed even more that you're picking up the tab.'

Jonah slapped Seb on the back as he made his way past him. Seb swung round in his seat to watch his friend walking out and spilt most of what was left of his glass of wine over the front of his shirt as he saw Gawn Girvin sitting alone at a table across the room. She was not looking in his direction and he didn't know whether she had seen him or not. Damn Jonah. He must have been able to see her from where he was sitting. Why didn't he say something? Thank God there was no way she could have heard what they were talking about. Could she? He had half-consciously noted a few people passing behind his chair making their way to their tables or the toilets. Was she one of them? Why was she here? Was she following him? Maybe he wasn't the only one who liked to play games.

Trying to be as unobtrusive as possible he waited until the waiter was beside his table, then walked to the exit using him as a shield. He paid his bill, barely looking at the amount, just throwing down three twenty-pound notes. It would be a generous tip, but he didn't want to be standing around waiting for change. He walked out of the bar without looking back but something made him sense he was being watched. Probably just an over-active imagination or maybe it was his guilty conscience.

Chapter 29

She hadn't wanted to spend the whole evening at home alone. She wouldn't admit it, but she was still feeling a bit jittery. If she had been sitting in the apartment by herself all night she would only have gone over and over what had happened. So, a meal out at Mooney's before she had to go back to Carrick had seemed like a good idea. She'd eaten there before and knew there was lots on the menu she would enjoy. She had taken her book with her – the biography of the tsar which she had half finished – and sat and read her way through her meal acutely aware that she was the only person in the restaurant eating alone.

But even though she was tired when she eventually got home, she hadn't slept well. She had tossed and turned all night. She was never sure which was worse – not being able to sleep or sleeping and being plagued by nightmares. Hopefully, the forensics people would have an update for her. She also needed to check with McKeown whether Schneider had identified anyone on the CCTV footage. The two had spent the whole day yesterday going through it and she had been glad to have the German out of her hair and made a mental note to thank McKeown for looking after him.

She was slightly later than usual arriving in the office. The traffic had been especially heavy. She had forgotten that there was some visiting dignitary, a royal she thought, in Belfast today. Some roads had been closed off and manpower had been diverted for traffic and protection duties. Most of her team were already at their desks and busy at work or at least pretending to be when she walked in.

Maxwell was the first to notice her arrival. He followed her into her office without knocking.

'Morning, ma'am.'

'Good morning, Paul.'

She noted his eyes which seemed to be shining with an intensity she had never noticed before. She just had time to take off her jacket when he blurted out, 'I think we might have a serial killer on our hands.'

If he had wanted to surprise her, he had certainly succeeded. Her face betrayed her shock.

'Are you serious? No, of course you are. Stupid question. You wouldn't joke about something like that.' She sat down and gestured for him to do the same. 'Tell me more. Why on earth do you think that?'

He recounted what he had discovered on the internet about the four murders and the link through the perfume bottles. He also detailed his visit to Munroe's office. Then he paused.

'Do you think I'm crazy? I mean serial killers are the stuff of American TV shows.'

'Oh, they're real enough, Paul. I have come across some before.' She shivered as she remembered one particularly gruesome series of murders of prostitutes she had investigated as a newly appointed inspector. 'But I don't think we should rush to conclusions. There do seem to be some similarities alright but I'm not sure our killing fits in. The others were all females...'

'But I thought we said Lucy could have been the target and Weil just got in the way.'

'That's one line of thinking, Paul, but we don't have hard evidence yet. Does she fit the killer's type?'

'Twenty to thirty, tall, slim build, attacked in a public park in the evening.'

'Pretty general stuff. What about hair colour?'

'Two blondes and two brunettes so not a definite pattern.'

'OK. It maybe sounds possible, but we'll need a lot more information on all four cases. We'll talk about it this afternoon and, if it seems a goer, you can present it to the team later and we'll work on from there. In the meantime, I'll flag up the possible line of enquiry to the Super. He needs to know. If it is a serial killer, we'll need more resources.'

She wanted to encourage him. She was pleased that he had taken the initiative and invested his own time in following up his ideas. He was shaping into a promising detective but it was a big jump he had made. They needed a much clearer connection. Before she had time to say anything else, her phone rang.

'Girvin.'

'Chief Inspector.'

She recognised the voice of Joe Lester, the Forensics expert.

'I have some news for you. We didn't get any prints off the bottle or the box. We didn't really expect to. Anybody organised enough to get into your apartment block without being seen would have been careful. But we did check it against the stopper found in your Botanic Gardens case.'

She waited. She knew what he was going to say.

'I couldn't go to court and say one hundred percent this is the bottle that the stopper came from. But… they're the same brand, approximately the same age – about fifteen years old we think from when that perfume was on sale – and they fit together perfectly. That wouldn't stand up in court, of course. A good barrister would run right through it, but I'd bet my pension they were together originally.'

'OK. Thanks, Joe. I don't know if that gets me much further forward, but I appreciate the rush job you did.'

'Take care, Gawn.'

'Alright, ma'am?' Maxwell's voice broke into her thoughts. It was what she had expected. The killer had left her a message.

'Yes. Fine. Now you've got a lot to do. Get Jack or Jamie to help you. Maybe Erin could help too if she's finished with our friend from Germany.'

As if the mention of the German had conjured him up, there was a knock on the door and Schneider's face appeared around the frame.

'I hope I am not interrupting?' His words were accompanied by a wide grin. 'Good day, Sergeant. I hope you do not mind that I made my own way here this morning.'

Maxwell had forgotten all about Schneider this morning. He had not made a definite arrangement to pick him up and had got too engrossed in his research to even think about him.

'I have hired a car. After all, I will need it to finish my holiday and see some of your wonderful sights.' He didn't seem put out that he had been forgotten.

'Any luck with the film, Norbert?'

'Yes. I have suggested a few names and we have taken stills from the film and a copy of the whole thing to send to my colleagues back home. I think Weil was part of the kidnapping in Salzburg and the murder in Phantasia Park. I would guess he was in Belfast to get hold of that film and your young witness is a very lucky lady that he did not get to her before someone got to him.'

Trying very hard to keep a sense of relief out of his voice, Maxwell said, 'So you'll be able to get about your sightseeing now.'

'Yes. I believe your Fermanagh Lakeland is very beautiful so I am heading over there. I used to go sailing with my father on the Wannsee so I am looking forward to doing a bit of boating.' He walked across and extended his hand to Maxwell. Then he turned to Gawn. 'Thank you for everything, Gawn. It has been a most pleasurable experience. I wish you success finding your killer.'

'Our serial killer.'

The words were out of Maxwell's mouth before he had thought through what he was saying and who he was saying it to. He had wanted to impress Schneider. Instead he had given away information to someone outside the investigation. Gawn would be furious and rightly so.

'Serial killer?' Schneider's voice held a note of what sounded like incredulity. 'You think this person has killed more than once. Have you had a lot of murders like this?'

Gawn did not give her sergeant time to answer. She tried to play down Maxwell's comment.

'It's just one theory we're working on. You know how it is. People come up with all kinds of crazy ideas.' She smiled in what she hoped was a disarming manner. 'Now don't let us hold you up. Go and enjoy the rest of your leave. And many thanks for all your help.'

'It has been a pleasure working with you. I hope our paths may cross again.' A smile spread across his face.

She didn't reply but merely shook hands with him, making sure to withdraw her hand quickly from his grasp.

Then Gawn and Maxwell stood at her office door and watched as Schneider walked through the room making an occasional comment to one or other of the detectives. He paused by McKeown's desk and handed her a small, wrapped box. She laughed and he kissed her on the cheek and then he was gone.

Reluctantly Maxwell turned back to face the DCI. Her face said it all. She was furious with him. He was aware of Gawn shaking with suppressed anger. Very deliberately she closed the door, not slamming it as he might have expected. Rather, she closed it especially quietly. He was reasonably sure she wouldn't give him a dressing down in front of the others, but he was expecting to suffer her wrath.

'What were you bloody thinking? No, scrub that. You weren't thinking, were you? Just wanted to impress him at the risk of information getting out about our investigation. What's to stop Schneider running to some journalist and giving them a story about a serial killer on the loose in Belfast before I've even mentioned it upstairs?'

It was a rookie mistake and he was so sorry he had let himself and let her down. He didn't say anything because he couldn't think of any words to say; any excuse to give. He was just glad that her back was to the outer office so no one could see the expression of disgust on her face.

'Wanted to impress the Kommissar, is that it? Bit of macho bragging? You've only got one murder and we've got a serial killer? I've had too many young men under my command playing silly buggers putting themselves or others in danger because they wanted to play the hero and ending up getting themselves killed. God, Paul, I really expected better of you.'

He had never heard her so angry before. Her look of disappointment dismissed him without her having to say anything more. Feeling like a puppy skulking off with his tail between his legs, Maxwell made his way back to his desk. No one made eye contact with him. He didn't know whether it was because they had heard what Gawn said – although she had kept her voice low and controlled – or they were all busy. He hoped it was the latter.

Chapter 30

Gawn had spent an uncomfortable half hour going over the case with Superintendent McDowell. There hadn't really been a lot of progress to report and he had voiced concern that someone now seemed to be targeting her. Eventually she had given him an outline of Maxwell's theory about a serial killer. At least he hadn't dismissed it out of hand. He took the same position as she had. They needed to get a lot more information before they could pursue that line of enquiry but he was prepared to let her run with the case until after the weekend to see what her team came up with. If no progress had been made by then, Maitland would be taking it over.

Back in her office, she had just bitten into a salad sandwich from the canteen when her phone rang.

'Girvin.'

'There's someone here asking to see you, Chief Inspector. His name is York.'

Gawn almost choked on her mouthful of lettuce and tomato. Surprise didn't come close to what she felt. What on earth could he want?

'I'll send someone down to get him. Thank you.'

* * *

York had seemed nervous as he and Grant walked along the corridor and now he sat fidgeting with three leather bracelets as they waited for Gawn to arrive. Grant didn't know what to say to him so he didn't say anything at all which only seemed to put York more on edge. Maybe the Chief Inspector was finishing her lunch, but Grant reckoned it was more likely she was making York wait deliberately, trying to fray his nerves a little before she talked to him. He suspected she might be watching them even now and the thought made him stand up straighter. Just as York seemed to be on the verge of getting up to leave, Gawn swept into the room. She carried a file and pen and a styrene cup of coffee. She set them down and pulled out a seat across from the academic and sat down. She straightened her top and, thinking of Schneider's mannerism which was a good way to take a few seconds to organise your thoughts, she flicked an invisible piece of fluff from her sleeve before she started to speak. All the time Grant noticed that York didn't take his eyes off her.

'Dr York, what can we do for you?'

She didn't smile and there was a hardness behind her eyes and a coldness in her voice. She fixed him with a stare. She made no attempt to put him at ease. If anything, she wanted to make him uncomfortable.

'I think it's more a case of what can I do for *you*, Chief Inspector.'

Now that she was sitting across from him, York seemed more at ease than he had been previously. Grant was fascinated. He didn't consider himself very sensitive to other people's moods but he was aware of a frisson of something between them. He watched as York leant back in his chair and crossed his legs as if he was making himself comfortable at home. Gawn had the impression this was some sort of performance. York was acting. But why? To what end?

'Well, what *can* you do?'

She tapped her middle finger on the desk in a show of impatience. She didn't know what game he was playing but she was convinced it was a game.

'I was thinking about Thursday evening and I realised I actually saw Lucy – Miss Armstrong – in Botanic Avenue.

She was just coming out of Tesco's. I was on the other side of the road. I was just about to go into the bookshop. I don't think she noticed me.'

'We know Miss Armstrong was in Tesco's. She told us that was where she'd been. Is there anything else useful you can add?' She stressed the word 'useful' to let him know she was not impressed with his helpfulness.

'Well…' He hesitated. Building up the tension, she thought to herself. With perfect dramatic timing he added, 'I think there was someone following her.'

York sat back in his chair with a smug look on his face and waited for a response from across the table. Gawn wasn't about to let him know they had already identified Weil on CCTV footage and knew he had been following the girl.

'Any idea who, Dr York? Could you describe him?'

'That's why I came in. I think it might have been the murdered man, Weil.'

He leant forward across the table, looking pleased. He could be so smug, she thought.

'Could you swear to that, sir?'

'Well, maybe. I'm not absolutely sure. There were quite a few people about and he was across the other side of the road and there was quite a lot of traffic coming and going and it was only a brief glance but I'm pretty sure it was him.'

Talk about not being particularly helpful. Gawn was puzzled as to why he had bothered to come to them, to her, at all with this.

'I see. Well, thank you, Dr York, you've been most helpful. We'll let you know if we need to speak to you again.'

She stood up and reluctantly, it seemed, he did too. They faced each other across the table. He seemed disappointed that she didn't want to ask him anything else, to prolong the interview. He extended his hand to her and without thinking, she took it. She was surprised at how soft and warm his hand was, but his grip was firm, not flabby as she would probably have expected, if she had thought about it at all. She couldn't help noticing those little laughter lines crinkling the sides of his eyes which she had noticed on the recording when he and Lucy had been having their fun day out at the theme park. She noticed his eyes too, a deep soulful brown. And she was aware of the musky scent of his aftershave.

'Glad to be of help to the police.' He smiled.

She was curt in reply. 'The constable will see you out.' She turned away making clear he was dismissed.

No sooner were York and Grant out the door than Maxwell came in. He had been watching the interview.

'What the hell was that all about?'

'I don't know, Sergeant,' she responded thoughtfully.

She was still referring to him as 'Sergeant' but at least she was speaking to him and she hadn't told him to get back to work so Maxwell was satisfied that she was beginning to thaw towards him.

'He must realise Lucy would tell us she was at Tesco's. Do you really think he's just remembered about seeing Weil? Nearly a week later?'

'I don't know what he would hope to achieve by coming in and telling us this unless…'

She left the sentence unfinished.

'Unless what, boss?'

'Well, there have been instances – quite a few actually - where perps tried to ingratiate themselves into an investigation, tried to get close to what was happening.'

'And you think that's what York might be doing? You think he's involved in some way?'

'I don't know, Paul.'

She didn't know what to expect from York, when to believe him and when he was playing with her. He puzzled her. There was something about him, his attitude, his behaviour, she found unsettling. She never seemed to know exactly where she was with him, always afraid of being caught off-guard. And the murderer was playing with her. That she did know. Did that mean York could be the man they were looking for? She didn't seriously think so.

'I can't quite see him as a member of a German criminal gang and we know he was at his book launch when Weil was killed so he can't have been lurking about Botanic Gardens hoping to kill Lucy or some other girl. So, what's his game? By the way, his alibi was checked, wasn't it?'

'I asked Billy to do it. He phoned the bookshop and spoke to the owner and he verified that the book launch took place and York spoke at it.'

'But he didn't actually visit the shop or check the time York was there?'

'Well, no, I don't think so.'

'Do it yourself, Paul, just to make sure.'

He wasn't certain if she was sending him on such a basic interview as punishment, but he didn't mind. He would be glad to be away from her gaze for a while.

Chapter 31

Maxwell had been glad to get out of the office and to have the chance to do something useful. Gawn was still livid with him he was sure, although she'd said no more about it. He was even more annoyed at himself. Such a stupid mistake to make. If Grant had done it, he'd have given him a right bollocking.

He had never been inside the famous crime bookshop on Botanic Avenue before, but he had heard of it. It was smaller than he expected it to be and, as he approached the door, he could see posters advertising new books, poetry readings and an evening with an author he supposed he should have heard of but hadn't. He pushed open the door to an Aladdin's cave of books. Books everywhere. Walls lined with books. Tables stacked with books. A customer was sitting in an armchair further up the shop, reading. A couple were browsing the shelves, their heads close together chatting and giggling over a book. A girl stood behind the cash register near the window. She seemed to be engrossed in whatever she was reading too, but as he approached her, she looked up and smiled broadly at him.

'Can I help you? Are you looking for anything in particular?'

He flashed his ID. 'DS Maxwell. I wanted to speak to the manager.'

'That would be me.'

The voice came from behind him, a deep friendly voice. He swung round and was faced by a smiling middle-aged man of about his own height. He was dressed in an open-neck check shirt and brown corduroy trousers and a pair of glasses hung on a chain around his neck. His skin was tanned as if he was not long back from holiday.

Maxwell held up his ID again.

'I think you spoke to one of my colleagues but we're just following up.'

'This is about the murder in Botanic Gardens?'

'Yes. We're double-checking everyone's whereabouts at the time of the murder and I just wanted to confirm that Sebastian York was here that evening.'

'Yes. That's right. As I told your colleague, Seb's new book was just out last week and we were having a bit of a launch event for it. *Inspector Darwin's Date with Death*.' He enunciated the title with dramatic emphasis. When he saw it meant nothing to the policeman, Thompson walked across and lifted a book from a pile sitting on the central table. 'Number three in the Inspector Darwin series. The first two have been really successful.'

Maxwell looked at the lurid front cover. It featured an attractive blonde woman facing a man brandishing a knife. It didn't look like his sort of thing, but Kerri might enjoy it.

'Is it about a woman being stabbed?'

'There is a woman stabbed in it near the beginning but that figure on the cover is Inspector Darwin. The series is about a woman police officer so it's really her solving the case.'

A lightbulb went off in Maxwell's head. He guessed York wanted to find out more from Gawn and about her for his books. That could be why he was hanging around and ingratiating himself into the investigation. The boss would be interested to hear that.

'I see. And Dr York was here last Thursday night between 6pm and 8pm for this event?'

He expected the man to confirm the times and was just about to thank him and turn to leave when his reply stopped him.

'That was the time of the event but Seb was running a little late. He'd almost arrived here when he realised he'd left something in his car and he had to go back for it and then he'd run into an artist friend of his, Jonty somebody-or-other, near the park so that held him up a bit. So, I'd say it was probably nearer 6.15 before he was here.'

'And he stayed till 8?'

'Yes. He was here. He stayed until well after eight talking and signing books.'

The timing of the writer's late arrival meant he could have spotted Lucy and Weil as he had claimed but it also made it possible for him to have been in the park at the time of the murder.

'Just one more thing, sir. You don't happen to know where Dr York's car was parked, do you?'

'He has a university parking space.'

'Right. That would be somewhere near the main building on campus then?'

'No. It's always been a niggle to him that he doesn't have a space on the main site. He's complained to me many times about it. His parking space is at the University PE centre. During the winter he hates the walk through Botanic Gardens in bad weather.'

'He parks on the other side of Botanic Gardens from here?'

'Yes.'

Maxwell had to try very hard not to show any reaction. He didn't want to make the same mistake again and give anything away. So, not only had York had time to commit the murder but he could have been right on the spot at his car. He thanked Thompson, told him they might need to speak to him again and then headed out onto Botanic Avenue glad to have something to report back. There was a smile on his face.

Chapter 32

By the time Maxwell got back to the office, Gawn had already convened a team briefing. As he walked in McKeown was talking and all eyes were on her. She glanced across to the door and paused in what she was saying.

'Here's Sarge now. It's really his line of enquiry. I just put together the background info.'

'Go ahead, Erin.'

He was happy to let her speak. She walked across to the murder board. There were now four new pictures pinned on it. She identified the four women and explained that they were murder victims from across Europe. The whole atmosphere in the office changed. The girl had everyone's attention. All four were between 20 and 30, with longish hair and had had their throats cut in a public park, she explained.

It was Jack who piped up, 'But our victim's a male and he was stabbed right enough but his throat wasn't cut.'

Maxwell stepped forward and faced the others. 'We think it might be possible that Lucy Armstrong was the intended victim, but Weil got in the way. Perhaps Weil was following Lucy and in doing so interrupted the killer's plans. In the heat of the moment our killer didn't have time to cut the throat the way he normally does.'

A murmur ran around the room and meaningful looks were exchanged.

'But, Sarge, it's a bit of a leap to connect our killer to these other four murders, isn't it?'

'You're right if it wasn't for the fact we have something linking them. This.' Maxwell tapped the picture of the perfume stopper on the board. 'All four victims were covered in perfume and a bottle was left with each body. Our killer dropped this bottle top.'

He looked across at Gawn and with an almost imperceptible nod of her head she signalled it was alright to give them the rest of the information.

'And on Monday night the bottle to go with it was left outside the boss's home.'

It seemed every eye in the room was turned on her then. The PSNI was long used to having terrorist crime invade their homes and families but a serial killer seeking out a senior officer was something new.

'We need to concentrate on the perfume bottle. Where did it come from, and how did the killer get into my apartment block. I think we can assume at the minute that Weil was collateral damage and if we get our serial killer, we will have his killer too, but I don't think there's any way to catch his killer through studying Weil. If we're right, he was a target of opportunity, not a planned killing. I doubt very much our killer knew him at all.'

'Poor bugger. You come to Belfast and get yourself killed first night by a psychopath.'

'Don't waste too much sympathy on him, Billy. Let's not forget we think Weil was here to retrieve evidence of a kidnapping and murder he was involved in, so he was no angel. Our killer was in Carrickfergus. We need to find out how he got in to leave his little gift for me. Billy, get down to Carrick and ask around. Check in at the local station. I'll phone ahead and clear it with them. We don't want to trample on any toes.' Then, turning her attention to Jack, she asked, 'How's the CCTV search from around Botanic going? Have you turned up anything yet? Anyone leaving the park in a hurry around the time of the killing?'

'Nothing yet. But we've more to go through.'

'Our killer is obviously well travelled. He's killed in four different countries. If we had any suspects, we could check if they were in those countries at the time.'

'Well, we have York.' This came from McKeown.

Maxwell chimed in, 'And his alibi doesn't hold up.' He explained what he had found out at the bookstore.

'I want everything we can get on Sebastian York,' Gawn said.

She remembered his visit to the station and her impression that he was playing games with her. Maybe the perfume bottle had been just another of his little games.

Chapter 33

Billy Logan had phoned in to say he was waiting to check CCTV footage in Carrick. She could hear laughter in the background and reckoned he was probably waiting in the pub next to the police station. He offered to go straight to Carrick in the morning to finish his interviews. He had questioned several of her neighbours but no one had seen anyone acting suspiciously. Most of them were out working during the day so he hadn't managed to see them all yet. He had also spoken to some painters who were working in the building. They claimed not to have noticed anything out of the ordinary but suggested he could check with a workman they had seen around the marina. So far, Logan hadn't been able to trace him. Gawn told him to check in to the briefing first in the morning. He could follow up in Carrick later.

As she sat in her office reading through the latest overtime figures and a memo about cutbacks, Maxwell put his head around the door.

'Bad time?'

'No, any excuse to put off the admin. It's the worst part of this job. Come in.'

'I've got the background check on York.' He was carrying sheets of paper which he reached out to her.

'I'll read through it later. Give me the main points.'

'OK. He was born in Belfast in 1984. Brought up in east Belfast in Braniel housing estate. Single parent family. Mother married an English soldier. He hung around long enough to father three kids – Sebastian's two older sisters and him – but then did a runner shortly after our POI was born and his mother brought the three of them up by herself with a bit of help from her father. York seems to have been close to his grandfather. He went to the local primary school. Then passed his selection test and got a place at grammar school.' He named a prestigious local school well-known for producing lawyers and successful businessmen. 'He seems to have done well there. Played for the first fifteen at rugby in the Schools' Cup final, prefect, that sort of thing. Four As at A level and a scholarship to Oxford.'

'"Local boy makes good" stuff, eh?'

Gawn sucked on the end of her pen as she listened to Maxwell's report. She realised they would have been at school at roughly the same time and within a few miles of each other. Her all-girls school had often held joint concerts and events with his all-boys school. Perhaps she'd even seen him. She didn't think she'd ever met him but then she hadn't had much time for boys then.

'I'm sure it must have been tough for him there. He'd have been very much the odd man out.'

Maxwell nodded.

'Probably. You would think so, but he seems to have got on well at school. He was popular with his classmates. Then he went to Oxford. Got his degree – first class of course – then took off around Europe on one of those train pass things. He worked in America, in California, got his doctorate at Berkeley and then came back here. He was teaching at Maynooth for a couple of years and then got the job at Queen's. He has no police record. Nothing. Not even a speeding ticket. Squeaky clean. And I checked into his teaching record but no hint of any scandal or trouble with students.'

'That's some CV.' She was impressed in spite of herself. 'And what about the book writing?'

'Apparently, he's a successful writer. I've never heard of any of his books, but Kerri has. He writes a crime series based on a female detective, Inspector Darwin, which I thought could be why he called in today, for a bit of research for his main character. He's had several published and one made into a series for some internet channel. Means he's made a bit of money out of it so he's doing alright. He travels quite a lot. No steady girlfriend. General reputation of being a ladies' man, a bit of a player.'

That didn't surprise her at all. He was a charmer alright.

'Female detective?'

A half smile played on her lips. She could just imagine the sort of rubbish York would write about some sex-mad policewoman falling into the arms of a hard-nosed cop who cast her aside in his climb to Chief Constable or even more unlikely, getting involved with one of the suspects she was investigating. Just the kind of thing she avoided reading or watching on TV.

'Nothing to link him to our murders?'

'Not yet but we're going to go back now and try to check his exact whereabouts at the time of the four murders. But do we really think he was trying to kill Lucy? Surely he could have killed her any time he wanted. He would have had plenty of opportunities.'

'Yes, but any other time and place he might have been an obvious person of interest. Here, he had an alibi.'

'So, are we saying he was lurking in the bushes waiting for her?'

'Maybe. Or that could just have been coincidental. Maybe Billy was right. It was some voyeur who was in the bushes, not our murderer. Anyway, we need to take an in-depth look at Dr York.'

Maxwell turned to leave but stopped when Gawn spoke again.

'Thanks, Paul. And, Paul, well done coming up with this link. That was good detective work. I did mention to the Chief Super that it was down to you.'

He couldn't help but beam. He knew other DCIs who, while they mightn't claim the kudos themselves, would certainly not go out of their way to let everyone know when it was someone else's work. And she had done it even though he had stuffed up with Schneider. He left the room with a spring in his step. Kerri would be pleased. He walked over to McKeown's desk and helped himself to a chocolate from a box lying open.

'I didn't know you were a chocolate lover, Sarge.'

'I could say the same for you.'

'Well, I'm not really. I didn't buy them. They were a present from Kommissar Schneider. He's a real chocoholic. He munched his way through about three bars of some awful chocolate he likes while we were going through that film. I told him I only like good old

Cadbury's not the fancy American stuff he eats so he bought me a box before he left.'

'Thank you, Hauptkommissar,' said Maxwell and popped an orange cream into his mouth as he walked away laughing. He was pleased with himself, but he couldn't help feeling he had missed something important.

Chapter 34

There was a pleasant level of noise in the restaurant. Gawn hadn't wanted to face an evening alone eating a plastic-tasting prepared meal from her freezer. Instead, she'd opted for Mooney's again. She was getting to be quite the regular. She liked it here. She had grown up not far away, gone to school just across the road and knew the area well. She could sit over her meal reading her book in peace but surrounded by people – just like the anonymity she had enjoyed in London.

A shadow fell over the page she was reading. She looked up expecting to see the waiter with the starter she'd ordered. Instead, the slightly diffident face of Sebastian York smiled down on her. She was stunned. What was he doing here? Her mouth fell open in surprise.

'Good evening, Chief Inspector. I'm sorry to disturb you. I wonder, could I ask a favour?' He ploughed on, not waiting for an answer. 'They're all booked up here for the evening and they tell me I'll have to wait at least an hour for a table. Could I join you by any chance... if you're not waiting for someone, of course?' This time he did wait for her reply.

Gawn was aware her mouth was still slightly open in surprise and closed it quickly – not a good look. She couldn't find the words; she was so astonished –

astonished that he was here and astonished that he would approach her like this. Eventually she managed to gather her thoughts and speak.

'I don't think that would be really appropriate. Do you, Dr York?'

He smiled, a sort of knowing smile. 'I'm not a suspect, am I? That's what you told me anyway. So, what harm could it possibly do? We would just be two people who have a passing acquaintance, sharing a table.'

He made it sound so reasonable. He was at his charming best. Whether this was because he genuinely wanted to eat here or whether he had another motive, another of his little games, she wasn't sure. She was just about to make it perfectly clear there was no way she would be sharing a table with him. Then she realised this would be the perfect opportunity to get him relaxed and talking; maybe get him to incriminate himself; at the very least a chance to do a bit more research about him. It would be unorthodox, which was very unusual for her, and the Super would probably have a fit if he found out, but they didn't have much to go on. So much for her 'by the book' reputation but it was worth taking the risk.

'Well, I suppose it would be alright,' she said dubiously, not wanting to appear too keen to get time to talk to him alone.

He didn't hesitate. He sat down immediately before she could change her mind, pulling his chair in close to the table, their knees almost but not quite touching.

'Have you ordered?'

'Yes.'

He turned in his seat and motioned to the waiter. 'I'll have whatever the lady's having.'

'How do you know you'll like what I've ordered?'

'I'm sure you have impeccable taste in food as you do in clothes. I can't imagine you'd choose anything I wouldn't like.'

Smooth, bloody smooth, Dr York, she thought to herself. She accepted the compliment with a shy smile, almost embarrassed at her own duplicity. It was too easy. He was playing right into her hands. If he thought he was fooling her, then he would learn she was fooling him. She looked at him closely. Tonight he was wearing a light blue denim shirt with button-down collar. She recognised the logo on the breast pocket. So, she wasn't the only one with expensive tastes in clothes. He was still wearing the three woven leather bracelets on his wrist she had noticed earlier in the interview room and a Claddagh ring on his right hand. Did this mean he was in a relationship? With Lucy? With someone else? A ploy to throw them off him as a suspect?

'Look, it's a bit strange sitting here sharing a meal and you calling me Chief Inspector. My name is Gawn.'

'What a lovely name. Unique. Like yourself.' He raised his glass of water to her as if in a toast. 'And, as you know, my name is Sebastian, Seb to my friends.'

'That's an unusual name too. Nearly as unusual as Gawn.'

'So how come you're called Gawn, then?'

'My great-grandmother's brother was called Gawn. The name's been in our family for years. My mother wanted to use it and I was born first. Simple as that. My brother's called Michael. He got lucky.' She laughed.

'And I'm Sebastian... Well, actually, I'm Jacob Sebastian York. I was named Jacob after my grandfather and he wanted me called Sebastian because he liked the name. He was a fan of Bach, you see. I ended up being called JS at school or Bach as a nickname. Parents have a lot to answer for, haven't they?'

They both laughed.

Their starters arrived speedily and they tucked in. It turned out he was a charming companion. She should have realised he would be. She found it easy to listen to him and was pleasantly surprised that he didn't spend all the time talking about himself and trying to impress her, as so many men tried to do. He wanted to know about her too and for every topic, what she learned about him, she had to reveal more about herself. They chatted about London, which they both knew well and about films they had seen and enjoyed. They laughed at some of the disastrous movie experiences they'd had to endure. They discussed music and she was surprised that he knew so much about Sixties groups. He also liked classical music and they found they had both attended the same Ulster Orchestra concert. No doubt he had been there with friends or maybe a girlfriend. She had gone alone. Neither of them strayed onto the topic of family.

Eventually the chat came round to travel and places they had visited and she saw her opportunity to find out where he had been and when.

'I love Venice and Paris. I think they're my two favourite cities, even more than New York. Have you ever been to either of them?' She smiled at him encouraging a response. She didn't quite flutter her eyelashes at him like a movie vamp but it came close. She was actually enjoying the subterfuge but hoped she wasn't overdoing it. It was like a game, she realised with a shiver, and York was obviously very good at playing it.

'Of course. They're both magical cities. But they shouldn't be visited alone. Paris, the city of love. I hope you had someone special with you, Gawn.'

He was fishing. She couldn't help but notice his quick glance at her ring finger. She didn't rise to the bait. The less he found out about her personal life, the better.

'Oh, of course.' She fluttered her eyelashes again and tried to look coy. 'My favourite type of holiday is the short city break. I'm not keen on beach holidays.' She almost added that she didn't like them because she never wore a bikini due to her scar but decided that was more than he needed to know. 'With my job I can usually only get away for a few days at a time but I've managed to get to Prague,

Berlin and Amsterdam all in the last couple of years. All great cities.'

'Yes. I've been to all of them too. And Barcelona, of course. Brilliant city. Great nightlife.'

'I was in Amsterdam just last year. Unfortunately, the weather wasn't great when I was there but I loved the Vondelpark. We had some glorious walks there. When were you there?'

She had never been to Amsterdam in her life and certainly never walked in the Vondelpark with anyone but remembered from Maxwell's report that victim number four had been found there.

'I went just before the start of term at the end of last summer. Maybe we were even there at the same time. It was a wee treat to keep me going until Christmas. I usually go skiing at Christmas. We got quite good weather when we were there.' She noted he had said 'we' so it seemed he had not been alone or maybe that was what he wanted to suggest. 'It was cold but dry but I'm afraid I didn't make it to the Vondelpark. I'm more of a museums and cafés sort of guy. If you know what I mean.' His smile challenged her to question him.

'By cafés, I take it you mean the brown cafés?'

'A little bit of weed never hurt anyone, Gawn.'

She filed it away in the back of her mind that it might be cause for a search warrant if they ever needed one.

'I think we'll have to differ on that one. I've seen too much evidence of the effects drugs can have.'

He raised his glass to her in a silent agree-to-disagree gesture.

She thought of the little white pills in her bag but pushed away any sense of hypocrisy she might be feeling. She wasn't some sort of junkie and her pills were just a temporary aid to help her through her anxiety. She could stop any time she chose.

Soon they had finished their meal. Gawn had barely noticed the time passing. He had been such an entertaining companion. It had been a long time since she had enjoyed an evening out so much or the company of a man. It had been a long time since she had had an evening out with a man, full stop. She glanced at her watch.

'Time for home.'

She surprised herself at the genuine regret in her voice.

'Yes, bed beckons.' She didn't know whether he was being serious or if he was propositioning her.

He stood up and moved round to pull her chair out for her in a show of old-fashioned chivalry.

'I suppose you wouldn't allow me to pay for your meal?'

'You suppose correctly.' But she smiled to demonstrate her appreciation of his offer.

'Or invite you back to mine for a nightcap or a coffee?'

'No.'

The word came out a little more forcefully than she'd intended but she felt things had gone far enough and she didn't want to encourage him. Even though she thought prolonging the evening with him could be pleasant. They asked for separate bills, paid, shared a tip and then he helped her into her coat. His manners are impeccable, Gawn thought to herself. A real gentleman. They paused just as they were about to step out onto the street. The night had turned chilly and there was a steady drizzle. Passing cars were splashing water out of the puddles onto the pavement. She hadn't brought an umbrella.

'Have you far to walk to your car?'

'No. It's just around the corner.'

'I'll say goodnight then, Gawn. Thank you for sharing your table with me and for a most pleasant evening.'

She didn't know what to expect from him. She wondered for one second if he was going to shake hands or even try to kiss her, but he merely smiled, nodded and started walking away. She watched him stride along, his coat collar turned up against the rain, hat pulled down low over his eyes, hands deep in his coat pockets. She was almost disappointed. Was it just a coincidence he had happened to be there tonight? Or was this another part of some game?

Chapter 35

When the explosion came, she was totally unprepared. She had been thinking about her time spent with York. It had been an unexpected pleasure in so many ways. She didn't notice the car. Wasn't aware of it slowing down and pulling closer to the kerb. She didn't see the firework thrown from the open passenger window. She knew nothing until it hit her back and exploded just behind her. The flash lit the path all around her. The bang seemed deafening; it was so close. She screamed. Instinctively, she dropped down on the ground. She was aware of it being wet beneath her hands and of pain in both her knees from the hard surface. Then she heard the sound of running feet.

'My God, what happened, Gawn? Are you alright?'

It was York kneeling beside her. To hear his voice was reassuring. She couldn't reply. She felt herself shaking and knew that very little would bring floods of uncontrollable tears. He gently took her by the elbow and helped her to her feet. She swayed and he put his arm around her waist to support her and started walking her up the road.

A crowd was gathered outside the restaurant and a voice exclaimed, 'Those bloody kids again. The wee buggers are always flinging fireworks about. It's only a matter of time until somebody gets seriously hurt. Is she all right?' The question was directed to York as they passed.

'She'll be OK. Thanks. I'll just get her home.'

He lived just round the corner and half-walking, half being carried, Gawn made her way haltingly there with him. The house was in a wide tree-lined avenue full of semi-detached and detached homes, typical 1930s style. He opened the front door and led her in, still holding her tightly round the waist.

'Sit down here. Take it easy. I'll get you something to drink. Do you want a brandy or maybe hot sweet tea would be better?'

He seemed to be slightly flustered now, not sure exactly what to do; not the self-assured man-about-town anymore.

'Tea would be fine. Thanks.'

She managed to find her voice although it was small and shaky. She sank into the chesterfield, her arms hugging her knees, her body rocking gently backwards and forwards as she listened to the sounds coming from the kitchen. She tried to concentrate on the normality of those sounds and close out any sounds and visions of other places and other times which kept flashing before her. She could hear the water tap running as York filled the kettle and the clatter of cups being brought out of a cupboard. Soon he was back clutching a steaming mug and a glass of amber liquid.

'I don't have any brandy.' He looked dismayed as he added, 'But here's a whisky. It should help steady your nerves.'

She almost laughed out loud. It would take more than that to control her nerves. He handed her the glass. She took it and without hesitation gulped the liquid down in one swallow. She wasn't particularly fond of whisky, didn't usually drink it so it caught her breath and she exploded into a fit of coughing. He waited until the coughing had subsided and took the glass back from her. Then he handed her the mug, placing it into her grasp as if she were a small child and cupping his hands around hers to make sure she had a good hold on it before letting go.

He was just about to sit down himself in an armchair opposite her when he seemed to notice for the first time the condition of her legs. Her trousers were ripped at the knees and there was grazed and bloodied skin showing through the gaps in the material. He left without a word and came back clutching a towel, some cotton wool and a bottle of something. He knelt in front of her and gently dabbed at the grazes. She winced.

'Sorry if it hurts.'

'It's OK.'

She watched his face as he carefully wiped the blood away to reveal deep scratches. He was concentrating so much on not hurting her that his tongue was peeking out of the corner of his mouth in what she assumed was an unconscious mannerism.

'I would suggest you take your trousers off, but you might arrest me.' He smiled up at her, his eyes crinkling at the sides, trying to lighten the mood, and she responded with a weak smile back.

'It'll be fine. Thanks.'

Then he seemed to notice for the first time her hands were scuffed and bloodied too. He took the mug off her and gently wiped the cuts. It was such a tender action she felt her eyes well up with tears.

'God. Sorry. Did I hurt you?'

'No. No, it's OK. It's not you. Just me being silly.'

She was so angry with herself for showing such weakness in front of him. If she could have, she would have run out, but she wasn't sure her legs would hold her. He set the towel and bottle aside and sat down in the armchair by the fire. He was watching her closely as he sipped his own tea.

'I don't know much about these sorts of things. You're not going to go into shock or anything, are you? Should I call an ambulance?'

She managed a weak laugh. 'No, I promise you I'm not. I don't need an ambulance. I just need to sit for a while and then, when I've got my breath back, I'll get out of your way.'

He nodded but said nothing and they sat in silence both sipping the hot sweet tea. Finally, York scowled. 'This is pretty horrible stuff, isn't it? I don't usually drink tea. I just keep some for when my sisters visit and I don't usually take sugar either.'

'It is pretty gross.' They laughed together.

Then they subsided into silence. It was not an uncomfortable silence. Gawn didn't feel the need to make conversation and evidently neither did York. He had lit the gas fire when they first entered the room and its heat had dissipated the chill, creating a cosy atmosphere. She was feeling quite sleepy now. She would just close her eyes for a minute or two.

* * *

She awoke with a start. It was light outside. She looked across the room but the armchair was empty. She looked down and saw that she was covered with a fleece blanket. He had obviously let her sleep and then fetched a blanket and tucked her in. Such a simple gesture. She glanced at her watch. She would be late and everyone would be waiting for the daily briefing. She needed to leave.

Just at that York walked into the room. She noted that he was wearing the same clothes as the previous evening, only his shirt was unbuttoned this morning and hanging loosely out over his trousers. She was aware of his bare chest and caught a glimpse of what might be a tattoo as his shirt swung open. His hair was tousled, reminding her of a small boy's first thing in the morning, and his feet were bare, something she found faintly erotic. He padded across the room in front of her and she caught the aroma of his aftershave. He had obviously taken time to shave before coming to wake her. He set a cup of coffee down on the table beside her.

'Good morning. How are you? Coffee this time – no more tea.' He laughed.

'I can't believe I slept here all night.'

'You were tired and you'd had a shock. I didn't want to wake you. I just hope it wasn't too uncomfortable.'

She was sitting up and stretching. She could feel a dull ache in both knees but nothing a couple of paracetamols wouldn't deal with.

'No. It was fine. I'm sorry to have imposed on you.'

'If I hadn't been happy for you to stay, I'd have thrown you out.' He noticed the look on her face and hurried on, 'It's not every night I get a beautiful woman sleeping over.'

This time her face registered a flash of anger as well as dismay. He raised both hands palm outwards in a gesture of submission.

'Look, just my idea of a joke and not a very good one. I didn't mean anything by it.' He hurried on, 'Why don't you go and tidy up? The bathroom's just at the top of the stairs and I've left a new toothbrush out for you.'

So, he wasn't used to women staying over but he just happened to have a spare toothbrush at the ready, she thought to herself. Gawn made her way upstairs. Her knees were sore, but she didn't think she'd done any lasting damage. At the top of the stairs, she couldn't help glancing into the first room – a bedroom. It was York's, she was sure. There was a masculine feel to it. The walls were painted light grey, the furniture was black and a large canvas, another one of Jonty Boal's perfume bottles, she noticed, dominated the wall opposite the bed. York really was a fan of his or he liked perfume bottles. The bed had not been slept in. Had York spent the night in the armchair? She couldn't risk taking any longer to look round, much as she would have liked to search through the drawers of his desk and see what his bedside reading was. She wanted to find out more about this man. There was something so intriguing about him. He was a paradox, and she didn't like it that she couldn't predict what he would do or how he would behave.

Ten minutes later, Gawn appeared back downstairs. She had splashed some water on her face, used the toothbrush he had left for her and brushed her hair into some semblance of order. She felt slightly more in control of herself.

'In here.' His voice called from the kitchen. 'I've made some fresh coffee. I happen to know you're a bit of a coffee fanatic. I hope you like this blend. It's Arabian and there's croissants or I can do toast if you prefer.'

She wondered how he knew about her love of coffee and the question flitted through her mind, what else did he know about her and how?

'Just coffee's fine. It's all I have time for.'

'How are you feeling?' His concern seemed genuine.

'I'm OK. Look, sorry about that wobble last night. It's just been a really crap week with one thing and another.'

'PTSD?'

She was shocked. Had he heard something? Was there talk?

He noticed her reaction.

'I'm not trying to pry. It's not any of my business. But I have come across it before in the States. A friend of a friend was kidnapped and she had a really difficult time afterwards. Just took her a while to get back to her old self.' He hesitated and then asked, 'Who's Max?'

'How do you know about Max?' she snapped back at him.

'You were talking in your sleep.'

He saw the worried look on her face and had the good grace to look sheepish.

'Look, Gawn, you don't need to worry. I won't be telling anyone. It's your business whoever he is and whatever happened between you. No one else.'

She wished she could believe that. For a start, if by some chance he was their serial killer – which she now found harder to believe although she couldn't really have explained why – he would obviously use it against her and, even if he wasn't, he would probably talk about it with someone, maybe even Lucy. God, what a mess. Why had she let him share her table last night? Big mistake.

As quickly as she could, she made her excuses. She thanked him for his kindness – and meant it. Then realising she must look a sight, she got back to her car as quickly as she could trying to avoid being seen by too many people and drove for home as fast as she dared.

Chapter 36

Bitch. Whore. How could she?

He had watched her in the restaurant pretending to be surprised. He had seethed inside as she had fluttered her eyelashes, those long eyelashes, hinting at seduction, promising more.

The firework had been planned for some time, another opportunity to watch her suffer. From her reactions when she had found his little present to her, he had realised she suffered from PTSD. That made her an easy target.

It had cost him only twenty pounds for those moronic teenagers to fling it out of the car window at her. They would never be able to recognise him again. He had been careful with his scarf across his face, his hat low over his brow and his fake American twang.

He had watched it all as if it was in slow motion. He saw her fall to the ground. He saw the state she was in, the look of terror on her face.

He had spent the night in an agony of being so near to achieving his goal and yet so far. Not yet. It could not be yet. It could not be here. But he knew where now. All he had to decide was when. But he knew it had to be soon.

The whore would pay. She was always going to pay the ultimate price, but now he would make her suffer first.

Chapter 37

She was flustered and trying her best not to show it. She had driven home – probably pushing a few speed limits if not actually breaking them – showered, dressed and back into the car and up to Belfast in under two hours. She paused outside the office door. Straightening her jacket, she took three deep breaths before pushing the door open. The team was all assembled, waiting for the daily briefing. She felt every eye on her. Totally exposed. She imagined they all knew what had happened; knew where she had spent the night; who she had spent the night with. But just as suddenly as they had looked up, they all returned to what they were doing.

She walked over to her office, consciously slowing her breathing and took time to put her coat and bag on her chair before stepping into the outer room and facing the other detectives.

'Good morning, everyone. Sorry I'm running a bit late this morning.'

One of the perks of rank, she didn't have to explain herself. They probably thought she had been meeting the Chief Super or something. Let them.

Maxwell spoke up. He had been busy. He repeated what he had told Gawn about York's background.

'We need to try to find out if he was in any of the cities where the murders took place at the appropriate time.'

'He has visited them all.' No one questioned how the DCI knew this. 'He was in Amsterdam last August or September, but we need to find out exactly when he visited the other three cities. Any word from the phone company, Billy?'

'Eventually.' He consulted his notebook. 'Only calls made by the victim on the day of his murder was to Doyle's taxi firm at 10.05 to get him from Dublin Airport to Connolly Street station.' So, he had come to Belfast by train. 'And then to Fast Taxis in Belfast to get him to the Titanic. No other calls in or out.'

'Anything new in Carrick?'

'Not yet, ma'am. I'm going back there this morning. I want to find the handyman from the marina.'

'Take a photograph of York with you. See if anyone remembers him hanging around. What about forensics? Any update?'

This time it was Jack who responded.

'They managed to find some DNA traces on that package. They've run it but it's not come up on any database.'

'So, we need a suspect to check it against.'

'And they've got fingerprints from your front door. But again, no matches.'

Gawn stepped back into her office and emerged with an evidence bag containing a comb.

'I'm not sure if they'll be able to get fingerprints from this but it's York's hair so they can check DNA. Get it over to them asap.'

She offered no explanation as to how she had come by the comb and no one was stupid enough or brave enough to ask her.

Several of the detectives had been trawling through hours and hours of CCTV footage. Jack and Grant had managed to source some residential security cameras as well as local businesses. There was a lot to go through. Nothing of interest had turned up yet.

Gawn was heading into her office when Maxwell moved up behind her and said in a low voice, 'Can I have a word, ma'am?'

His voice and his manner were both secretive and Gawn wondered what on earth he was going to say. She closed the door behind them before he spoke again.

'I have something to confess.'

Gawn wondered what was coming next. Was he splitting up with Kerri? She suspected that he had a bit of a thing for her and hoped he had not done something stupid. She could see he looked pale and strained.

'When I was in Munroe's office, I took photos on my phone of his perfume bottles.'

Relief surged through her. Was that all? She immediately thought of how she had spotted York's comb sitting out on a shelf in his bathroom and taken it. It couldn't be used in court if he ended up being charged but it could eliminate him from their enquiries and, if it didn't, they would be able to get his DNA officially.

'Hardly a hanging offence, Paul.'

He was hesitant, not like himself at all.

'Erin and I were looking at it.' He paused and then in a rush added, 'He has all the bottles from the four murders.'

For a second her blood ran cold. Then she spoke reassuringly, 'Not the actual bottles, Paul. You mean he happens to have four bottles of perfume which match the perfume used in the four murders. But he has a lot more than that. It's probably just a coincidence. They're probably quite common and if he still has them, he can't have left them at the scene of the crime, now can he?'

'Erin says they're not. She's checked them. They're all expensive and quite unusual and quite a few of them would originally have come in paired sets but he only has one of each.'

Gawn needed a minute to take in what Maxwell was implying. She slumped down in her chair.

'You're suggesting, our chief pathologist is a serial killer?' Her intonation rose with her incredulity.

'There's more.'

His face was pale. She looked up at him. He was scared about what he was saying, and that was rubbing off on her. She wondered what he was going to tell her next.

'We did some research and found a photograph of Munroe in Berlin at the time of the murder there. He was at some medical conference – a keynote speaker.'

He handed her his phone where he had downloaded the picture. She looked at it and saw the pathologist standing, champagne glass in hand, sandwiched between two other men, all three smiling for the camera. The caption under the picture identified the three doctors and the date and venue of the conference.

Gawn paused a second. She needed to think. This was not the time to rush to any kind of judgements or action. She interlocked her fingers reminiscent of someone in prayer as she leaned her elbows on her desk. If she had prayed much, this would have been the time to do it.

'I would need to run this past the super before we do anything. I don't need to tell you Munroe's position – he's well respected by everybody. He's famous, for God's sake – that's why he would have been invited to that conference. If he turns out to be a serial killer that would have all kinds of implications for any investigation where he has given evidence – so basically virtually every murder here for the last twenty years.'

Her voice trailed off as she got to the end of her sentence. The implications were huge. The possible repercussions – even of him being a suspect if the press got wind of it – would be horrendous. Gawn wasn't prepared to carry the responsibility for that. She would need to speak to the superintendent urgently if they were going to do any follow-up investigation. But did they have enough evidence? Would McDowell knock her back, tell her to keep her sergeant and his wild imagination under control? Everything was only circumstantial.

As her thoughts bounced around from certainty to confusion to disbelief, McKeown tapped on the door.

Gawn waved her in. She obviously knew what they had been talking about.

'Sorry to disturb you, ma'am.' She looked at her boss and thought she looked as if she had aged ten years since yesterday.

'What is it, Erin?' Gawn's voice sounded sharp. She wanted time to think. Whatever it was could wait.

'I know what the sergeant has been telling you and I thought you'd want to know that I've just overheard Jamie and Jack talking.'

Both Gawn and Maxwell looked at her quizzically.

'And?' the DCI said impatiently.

'They were joking about how it was funny that Munroe had shown up on the CCTV footage.'

Gawn remembered how surprised she had been to see Munroe at the crime scene that night.

'I asked them when and the time stamp showed he was there just before the murder was phoned in to control.'

'Christ.'

It was Maxwell. Suddenly his suspicion was becoming very real.

Chapter 38

Gawn looked serious as she walked into the office. Maxwell kept his head down afraid to catch her eye. He didn't know what McDowell had said but he could guess. He was infamous for his foul-mouthed outbursts when he lost his temper. When she had first arrived, Gawn couldn't understand why McDowell had the nickname 'Edna' until she learned they were calling him 'Etna' because of his volcanic temper. Normally he kept it under control, but

Maxwell could imagine Gawn might have felt the full blast of it this time.

She headed straight for her inner office. She felt exhausted as if she had faced an interrogation for the past hour. McDowell had been first dismissive, then incredulous and finally apoplectic. He shouted as if it was her fault Munroe might be a serial killer. She had felt like asking him if he would have preferred that she hadn't followed up Maxwell's suggestion, but she didn't. She simply sat and took all that he said to her. But that had not been the end of it. McDowell wasn't going to be the fall-guy either if this turned into a disaster, so he had marched her up to Chief Superintendent Reid and Reid's reaction was to go right to the top. Gawn was thankful that the chief constable was away at a conference in London, so it was Assistant Chief Constable Norman Smyth that she had to speak to instead.

Smyth was her godfather. He had been her father's best friend. They had walked the beat together in Ballymena as young men before their careers had taken Smyth to a posting in Newry and her father to Belfast. He had been the kindly figure who appeared at Christmas and birthdays with a present for her. He had been a support to her mother after her father was killed and she suspected that their relationship might have developed into something more than friendship after she had left home although nothing had ever been said. He had comforted her at her mother's funeral and had encouraged her when she had contacted him about moving back to Belfast. Even so, she didn't expect any favours from him over this.

It seemed she had had to go over and over what they had found out and what they suspected. Sometimes she thought it sounded very circumstantial and flimsy; other times she was certain they had to follow up what they had found so far. And eventually all the men agreed but also stressed that it had to be kept to a very small circle of people. Maxwell knew and so did McKeown but no one else was to share their suspicions. It would be down to Gawn to question Munroe and to do it as quickly and as diplomatically as possible.

The phone rang on Maxwell's desk and he was surprised to hear Gawn's voice.

'Can you come into my office now, please, and bring Erin?'

She hadn't wanted to attract the attention of anyone else in the office by summoning them in person.

'Close the door. Have a seat.'

She looked at them and the signs of strain on her face were clear for all to see. Her skin was the colour of putty. She looked ill. She was fiddling with her pen, but Maxwell suspected it was to disguise that her hands were trembling. Of course, they didn't know about her experience the previous evening. They just put it down to her being under a lot of pressure about the case.

'This must stay strictly between us. No one else must get wind of it. Understood?'

They didn't speak; only nodded aware of the gravity of what they were involved in. She outlined what had been decided omitting any mention of all the questions and unpleasantness she had gone through.

'It is *crucial* that we find out if Munroe was in those other three cities when the murders took place. If we can establish that he was somewhere else for sure then the perfume bottles are probably just coincidence. In the meantime, I'm going to question him about his whereabouts on Thursday evening. I want you with me, Paul. It's not going to be an official interview, but I'd still prefer a witness. Erin, you can get on with finding out Munroe's whereabouts on the dates of the other three murders.'

The two detectives looked serious. They knew, or at least thought they knew, what was at stake here.

'I'm going to phone Munroe's office now and see if I can get an appointment as soon as possible. That's all for now. You two get started.'

Without a word, they left. If any of the others had looked up, they might have noticed a very serious-looking pair walking back to their desks; they might have suspected that they were in trouble and the DCI had been giving them a talking to. But no one looked up; no one suspected what was going on; everybody was busy with their own little bit of the investigation, oblivious to the potential drama unfolding.

Chapter 39

Gawn and Maxwell had made the journey across to the RVH in almost total silence. She had phoned ahead to arrange an appointment, making sure not to talk to Munroe himself as he would have questioned why she wanted to see him and she didn't want to reveal that yet. She pulled her car into one of the designated parking bays and shut off the engine. She sat with her hands on the steering wheel obviously gathering her thoughts. Her eyes were closed and Maxwell wondered for one second if she was praying although he didn't think she was religious. She opened her eyes.

'I'll take the lead. We've got to tread carefully. Just watch and listen, Paul.'

They walked over to the building both feeling nervous, as if they were marching to the gallows. Gawn was surprised her voice sounded so normal when she explained about her appointment to the receptionist. They were directed to Munroe's office, a journey they were getting used to. Gawn paused at the door and Maxwell waited, saying nothing. He saw her breathe deeply, straighten her shoulders and then knock.

'Come in.'

The pathologist was sitting behind his desk. He seemed pleased to see them, well, see her anyway. His smile faded a little when it rested on Maxwell walking in behind her.

'Good afternoon, Chief Inspector. A most pleasant surprise. I thought we had concluded our business but, if there's something more I can do to help, I'd be delighted. Good afternoon, Sergeant.'

The greeting to Maxwell seemed to be an afterthought.

'Well actually there is something you can do to help me.'

Maxwell noticed she had used 'me' rather than 'us'. He watched the older man's face and thought he detected a certain wariness. But he waved his hand expansively to them in a gesture to sit.

'Please sit down. Tell me, how can I help?'

Maxwell took his lead from the DCI. She took a seat and he sat in the chair beside her. Munroe's words had been friendly, but Maxwell thought the man's smile was a little forced as he faced them.

'You'll know, of course, that we've been trawling through a lot of CCTV footage from around the Botanic Gardens.'

She paused and tried to look embarrassed hoping she was a good actress. She wanted to convince Munroe this was all routine. The pathologist's eyes darted from Gawn to Maxwell and back again. Did he know what was coming?

'I'm afraid you, or someone very like you, was seen on Stranmillis Road at the time of the murder. We have to follow up on the sighting, of course, so, if you could just confirm where you were last Thursday evening that would be great. We'll get it all cleared up.'

She smiled encouragingly.

'You know where I was. I was there. I attended the scene. You met me there.'

He sat back in his leather chair, steepling his fingers, looking relaxed again.

'Yes, of course, we met there but I'm referring to earlier in the evening, say between 6pm and 8pm. The time on the surveillance footage places you on Stranmillis Road outside the park just before the call came through to the control room about the body being discovered.'

The smile disappeared off Munroe's face, like a sheet of ice sliding off a mountainside in the sunshine. He stood up seeming to try to bring himself to his tallest to try to dominate the situation.

'Are you seriously suggesting, my dear Chief Inspector, that I was involved in the murder of this man? That's just ridiculous. Who came up with such nonsense?'

His eyes flicked from Gawn's face to Maxwell's and back again. The soft musical Edinburgh accent had deteriorated into something more akin to Glasgow at pub closing time on a Friday night. A vein pulsed in the doctor's temple and red suffused his face. He was struggling to keep his temper. His hands were shaking but was it with anger or was it with fear?

Gawn's voice, when she spoke, was calm and reassuring.

'Of course, I'm not suggesting that, Al. It's just we've got to cross all the T's and dot all the I's. You know what it's like. Due diligence and all that. If the Super found out I hadn't checked, I'd be for the high jump and if the press found out we'd all be in trouble.'

At mention of the word 'press' Munroe collapsed back into his chair. He seemed to have grown suddenly smaller as if he had shrivelled up in front of them like the wicked Witch of the West in *The Wizard of Oz*. He didn't speak and Gawn let the silence hang between them. He'd obviously been thinking things over and had come to a decision. She had watched his face closely all the time and could almost hear his thinking. How much should he tell them? How much could he lie or at least keep to himself?

'Could I speak to you alone, Chief Inspector?'

The words were accompanied by a nervous smile as his eyes flicked to Maxwell.

'Of course. Paul, give us a couple of minutes.'

She nodded to the sergeant to assure him it was alright. Once Maxwell had closed the door behind him, Munroe started talking, at first hesitantly.

'I was there. On Stranmillis Road. I meet up with people there.'

'Meet up? People?'

She could make a guess at what he was referring to, but she needed him to tell her directly, so she simply waited. Seconds ticked by. Munroe was almost physically squirming in his seat. He seemed to be struggling, not sure how to explain, fearful of putting it into words. Eventually he asked, 'You're familiar with BDSM?'

He spoke as if the very sound of his words disgusted him. Whatever she had been expecting him to say, it wasn't that. She knew the reputation of various toilets round the city for prostitution and cottaging so had expected something along those lines. So, Billy Logan hadn't been too far wrong then. She kept her responses short, letting Munroe do the talking.

'Yes, of course.'

'I meet people there… sometimes near the park. The toilet block in the park – people leave their business cards there.'

He was trying to make it sound like a normal business arrangement, but he was speaking in so low a voice that she could barely make him out and it was obvious it was not something he wanted anyone to know.

'I have a dominatrix I visit in that area. On Thursday night I was with her in her flat on University Street. I stayed with her maybe about an hour and when we'd finished, I left and went back to where I'd parked my car

182

further up Stranmillis Road. 'That's when I must have been caught on the camera.'

'But we didn't have you arriving near the park.'

'I wasn't in the park that night. On Thursday I'd had business meetings in Belfast in the afternoon. I'd parked at Stranmillis and walked into town. Then, when my meeting was over, I came up by taxi to Madame Katarina's. If I'd needed to get into the park, the fence behind the toilet block is broken and it's easy enough to get in and out that way when it's locked up, but I'd already made my arrangements.'

He couldn't help himself smiling at the mention of his dominatrix even in these circumstances.

Gawn digested what she was being told. She would speak to whoever had been in charge of the search in the park. Why hadn't they found a gap in the fence? It was sloppy work. It would be easy enough to check what Munroe had told her about his meeting and the taxi. She wondered if Madame Katarina would be forthcoming as a witness. She wondered too about that gap in the fence and who else might have been able to get in and out of the park at night.

'I haven't done anything illegal, Chief Inspector. We didn't do anything in public. We are two consenting adults. I just don't want my private life becoming public knowledge. I know there's enough speculation about me already.' His voice had taken on a plaintive tone.

'If what you say is true, Al, then it's not any of my business or anything to do with the investigation. But I will need to verify it, of course.'

Munroe looked horrified.

'This mustn't get out. My mother doesn't know.'

He was almost on the verge of crying. She could see the tears sitting on his eyelashes.

'I only know her as Madame Katarina. I have no idea of her real name, but I can show you the house.'

'OK, Al. I'll check it out myself. No one else needs to be involved. But there's something you can do to help me.'

'Anything.'

He seemed just a little too quick to justify his behaviour. Almost despite herself, Gawn couldn't help feeling sorry for the man sitting in front of her. So prim, so proper, driven to seeking out sexual satisfaction with strangers. Paying for his humiliation. She could understand his concern. He was already a target for speculation and the butt of jokes, which he obviously realised. If this got out, he would no doubt have to resign.

He had agreed with such vehemence to her request she was sure that no matter what she had asked of him he would have said yes. She couldn't help herself thinking, perhaps he would even enjoy being ordered about by her. Then her mind wandered to times when he had remarked on the shoes she was wearing and she knew shoe fetishism was a popular form of BDSM. She didn't let her thoughts go any further along that line.

'I'll need to get your fingerprints for cross-referencing and elimination. We'll borrow one of your perfume bottles. You can handle it and we'll get the prints without having to do a formal fingerprinting or my sergeant knowing anything about it.'

Under normal circumstances she knew he would have refused but he was so relieved that his secret could stay hidden with her, she could have asked anything. He walked across to the shelves and lifted down the blue bottle nearest them making sure that his fingerprints would be on it. Then she called Maxwell back into the room and, wearing gloves, he removed the bottle from Munroe's desk and placed it into an evidence bag.

'We'll take good care of it and get it back to you as soon as possible. I'll be in touch if I need to get details of your friend.'

Maxwell looked back as they were walking out the door. The picture of Munroe in hunting gear hanging on the wall behind the desk caught his eye. Then his gaze turned to the man himself. Munroe was sitting at his desk. He looked distraught. He wondered what Gawn had said to him and what he had told her. Obviously, whatever it was, she was not going to share it with him.

Chapter 40

They had dropped the perfume bottle off on the way back to the office. Maxwell didn't question what had gone on while he was out of the room and Gawn had volunteered no information. It was not late but Gawn sent Maxwell home and headed home herself. There was nothing more they could do about Munroe until Monday when hopefully they would have some results. She felt wiped out. Was it only last night she had spent the night on York's sofa?

Once home, she couldn't face cooking, but she was quite hungry. A local restaurant was within sight of her apartment so she rang to see if they had a table free. Half an hour later found her tucking into a plate of crispy chilli chicken strips and chunky chips. She was enjoying the food. No book with her this evening but there was plenty of activity all around her to hold her attention. The restaurant was busy, all the American-style booths packed with couples and family groups. One table at the top of the room was obviously a birthday party with helium balloons floating in the air for the birthday boy. The big screen on one wall was showing music videos – thankfully not too loudly – and she watched the people all around her enjoying their evening in the company of family and friends. She even joined in the clapping when a birthday cake was brought out and Happy Birthday was sung to an embarrassed-looking teenager.

It was still not late when she had finished her meal. She paid the bill and made her way outside glad to see there was still some light in the sky although the floodlights were illuminating the castle, soaking it in a yellow glow. The lights along the walkway on the Marine Highway were already lit too with the strings of Christmas lights swaying between them still dark until the switching-on ceremony weeks away. Even at this distance she could hear faintly the jangling of some of the rigging in the harbour. She walked towards the restaurant exit and was immediately aware of a man sitting with his back to her on the low wall which surrounded the restaurant car park. That hat. She recognised it. It couldn't be. She wasn't one hundred percent sure until she had walked quickly across the car park and faced him. It was who she thought it was – York. He was sitting looking quite relaxed clutching two paper cups, she presumed, of coffee.

'What are you doing here?' she demanded angrily.

'And good evening to you too, my dear Chief Inspector.' Seeing his quip was not having the desired effect, he continued, 'We never got the chance to finish our talk this morning. You were rushing off to work so I thought I would come and bring you coffee and we could talk now.'

She was annoyed. She was surprised. She was frightened that he had been able to find her so easily. Had he followed her? Was he the stalker who had planted that package at her door?

'Did you follow me home?'

'Certainly not.' Now it was his turn to be annoyed and it showed in his voice. 'This is a very small place. You must know how it works. If you don't know someone, you know someone else who does. Surely, you've realised that by now. It only took a couple of phone calls to find out where you lived.'

He smiled, seeming to be unashamedly pleased with himself.

'Coffee? I have a latte and I have an Americano. Take your pick.'

He stood up and proffered the two cups. She was mesmerized. His audacity was breath-taking. She didn't speak but almost automatically she reached out and took one of them.

'How about a walk? We could walk and chat at the same time.'

It would certainly be better than standing out in the street at a major roundabout for everyone to see. She thought of the first time she had set eyes on Sebastian York, at the traffic lights in front of the university with traffic all around. There was a bit of a recurring theme going on here. She started walking, crossing the road when the lights changed at the pelican crossing and headed to the harbour. York followed by her side. Only when they were well away from everyone else did she speak again. She stopped, swung around and faced him.

'Look, I don't know what you're up to but you're a person of interest in a murder case.'

'I thought I was just a witness. That's what you said. Haven't you eliminated my DNA from your enquiries yet?'

He smiled, or was it a smirk?

'What do you mean, "yet"?'

'Well, you did take my comb from the bathroom to get my DNA, didn't you?'

He seemed so pleased with himself. She didn't deny it; didn't respond at all.

'I'm a crime fiction writer after all, Gawn. I know all about DNA and the underhand ways you cops go about getting it.' He paused, smiled, enjoying teasing her, then, almost as an afterthought, said, 'Or *was* it my comb?'

He had known she would take the comb; had left it out deliberately. Had he planted someone else's hair on the comb to trick her and give the wrong result?

'You bastard. You didn't switch combs, did you?' Her voice rose in anger dreading that she had been duped.

'I could have… but I didn't.'

He tried to look convincing but there was a gleam in his eye which she couldn't quite interpret. My God, he was infuriating. Could she believe him? He hadn't needed to tell her he knew about the comb but maybe it was a double bluff. She found him impossible to read. One minute he was imperious and difficult to deal with; other times he was gentle and thoughtful. She couldn't forget how he had tended to her cuts. But she knew he had a high opinion of himself. He thought he was very clever, cleverer than her, and she had already suspected that he liked to play games and had been doing that with her from the very beginning. She thought back to the interview in his office when he had pretended not to recognise the photograph of Weil.

'Look, Gawn, let me be frank with you.'

She thought he was going to reach out and take her hand, but he didn't.

'No games this time. I really like you. You're a beautiful woman and I was hoping you might like me too. I thought we got on really well last night over dinner. Didn't we?' He paused, obviously expecting a reaction, but when she didn't respond he continued. 'We share a lot of interests and I'd really like to get to know you better.'

She thought his voice was different – softer, less confident, more diffident. If she hadn't seen how he could change his attitude in an instant, she would have said he seemed vulnerable but it was probably only another ploy.

It was when he paused again trying to gauge her reaction to what he had said that she exploded.

'Are you bloody serious?'

It was almost laughable. Was he coming on to her in the middle of an investigation? The arrogance of the man.

'I'm a Chief Inspector, for God's sake. You're, at best, a person of interest in the investigation, at worst a murderer and you're hitting on me!'

It was crazy. He was crazy. It was impossible.

Before she had time to realise what was happening, he had moved closer to her and was trying to kiss her. His arm was around her, holding her body close to his. His mouth was soft against hers and she felt his tongue move along her lips. She pushed him away spilling what was left of her coffee over his jacket and slapped him hard across the face. She had never slapped a man before. Yes, she had punched them, even kicked them when it came to defending herself at an arrest, but she had never had occasion to slap a man trying to kiss her. York looked at her, stunned. She didn't think it was because she had hurt him except maybe his pride. She guessed he wasn't used to having his advances rebuffed; more used to women falling at his feet. He looked livid. His eyes flashed.

'I don't know who the hell Max is, but he's well rid of you.'

He spat the words out at her. If he had slapped her, he couldn't have stunned her more. His words stung her. Tears welled up in her eyes. God, not again; not with him; not again. She was not going to dissolve in tears in front of this man. She flung the cup down at his feet splattering what little was left of the coffee over his trouser leg and ran off. She needed to get away. She didn't stop running until she had banged her front door shut behind her.

Chapter 41

Thinking about it later, he realised he had been stupid. He should never have gone down the subway to get back to the car park. There wasn't much traffic on the road. He could easily have waited and just walked across the Marine Highway at Fisherman's Quay whenever the road was clear. But he had been preoccupied. He had wanted to keep walking to get back to his car as quickly as possible and put as much distance between himself and Gawn as he could.

He was so angry at himself for misreading the situation with her. He had been attracted to her from that very first day she had chased after him and Lucy. His fascination with her had grown and their shared dinner had been fun. At least that was what he had thought. He'd enjoyed it and he'd thought she had too. He had spent most of the night while she slept on his sofa watching her, tracing the moulded contours of her face; the sheen off her red locks as they reflected the light from the fire; the gentle rising and falling of her chest as she slept. He had caught a glimpse of a silver scar between her breasts as he had tucked the blanket tightly around her and remembered Jonah's phone call with more information about her. This must be part of the injury which had led to her leaving the army. He now knew she had been caught up in an IED in Afghanistan and had lost two of her fellow soldiers as well as suffering serious injuries herself. Jonah had said that they thought they might lose her too and she'd been in hospital for a long time.

He had really thought she liked him and that crack about swapping the comb had just been a silly joke – not a good one as it turned out. He was stunned when she slapped him. It was not that it was so very sore, though she could pack quite a punch, he thought. But it had never happened to him before. He would never force himself on any woman. But what he was most sorry for was what he had said to her afterwards. He didn't think he would ever forget the look on her face when he had mentioned Max. He had been thinking about that when the blow came.

The subway was poorly lit, made worse by one of the bulbs obviously being smashed and providing no illumination to the far end of the passageway but he could see the light streaming in from the bright streetlights and he was heading towards it. He had made it more than halfway along when it happened. He didn't hear any footsteps behind him to warn him. The blow came out of nowhere, so he was totally unprepared. For one crazy second, he thought it might be her, coming after him, attacking him. The blow had caught him on his right shoulder just to the side of his neck, partly deflected by the brim of his hat. He went down in a heap face first but managed to put out his hands in an automatic response to stop his face smashing into the rough cement floor. Then some primitive instinct, or maybe it was research for one of his books dredged from the back of his mind, led him to curl up into a ball. It meant the second blow, a kick, connected not with his head where it had been aimed but with his leg and arm. Its force knocked his prone body back into the wall. He was anticipating a third blow, tensing himself for it, when he heard voices. His attacker heard them too for just as suddenly as it had started, so it ended. With what sounded like a hiss he was gone, the sound of his feet running back in the direction he had come, a welcome noise to Seb's ears. He was still alive but wasn't sure he could move. In fact, he was pretty sure he couldn't.

The new voices came closer. Two pairs of scruffy trainers, one pair black and the other which had once been white but was now scuffed and muddied, came into his line of sight. He felt hands moving him roughly onto his back. He couldn't make out their faces clearly but he recognised the unmistakable sickly-sweet aroma of cannabis. Hands went through his pockets. He could do nothing to help himself; to prevent their plundering. He had never felt so vulnerable. He felt the bulk of his wallet disappear from his breast pocket and his mobile phone from his trousers. Then a cold slimy hand grabbed his wrist and jerked his arm up causing a stabbing pain to shoot up into his shoulder. His watch was wrenched off with a yank. He wanted to yell 'no' but couldn't find the word and knew it would have no effect anyway. They pushed him carelessly back down, banging his head off the wall, and then ran off laughing. At least they hadn't hurt him deliberately.

He couldn't be sure how long he had lain there aware of the cold wet ground beneath him and the stench of urine and excrement – animal or human – in his nose. His eyes focused on a used condom and wrapper carelessly discarded just inches away from his face. A scuffling noise caught his attention. He shuddered, whether from the cold or shock he wasn't sure, but he knew he needed to get up onto his feet, make it out to the street, get help.

Getting to his knees was a struggle. His right arm wouldn't support his weight. He guessed it might be broken either from the blow or the kick. After what seemed like hours, with the sweat sitting thick on his brow from the effort, he got to his feet lying back against the wall to support himself. The journey to the opening at the other end of the subway was probably only about five metres but it might as well have been five miles. Slowly, inch by inch, dragging himself along the wall, stopping between each movement to recover and allow the pain to subside a little, he made it. Now to climb the ramp up to street level. At least now there was a railing he could cling on to.

'Hey, mister, are you alright?' The voice was young. Interested. Not threatening.

'He's drunk, can you not see? He can't even stand up.'

'No. Look. He's hurt. Here, mister.'

A hand went round his shoulder and he winced in pain. He looked round at the group of boys. They were in some sort of uniform and then he recognised it. It was the Boys' Brigade. His mother had made him join as a boy. Incongruously all four were clutching colourful ice creams. They got him to a patch of green grass beside some kind of medieval figures, knights he thought, and helped him sit down. One of them phoned for an ambulance and after he had managed to tell them he had been attacked, asked for the police too. They stayed with him until the police car arrived, sirens blaring, its lights visible along the length of the Marine Highway.

Then things started happening. In one sense it was so quick. Policemen with questions, a passing nurse offering help, the paramedics arriving, the transfer to an ambulance. He was conscious but in pain as they sped to the nearest hospital but was alert enough to reason that, seeing they didn't deploy the siren, his condition mustn't be life-threatening. At least that was what he hoped. In another way it had all happened in slow motion, like a dream or maybe more like a nightmare.

A&E was busy – the usual quota of drunks for one thing. Then a major traffic accident resulted in a flurry of activity. At first, they might well have categorised him as another drunk who needed to sleep it off but the policeman who had accompanied him in the ambulance filled the medics in on what had happened to him. They were all rushing around dealing with much more seriously ill people than he must be, but he was touched by their kindness. They patched him up, sent him to X-ray, declared there was nothing broken and discharged him with a supply of strong painkillers and a prescription for more. A bright wee nurse who had dabbed his face clean told him he would have a lovely black eye in the morning and that was the first time he had realised he had not been totally successful in shielding his face. He asked for a mirror and saw with surprise a bruise developing on his cheek and the puffiness under his eye.

Jonah had come and picked him up from the hospital after he had asked the nurse to ring his friend. He had wanted to take Seb to his sister's house, but he refused. He didn't want to worry her. He just wanted to get to his own bed and curl up and sleep. The bruises and pains would go away. With time. What would not go away any time soon was the feeling of powerlessness he had experienced, the terror of knowing there was nothing he could do to stop what was happening. Nor would he forget the feeling of the watch being taken from his arm. It was not an expensive watch. He had others worth a lot more. But it was special. It had been his grandfather's. He knew he didn't need a watch to remind him how his grandfather would expect him to behave; the kind of man he would want him to be, but it still hurt to lose it. He allowed himself to imagine what he would do if he met his attacker face to face, but it didn't help. He just wanted to forget all about the events of the night and that meant forgetting Gawn Girvin too. So be it. He determined to do just that.

Chapter 42

It had taken her a long time to pull herself together. She just wanted to cry. But she couldn't. She didn't think she had any tears left for Max. Her tears now would be tears of anger and frustration. She was angry with York. He was Mr Cool. He thought he could charm his way into her bed with a cup of coffee and a cheeky smile. She didn't believe he was the murderer, but she was angry that they hadn't made more progress on finding the actual killer and really angry that the bastard had invaded her home and life and was playing tricks with her mind.

Gawn was in her office next morning before it was fully light. She had slept badly. Munroe haunted her dreams. She had woken about 5am her heart pounding, visions of a maniacal Munroe brandishing a huge knife chasing after her. Then York had suddenly appeared and come between her and Munroe, so it was York who ended up stabbed. She had watched the blood spurt out of his neck and screamed. That was what had woken her up. She hoped she hadn't really screamed out and disturbed her neighbours.

At first, she had tried to get back to sleep, then given it up. There was no way her mind would settle to sleep again. Even showering, dressing and driving as slowly as she could, she had reached the office before 7am and surprised the night duty desk sergeant.

She allowed herself to feel excited. She was sure there was going to be a breakthrough today. Knowing now what Munroe had told her about the toilet block in the park she had decided to send some officers to check the fence between the back of the block and the back of the university building and see if they could find anything useful. She doubted that area had been searched previously and could find no mention of it in any of the reports she was wading through.

She was still sifting through reports when Maxwell arrived. He was obviously keen to get started to work too. He logged on to his computer before he waved to Gawn to acknowledge her presence. He had wanted to begin trawling through documents and websites trying to verify the whereabouts of both Munroe and York, the chief suspects, the previous evening but Gawn had insisted he go home. Kerri had been pleased to see him at first but complained that he might just as well not have been there because his mind was somewhere else and that was true. He couldn't wait to get started again. His money was on Munroe as the killer. He had always thought him strange and seeing him yesterday after his interview with Gawn, he was convinced he was hiding something.

When McKeown arrived, she joined Maxwell in his search. They divided the work between them. Maxwell focused on Munroe, McKeown on York. It was slow-going. Gawn had made it clear they had to be absolutely sure before they made any moves. She was sitting over a report from Billy Logan about his investigations in Carrick – he still hadn't traced the mystery handyman – when her mobile phone rang, and she was surprised to see Schneider on her caller ID.

'Hauptkommissar, what a surprise. I thought you'd be too busy sightseeing to be thinking about us.' She tried to keep her voice light. She couldn't think why he would be contacting her.

'Oh, I'm having a great time. Belfast is a very interesting city. I have done one of your black taxi tours and seen your murals. Not quite as impressive as our Berlin Wall.' He laughed. 'Have you ever seen it?'

'Yes, of course. Some time ago.'

'I hope you enjoyed it. Berlin is my hometown. Nowhere ever compares to your own hometown.'

Gawn didn't have the time or the inclination for this chitchat with him and wondered why he was really phoning. She didn't want to be rude, but she did want to get him off the line.

'I am moving on tomorrow, but I thought we might meet up for a drink tonight.' She was about to make her excuses when he added, 'Then I could bring you up to date on the fire inquiry. There have been developments.'

He did not elaborate and she realised it was a deliberate ploy on his part to make sure she would agree to meet him. She could try asking him directly but as it was a German investigation and not hers, she couldn't really insist. She could invest half an hour and have one drink.

'I suppose I could spare a short time for a drink. Where and when?' It was a slightly ungracious reply but the best she could manage.

'How about the hotel in Bedford Street? It's supposed to have a wonderful bar on the top floor with a panoramic view of the city.'

She knew of it but hadn't been there. She was interested to see what it was like.

'Fine. Shall we say seven o'clock? I should be cleared up by then.'

'Perfect. And you can bring me up to date on your serial killer.'

He laughed but she sensed he meant it. No way would she be sharing any information with him.

'See you tonight.' And she rang off.

* * *

She was late. She hadn't been able to get rid of McDowell. He had appeared in her office unannounced and sat talking for ages. He was concerned about the investigation and wanted to make sure Gawn had everything under control. The stakes were high, he kept repeating. When he had eventually left, she realised she was going to be late for Schneider. She hated being late.

Finding a parking space nearby had proved impossible. The crowd lining up outside the Ulster Hall meant there was a concert there tonight, so she had to resort to a car park at the end of the road. It meant she arrived breathless in the hotel foyer having run all the way from her car. She cursed herself for choosing her Manolo Blahnik shoes this morning to complement her plain black trouser suit. She loved them but tonight as she ran along the darkened pavement in Bedford Street shining after an earlier shower of rain, she wished she had chosen something else.

She spotted him immediately, casually leaning across the desk at reception chatting to an immaculately made-up blonde. The girl giggled at something he said to her and Gawn saw him lean closer and whisper something in her ear. Even from the doorway she could see the blush rise up the girl's face. She took a second to catch her breath before she approached him.

'Good evening, Norbert. Apologies for being late. You know how it is.'

He placed his hand on her arm and leaned in kissing her on the cheek. She was surprised but this was outside the office and they were off duty, in fact he was on leave, so she supposed he thought it was alright. Anyway, it was just the continental way of greeting. He didn't mean anything by it. She hoped. She didn't want him to get the wrong idea.

'I have arranged for us to have a drink in the Observatory.'

He continued holding her by the elbow and guided her towards the elevator. A concierge stood ready obviously expecting them. He pushed the button to open the elevator doors and followed them inside.

'You're in luck. We're not too busy yet this evening. Have you been up to the bar before?' His modulated Belfast accent would be a hit with the tourists, she was sure.

'No.' Gawn and Schneider responded in unison.

'You'll enjoy it. The views are spectacular.'

The elevator arrived at their floor and the concierge pushed the button to open the door. Schneider gestured for Gawn to walk out before him and as he passed the young man he put something into his hand.

'Thank you very much, sir. Enjoy your evening.' The two men shared a conspiratorial smile.

And with that he was on his way back down to the foyer leaving Gawn and Schneider to walk through a set of glass doors into the cocktail bar. The concierge was right. It was not overly busy yet. Gawn took in the whole room as was her custom. She wanted to get her bearings. The décor was tasteful, the lighting subdued, and the music set at just the correct volume for conversation so long as you were not sitting too far apart. Couples – it was all couples, she noted – were grouped at tables, dotted around, all seeking their own pod of privacy. The centre of the room was taken up by the bar. Its glass-backed display of colourful bottles gave notice of the selection of drinks available. Checkered panelling filled the wall under the bar counter and reminded Gawn, along with the strategically placed couples, of a game of chess. What was it with bottles and games, she thought. They were following her everywhere.

There were several free tables and Schneider selected one beside one of the panoramic windows and guided Gawn to it, his hand this time resting on the small of her back. The view was spectacular, taking in a vista of north Belfast, lights twinkling in thousands of houses and streets and the red brake lights of cars illuminating the scene like glowing insects floating in a black sea.

'What would you like to drink, my dear?'

She was not happy to be addressed as 'my dear'. She was no one's 'dear', but she let it pass. This was a one-off meeting; she would never see the man again and she wanted information from him. No point in making an issue of it. She scanned the drinks menu. There was a selection of cocktails all given appropriately Belfast-related names. She was amused to see that one was named Botanical Gardens and was tempted to try it. It was gin-based which she knew she would enjoy but she wanted to keep a clear head. A glass of wine would be better. She could take a few sips and leave the rest.

'I think I'd like a glass of Châteauneuf-du-Pape.' She smiled at Schneider.

'Perfect. I think a bottle would be best.'

He ordered a bottle when the waiter came to their table bringing a bowl of nibbles.

'I'm sure you haven't eaten yet. Perhaps we could have dinner in the restaurant?'

His intonation indicated this was an invitation rather than a suggestion.

'No.' She spoke a little too hastily and a little too vehemently. 'I mean that's very kind but I'm fine. I can only spare a short time. I have to get home.'

'Of course. Just an idea.' He didn't seem too disappointed. Perhaps it had been just a spur-of-the-moment thought with no suggestion of anything other than being hospitable.

While they waited for the wine to arrive, Gawn tried to make conversation. She didn't want to give him the impression she had only agreed to meet him in order to pump him for information. Even though that was the truth. But she found he was difficult to talk to when it wasn't about work. They seemed to have such different interests. It was a relief when the wine arrived and Gawn felt she could broach the subject of the fire.

As Schneider poured her a rather large glass of wine, she asked, 'What are the new developments in your case that you mentioned?'

'Well, it's not my case, of course, but my colleagues are keeping me up to date with it. They have gone through a lot of the CCTV coverage now. The stuff they got from you was very useful because it helped them pinpoint the time they needed to focus on. They were then able to identify several members of the Schwarzer Adler including Weil and one of the leaders, a man called Schaepe. He doesn't usually involve himself directly so having him on film is great. They have been able to pull him in and are questioning him, so they are delighted. Someone will be contacting your Chief Constable directly to thank the PSNI officially.'

Gawn was glad they had been able to help and that the Germans were making progress. Her only concern was, if Weil was involved in this, did it mean his murder was more likely to be because of that and their theory about a serial killer was less likely?

'And what about your serial killer, Gawn? Any progress finding him?'

'We're exploring several interesting leads.'

Even as she spoke the words, they sounded like stalling tactics, the kind of thing she would say to a reporter to give them something to print without giving them anything at all. He didn't push it.

'I wish you every success, Gawn. I hope you get face to face with your killer soon.' He smiled and raised his glass to her.

It seemed like a strange way to put it and she shivered as if someone had walked over her grave. Of course, he was speaking in a foreign language. Sometimes vocabulary or idioms could be misused. She had once found herself facing a plate of eggs in a restaurant in Germany when she thought she had ordered spaghetti.

'Thank you.' They clinked glasses. 'I hope so too. Cheers!'

She took a mouthful of wine. It was very good quality and under different circumstances she could have really enjoyed it. One more sip and she got to her feet.

'I must go. It's been nice seeing you again, Norbert. I hope you enjoy the rest of your stay.'

He was about to get to his feet too.

'No. Stay. Please don't get up.' She placed her hand on his arm as much to physically stop him from getting up as to preclude any intimacy between them. 'Finish the rest of the wine. I can manage. My car's not far away. Goodnight.'

She walked off before he had the chance to kiss her again. Once was enough. At the door she turned back to wave. He had been watching her and a weak smile formed on his face as she waved at him. He did not wave back.

Chapter 43

Gawn had not left her apartment all weekend. She had barely left her bed. She had cried herself to sleep on Friday night when she got home from her meeting with Schneider. She woke up late on Saturday morning with red swollen eyes and a pounding headache. She just took her tablets and climbed back into bed, sleeping off and on for the rest of the day. She just wanted to close the world out.

Sunday passed mostly in a haze. She forced herself to get up and make some tea and toast around noon which she managed to keep down even though bouts of nausea threatened to overwhelm her. By eight o'clock her despair had begun to change to anger. She was not going to be beaten. She had faced worse than this. She had a job to do. There was a killer out there; a threat to young women and whether it was York or Munroe or whether it was someone else, she had to find out and stop him.

She woke before her alarm clock went off on Monday morning. It was as if she was revitalised after a weekend of despair. She was in the office, having already arranged to call with Madame Katarina later in the day, and was sitting sifting through reports when Maxwell arrived. Gawn had made it clear they had to be discreet. In normal circumstances Maxwell would have questioned other staff in the mortuary, especially Munroe's assistant and checked his work diary. Instead, he had to use more roundabout methods like checking pathology conferences – when and where they'd taken place and who had attended. It was amazing what was available online these days.

Erin McKeown had been tasked to make a preliminary check on York's and Munroe's movements. She had started with York as she knew Maxwell was looking at Munroe. She began by scrutinising CCTV footage to see if she could pinpoint exactly when the lecturer had arrived at the book signing. Because she knew approximately when he was supposed to have been there, she was able to confirm the time quite quickly. She reckoned he would just about have been able to carry out the murder and get to the bookshop even though she caught him on the traffic camera at University Street stopping briefly to talk to some man in a pork pie hat. He looked flustered and out of breath when he arrived for his book launch. It could simply have been that he was late or he might have been excited after committing the murder.

Gawn signalled for Maxwell to come into her office.

'Paul, any word from Forensics?' She asked not really expecting that there would be.

'Too soon to have results on the DNA yet but they have identified the fingerprints. There were two sets on the bottle and one of them matched the prints on your front door.'

Gawn couldn't believe what she was hearing. Was Munroe their killer? She was really losing it if she had misjudged both York and Munroe so badly.

'Should we pick him up, ma'am?'

This was a big decision. She hesitated. What if they had got it wrong? But what if they left a killer on the loose to kill again? If Weil had not been the intended victim, some poor girl was in danger. Right now.

'I think we definitely need to question him under caution. Can you do it, Paul? Pick him up at his house. At least we can try to keep it quiet for a while if we don't arrest him at his office. Take Billy with you to bring him in. Billy has plenty of faults, but he can keep his mouth shut.'

Before Maxwell had a chance to call Logan over, McKeown appeared at the door.

'I managed to check some of Dr Munroe's whereabouts at the time of the murders. I haven't got dates for all three but for two of them he has definite alibis. When the girl was murdered in London, he was speaking at a conference in New York, and for the killing in Amsterdam last year, he was in hospital getting his appendix out. You remember, ma'am, he collapsed in court and had to have an emergency operation. It was the talk of the place that day.'

Of course she did. So how did his fingerprints get on her door?

'OK, Paul. Looks like we're not arresting Munroe – at least not yet – but we do need to talk to him. Phone him. Ask him to come in for a chat today.'

She hoped that Munroe was out of the picture but she would need to check his alibi with Madame Katarina. And, if he was, that would leave only York.

Gradually the others began straggling in. Seeing both Maxwell and McKeown were already at their desks working, they went straight to work too. The normal coffee and chat before starting was not an option today. Even Logan sat down and began typing up his report of his findings in Carrickfergus. He hadn't been able to trace the workman spotted in the marina. But he would keep looking.

Chapter 44

Gawn, Maxwell and McKeown stood watching Munroe on a screen. He sat at a bare table in a bare room with a paper cup of lukewarm tea in front of him. Logan had brought it in and now stood behind the pathologist examining his fingernails in a bored manner. There was no doubt the doctor was uncomfortable. His shoulders were shrugged as if he was cold even though the room was well heated. They could see his hands were shaking as he lifted the cup to his mouth.

'OK, Paul. You take the lead.'

Gawn stood watching as the two moved to the door. Munroe's head turned sharply when he heard the door open behind him. His expression didn't change as he saw Maxwell although he didn't recognise the woman with him.

'Thank you for agreeing to come in and help us, sir. Sorry to have kept you waiting. This is DC McKeown.'

'Did I have a choice, Sergeant?'

The pathologist looked up at the camera placed as discreetly as possible in the corner of the room at ceiling level. Its red recording light flashing, Munroe knew he was being recorded and no doubt suspected that the Chief Inspector was watching.

But the sergeant's deferential tone seemed to have had the desired effect on Munroe. He took another gulp of the tea and looked first at Maxwell, then at McKeown. He seemed to relax, realising or at least hoping that his alibi had checked out and he was no longer under suspicion. He smiled at them.

'We really just wanted an explanation of how your fingerprints happened to be on the Chief Inspector's front door, sir.'

Munroe's face revealed his utter astonishment. He wouldn't make much of a poker player, Gawn thought to herself.

'My fingerprints? On the Chief Inspector's door?' His intonation rose almost to a squeak as he repeated Maxwell's words.

'Yes sir. The prints on your bottle match prints we found on DCI Girvin's door.'

'But I've never been near her door. I don't even know where she lives.'

He directed his response to Maxwell, his eyes wide in confusion. He didn't react, just held his gaze.

'Could anyone else have handled the bottle, sir?'

'No, Sergeant. Definitely not. I'm very particular. My staff are never in my office when I'm not there and the cleaners know to leave the cabinet alone. I dust it myself.'

Unbidden, an image of Munroe dressed only in a pinny with a feather duster cleaning his cabinet came into Gawn's mind and she wondered if Madame Katarina had him dusting as part of his humiliation. She dismissed the thought quickly.

He had shaken his head from side to side as he spoke to emphasise his words. He seemed genuinely bewildered. He placed his hands palm down on the table, splayed his fingers, then opened and closed them in a gesture of anxiety.

'I just don't know how anyone else's prints could have got on to the bottle. Unless they were yours when you collected it, or someone made a mistake in the lab.'

He offered the suggestions but not with any degree of confidence.

Watching the interview, Gawn didn't really think either of those suggestions was likely. She had watched as Maxwell had placed the bottle in the evidence bag and she was confident that the lab techs would not have made such an elementary careless mistake, especially on a murder enquiry.

'Well, just to help us eliminate you from the enquiry, sir, would you provide a DNA sample?'

McKeown readied a swab. She prepared to open its sterile wrapping. For a split second, Munroe seemed to hesitate. Then emboldened by Gawn's absence and his secret apparently safe with her, he stood up.

'I think I have been more than cooperative. I have no intention of providing a sample like a common criminal. If you wish to speak with me again I will require my solicitor to be present and I would be grateful, Sergeant, to have my bottle returned to me as soon as possible.'

Seeing that they were not going to prevent him, Munroe made his way to the door. At a nod from Maxwell, Logan keyed in the number on the entry pad to open the door and followed Munroe as he walked out. He was barely out of the room, when Gawn walked in.

'Sorry, ma'am, that didn't help much.'

'Only got his back up,' added Maxwell, apologetically.

Gawn looked troubled and the other two picked up on that.

'On the contrary. Dr Munroe was very helpful. It would have been unhelpful if he had said anyone in his building could have handled the bottle. Then we'd have had a load of possible suspects to try to check out. But he said no one handled it. But he was wrong. He may not remember someone else handling that bottle, but I do.'

Maxwell raised his eyebrows in query.

'Who?'

'Schneider. The day we went over to identify Weil's body, we were in Munroe's office first and Schneider picked up a bottle. I would be prepared to swear it was that particular bottle.'

She looked at the two detectives. It was Maxwell who voiced their thoughts.

'So, we may have eliminated our Chief Pathologist as a suspect but now we're suggesting a senior German policeman is our serial killer?'

'Yes. And we have absolutely no idea where he is.'

Chapter 45

The next few hours were a whirl of activity. When Gawn had called the team together and given them the news about her suspicions of Schneider, they were astonished and then they were furious. He had been among them. He was supposed to be one of them. They had welcomed him, shared a joke with him, regarded him as a colleague.

Jack got the job of finding out where Schneider had hired a car and what make and model it was. Grant was busy contacting the airport and getting details of Schneider's booking for his flight back to Germany so that, if they couldn't trace him before then, they would be able to pick him up at the airport, always supposing he hadn't already left the country. Maxwell helped Logan to go through the CCTV footage around the time of the murder for anyone looking like Schneider. No one was wasting time. They were all aware that they had had this man among them and then just let him walk out. McKeown in particular was upset. She was the one he had spent the most time with, apart from the DCI herself. He had seemed charming and friendly and his goodbye peck on the cheek she regarded as a terrible failure on her part.

The first shock they got was when Grant found that Schneider had no booking for a return flight from Belfast but, more shocking still, that he had never flown into Belfast from Heathrow or anywhere else.

'But I picked him up at the bloody airport,' Maxwell nearly wailed.

'Did you actually see him getting off the plane?' asked Gawn.

He nodded his head puzzled.

'Or picking up his luggage?'

'Well, no. I just thought I'd missed him in the crowd. He came across and spoke to me.' He was miserable. He had been tricked. 'He just appeared at my side.' He hadn't liked Schneider at first sight and now he felt vindicated in his reaction.

'So where did he come from and when?'

That was the next thing to find out and it was Grant who managed to find a booking not for any airline but on the ferry from Scotland. He had tried every airline and both Belfast City and Belfast International airports as well as Derry and Dublin. Then he remembered the old Sherlock Holmes quote, "When you have eliminated all which is impossible, then whatever remains, however improbable, must be the truth." So, he had rung the ferry line and found that Schneider had travelled with a car from Scotland to Belfast nearly a week before Weil's murder.

'He was here for nearly a week before Weil was killed. What was he doing? Where was he staying?'

There were plenty of questions and not much in the way of answers. But at least they now knew his car registration.

'Erin, did Schneider talk about where he might visit?' Gawn asked. 'We'll put out a general call but if we could narrow it down, that would be good.'

'He mentioned the Giant's Causeway a couple of times. Said he was keen to see it for himself – he'd seen photos – and he talked about Fermanagh, but I don't remember anything more specific. Sorry, ma'am.'

Then a look of horror came across her face.

'The chocolate!'

The chocolate? What was the girl talking about? They watched as she searched frantically through the reports on her desk. She pulled one out and scanned it.

'Fuck! All the time we were looking over the camera footage, Schneider was eating chocolate. We even joked about it and he bought me a box of chocolates when he left because I said I preferred normal chocolate to his fancy American stuff. I never made the connection. I hadn't noticed the brand of chocolate on the wrapper found in the park. He was eating that chocolate.'

She was distraught. Why hadn't she noticed it before?

Gawn patted her on the shoulder. 'Don't worry about it. We all missed it. We'll get him.'

Now for the difficult bit. First, she had to inform Superintendent McDowell about the latest developments. She expected a rollicking and that was what she got. He was furious. The fact that the German had managed to carry on his murderous plans for ten years and evaded police forces in four countries meant nothing. McDowell wanted him found and arrested in Northern Ireland. On no account was he to be allowed to get out of the country. With miles of border crossing roads between the north and south of the island, that would be no easy task. Gawn was confident they could cover the airports and ports in the north, but Schneider was obviously clever and devious. For all they knew he had other passports.

McDowell had ordered her to hold off informing the German authorities for now. He didn't want one of Schneider's friends tipping him off. She headed back to the office to meet with Maxwell and discuss their next move. The two were together in her office when an unusually animated Logan came to the door.

'Ma'am, I've just heard from Carrick. They've managed to get a sighting on CCTV of Schneider dressed in workman's clothes. At least he was.' When he saw their puzzled expressions, he continued, 'At least he was in overalls when he went into the public toilets at the castle car park but when he came out he was in his normal clothes. The camera was quite far away outside a shoe shop across the road but a sharp-eyed constable noticed him. He had seen the guy go into the toilets but not coming out so then he watched it again and noticed a well-dressed man coming out but never going in. They were then able to watch him get into a red Hyundai and drive off.'

'And Schneider's rental car is a red Hyundai,' added Maxwell although they were all already thinking that.

'Good, Billy. Thanks.'

'There's something else, ma'am.'

'Yes?'

'It seems Dr York was beaten up in Carrick on Friday night.'

He stated this in a matter-of-fact manner not aware of the effect it was having on the DCI.

'He's lucky we've got Schneider in the frame now or we'd be looking at him for the killing and wondering what he was doing in Carrick – maybe targeting you again.' Maxwell's comment was directed to Gawn.

'Was he badly hurt?' Gawn asked, keeping her voice steady.

'Just cuts and bruises, I think.'

'Did they catch who did it?' asked Maxwell.

'No. Just a mugging. They got his wallet, phone and his watch. The locals have a couple of yobs who they like for it but no proof yet and York wasn't able to give a good description.'

'Poor guy,' said Maxwell with mock sympathy. 'His girlfriend nearly gets murdered and he gets mugged. A lot of bad luck going around.'

'She is not his girlfriend.'

Gawn's voice was unusually strident. Realising she might have been too definite and reacting to the look which passed between the sergeant and the veteran detective, she added, 'We've established they are just old friends but I think we should follow up on his assault. It's just a bit too unfortunate that in the midst of all this, he's attacked. We know Schneider was in Carrick at least once so he may have been there again.'

'But why would he attack York and what on earth was York even doing in Carrick?'

'Your guess is as good as mine.'

Which wasn't true of course. She knew perfectly well why it had happened.

Chapter 46

They had not spoken as she drove along the outer ring on her way to Ballyhackamore. Gawn's demeanour did not invite conversation. Maxwell wasn't sure what was going on between her and York, but he was sure there was something. She negotiated her way through a narrow opening to a small car park behind the public library and a row of shops and cafés. She killed the engine and turned to him.

'Wait here, Paul. I'll talk to York myself.'

Maxwell was surprised. They were supposed to be checking if York could identify Schneider as his attacker. Why had she brought him if he was going to be left in the car twiddling his thumbs?

Gawn looked around her as she headed up the leafy avenue. She hadn't been able to take much in the last time she had been here. It had been dark and then her eyes had been blinded by tears and her mind in a state of confusion, more in Afghanistan than Belfast. The street was quiet, a typical suburban road populated by young families and aging couples. As she approached York's house she noted the neat garden, the carefully tended flowerbed, the colourful autumn-flowering shrubs and the manicured bay trees either side of the glossy black door. It was what she considered a typical family home, not a trendy bachelor's pad. She would have thought his choice of home would have been a serviced apartment in the city centre. Then she realised that was more like her choice of home than his. She spotted the bell and pushed it listening for the ringing inside. For what seemed like a long time, there was no sound of movement in response. Then she saw a tall shadow through the stained glass in the upper half of the door and it slowly started to open.

They had said he had not been seriously hurt. She had expected some cuts and bruises. She did not expect his arm in a sling and a puffy black eye.

'Oh, it's you.' Not exactly an enthusiastic welcome. 'They said someone would probably be coming to interview me again. I didn't think it would be the big boss herself.'

'May I come in?'

He didn't respond but turned and started to walk away into the living room where they had slept just a few nights ago. He didn't invite her to follow but she did, noting his

212

slight limp as he walked. Once in the room he perched on the arm of the sofa. The same sofa she had spent the night on. He looked uncomfortable, in pain.

'It's easier to get up from this position. I'm not very flexible or mobile at the minute,' he said by way of explanation. His face remained impassive. He wasn't going to make this easy for her.

'Look, maybe this isn't a good idea just now. I could come back another time.' She left the sentence hanging, hoping he would not take her up on the offer. She wanted to get this over with, not have it hanging over her.

'You're here now. Might as well get it done. Save you having to come back. What do you want to know? They took my statement already. I don't think I've anything to add. I was mugged. One guy hit me and gave me a kicking, the other two took my stuff. End of story.'

Gawn stood in front of the fireplace, facing him. She didn't want to sit down for then he would be looking down on her and she didn't want to give him that advantage.

'We think your attack has something to do with the murder in the park.'

She could see he was surprised. The idea had obviously never occurred to him. Why should it?

'What on earth could that have to do with me? Why would someone want to attack me? I didn't know your victim. It was Lucy who was there, not me.'

'This isn't general knowledge, but we think... no, we know that the killer is now targeting me.'

This time there was no disguising his surprise. His mouth dropped open and his eyes grew wider.

'Dear God. Have you been attacked too?'

'Not physically. There was an incident at my home, and I suspect the firework was the killer's handiwork too. I haven't told anyone else about that, but I've checked with the local police, and they haven't been able to trace any kids going around in a car throwing fireworks, so I don't think it was random. I was the target.'

She saw he was digesting what she had said.

'But why would the killer attack me?'

She hesitated. 'Because you were with me… I think. He must be watching me and he saw us together. When you tried to kiss me either he was angry or he was protecting me in his own warped way of thinking. Either way he took it out on you.'

She hadn't apologised to him but her face told him she regretted that he had been dragged into the case and been hurt because of her. He seemed to be digesting this new perspective on his attack. Then he surprised her with what he said next.

'I didn't say anything to the cops who interviewed me but there was one second when the attack started that I thought it might be you.'

'Me!'

'Stupid, I know, but you were so angry with me and I saw the look on your face when I talked about Max.' He hesitated before adding, 'I shouldn't have said what I did. I'm sorry.'

Amid everything, he was apologising to her. He was in obvious discomfort, pain even, he looked crap and probably felt that way too. She had just told him he had been targeted by a killer because of her and yet he was concerned that he had hurt her feelings. There he went knocking her off kilter again, surprising her. She never knew what to expect of him next.

'Well, at least we now know for sure you're not the killer.'

'How do you know I didn't arrange to be beaten up to deflect suspicion? That's the kind of thing the characters in one of my books would do.'

He managed a weak smile. For one fleeting moment she allowed what he had said to plant a seed of doubt. Like the comb, was he playing games? But if he had done that, surely, he wouldn't suggest it? No, it was just his idea of a joke.

'I wouldn't go saying that to anyone else. They don't know you like I do. They might think you're serious.'

'And do you know me, Gawn?' There was a teasing, almost playful tone to his question now.

'I think I'm beginning to.' Their eyes locked, just for an instant. It was Gawn who looked away first. 'Are you sure there's nothing else you can tell me about your attacker? Height? Smell? Was he sweaty? Was he wearing aftershave? How was he dressed? Did he say anything? Anything at all?'

As Gawn was barking out her questions, York had nodded his head from side to side to show he had nothing new to add.

'He was tall. Taller than me, I think. I don't know about any aftershave. I was too busy inhaling God knows what in that passageway. And the only noise I can remember him making was like a hiss. Or…' He paused thinking. 'I wonder, could it have been "Scheiss"?'

She knew at once what he meant and what it implied. It was further corroboration that Schneider was the man they should be looking for, but she couldn't tell York that.

'But that doesn't make any sense. Why would he be swearing in German? Your victim was German, maybe his killer was too? But I could be sending you off in the wrong direction. Maybe it was just a hiss. I don't really know what I heard. I was half out of it and scared to death.'

'Well, it's something to think about, anyway.'

She made a quick decision. Taking a photograph from her pocket, she held it out to York.

'Have you ever seen this man?' It was Schneider's photo from his temporary PSNI pass. York looked at it closely but showed no sign of recognition.

'No. I don't think I've ever seen him. Who is he?'

Gawn decided that he deserved to know about Schneider especially in case the German came after him again.

'His name is Norbert Schneider. We think he's the killer and probably also the person who attacked you. If you see him, stay out of his way. He's dangerous.'

He handed her back the photograph.

'Thank you for your help, Dr York. I'll leave you in peace.'

'Really? We're back to *Dr York* again?'

She needed to get away as quickly as possible. She didn't like to think that he had been half beaten to death because of her. Gawn made to walk out of the room, but York stood up and blocked her way.

'You might think you know me, but you don't really, Gawn. When all this is over, I'd like you to get to know me better. Whatever Max did, however he hurt you, I'm not Max. I would never hurt you.'

She looked at him and when she spoke her voice was low. He had to strain to make her out at first.

'But you don't know *me* at all. Max wasn't my lover and *he* didn't hurt me. Max was my daughter. She was killed last year.'

She paused, unable to go on, her voice breaking. Tears welled up in her eyes.

His shock was evident as he almost spluttered, 'I didn't know you were married. I didn't realise you had a family.'

He took a step towards her, his natural reaction to hug her and then stopped, aware she needed space. All that was expected of him in this moment was to listen.

Having started, it seemed Gawn needed to go on, to tell him what she had kept hidden for so long from everybody.

'I wasn't. I don't. I had Max... Maxine. I had her when I was 17. I went over to England, had my baby, gave her up for adoption and never came back here. Sounds so simple, doesn't it? But it changed my life, changed me forever. No one knew except my mother. We never talked about it, about her,' she corrected herself. 'Then two years ago Max found me. Her adoptive parents had told her about me and she traced me. We had ten months together. We were just enjoying getting to know each other. Then she went off and never came back.' She paused and took a deep breath. 'I survived Afghanistan, she didn't.'

She spoke in such a matter-of-fact manner. No histrionics. Death was so commonplace where she had been but for Gawn it felt so good to tell someone, not to have to hold it all in anymore. The tears had started to trickle down her face as she'd been speaking. York didn't say a word. Now he did reach out with his one good arm and pulled her tightly into him. When she started sobbing, he merely hushed her like a baby and stroked her hair. When her sobs had started to subside, she moved back from him.

'I've never told anyone that.'

'Thank you for sharing it with me. I am so, so sorry, Gawn.'

Before either of them could say anything more, Gawn's phone rang. She pulled it out of her pocket, ran her hand over her eyes and answered the call.

'What is it, Sergeant?'

Whatever he had said, she replied, 'OK. Give me two minutes.' She replaced the phone in her pocket. 'I have to go.'

'Are you alright?'

'Yes. I'm OK. Just something I need to follow up.'

She ran her hand over her eyes again.

'Can I see you again?' He could not disguise the eagerness in his voice.

'Maybe we should wait until all this is over.'

'Or maybe we shouldn't. It's a cliché but that doesn't mean it's not true, carpe diem.'

He thought of adding that she above anyone should know that from her experience but decided not to. That would be manipulative, and he didn't want to trick her into his life or guilt-trip her because he had been hurt because of her. He wanted her to want to be with him as much as he wanted to be with her.

'I'll phone later, if I get the chance. It's just crazy at the minute. We need to get this guy before he kills someone else or gets away.'

He knew she didn't really mean it. She wouldn't phone and she knew it too but as she walked past him, she allowed her hand to brush against his. It wasn't much but it was something. She walked into the hallway, York following. Just at that moment, a voice rang out from upstairs and a young blonde, wearing only a long Oxford University T-shirt which barely met the top of her long legs, came bounding down the stairs.

'Where did you put my jeans last night, Seb?' She noticed the two standing there. 'Oh, sorry. Didn't know you had company.'

Gawn turned from the girl to York. She didn't say a word, only registered the look of confusion on his face, and quickly turned back and walked out the door without looking back. He didn't come after her or call out. As she walked away, she heard the door slam shut.

Chapter 47

How could she have been so stupid? He had been busy trying to convince her of how sincere he was while his latest conquest was upstairs getting dressed after spending the night with him. And she had fallen for it. So bloody naive. He was smooth. Did sincerity so well. She had to give him that. But she'd been right all along. Never get involved; don't let it get personal. Work is work. Don't mix it with pleasure. Just do the job and walk away.

By the time she'd reached her car, she was confident Maxwell wouldn't notice how upset she had been. Her tears had given way to anger. She was furious with York and even more furious with herself.

'OK, Paul. Schneider's been sighted?'

'Yes. On the North Coast. He was spotted near Coleraine and they traced where he was staying in an Airbnb in Portstewart but they missed him. I remember now he mentioned the Giant's Causeway to me when I met him at the airport and he talked to Erin about it too so he must have had it in mind to go there. Anyway, they're searching the property now to see if he left anything interesting behind.'

'Great.' She added sarcastically, 'Maybe he left us a map showing where else he was going.'

'Funny you should say that, ma'am. Erin told me he had mentioned Fermanagh too as somewhere he'd like to visit. And remember he told us he liked to go sailing with his father, so he likes boats.'

'You think he was planning a sightseeing tour after he killed Weil and threatened me?'

Maxwell didn't like her sarcastic tone. He knew she was under a lot of pressure, but they were all doing their best. They just needed a lucky break.

'I think he's a bloody maniac, ma'am. That's what I think. But I also think we'll get him. We've got his car reg. and they only missed him by a few minutes in Portstewart. He can't know all the back roads like the local boys do so he'll probably be on one of the main roads and they already have the chopper up too. They'll get him.'

He sounded confident. He was upbeat but his boss seemed strangely subdued in comparison and he had wanted to give her some good news.

'Let's hope so. Let's get back to the office, Paul.'

Chapter 48

Early on Tuesday morning, before she had time to leave home, Maxwell phoned. She hoped it was good news. It had all gone strangely quiet after the initial sighting of Schneider yesterday. Obviously, the locals hadn't been just so quick as they had hoped. He had either got away or gone to ground somewhere. She hoped Maxwell had good news for her.

'You're in the office early, Paul.'

'I got a call from Forensics. They didn't match Munroe's prints from the bottle to the door in the Botanic toilets, but they did match another set. Schneider was in the park around the back of the toilet block as well as at your apartment and in Munroe's office.'

'Great. That's enough for us to contact Germany and get Schneider's prints officially as well as informing his bosses, and we should be able to get a European arrest warrant issued for him so if he does manage to get away from us, they'll be able to pick him up wherever he goes. Great news, Paul. Thank you for letting me know.'

'There's something else. Billy was planning to be in Carrick this morning. They have tracked down CCTV of Schneider around your apartment block. You might want to have a look at it yourself.'

'Yes. I'll call in to the barracks here. Let Billy know I'm on my way in case he's doing something he shouldn't be. He's done some good work on this. I don't particularly want to catch him out at something.'

Maxwell was surprised. He hadn't thought Gawn was aware of Logan's drinking and he had thought she wouldn't cut him any slack if she ever found out but obviously he was wrong. Maybe she wasn't just quite so 'by the book' as everyone thought.

She took her time getting ready. She wanted to give Logan time to tidy himself up; maybe even sober himself up. She knew he was a heavy drinker; had realised it some time ago. So far, it hadn't impacted his work. She hoped to keep it that way. She wanted to see him get safely to retirement and his pension.

Half an hour later, she was seated in a claustrophobic office at the back of the local police station. She, Logan and one of the local detectives, Harry Sloan, were watching black and white footage taken around the front of her building.

'Any idea where he was coming from or going to?' she queried.

'No. He just disappears. He doesn't show up heading into the town centre or towards Belfast. It's as if he just vanishes into the lough.'

'Can you get a copy of this sent over to my office? And I'd appreciate it if you could have someone watch the days either side of this. I'll only be happy when Herr Schneider is safely in custody.'

Like all the local policemen, Sloan was aware of the bomb hoax at Gawn's door. He wasn't privy to all the details about the perfume bottle but he knew enough to want to catch this man.

'I'll get that arranged.'

'Thank you.'

Gawn was shaking hands with Sloan as she stepped out of the office into the hallway.

'Thank you, Constable. I appreciate it. And thank you for retrieving my hat. I assumed I had lost it forever.'

She knew that voice. It was Sebastian York's. She turned round. York and his girlfriend were exiting the main door. He hadn't noticed her or at least he hadn't made any sign of seeing her.

'What was that about?' she questioned the constable he had been speaking to.

'Mr York was beaten up in town last week, ma'am. We've got a couple of guys for it and we've recovered a watch they stole. He was here to identify it. Funny, it's a battered old thing only worth a few quid and I noticed he was wearing a Rolex, but he seemed really pleased we'd got it back for him. Oh, and his hat. It was left in the subway, but we gave it back too.'

Simple enough. This case was riddled with coincidences. It had started with one and kept going from there. Now here was another one. He had happened to be here when she was too. This was her first ever time in the police station in Carrick and he was here too, with his new girlfriend.

'Poor guy took quite a hammering. He can't even drive at the minute until the doctors give him the all-clear. Lucky he has his sister to ferry him around.'

'That's his sister?'

She'd been thinking this but hadn't realised she had spoken the words aloud. She hoped that Sloan and Logan hadn't picked up on her reaction.

Chapter 49

She sat in her office and stared down at the document on her desk. It was background information on Schneider which the German police had provided. She had started to read about his secondment to New Jersey police which coincided with a gap in the timeline of the murders in Europe. The Americans were checking to see if anything similar had happened there when he was in the country. So far, they had found one possible murder.

She learned too that Schneider was not his real name. He had changed it officially from Rosenmeyer. That had brought a cynical smile to her face. Of course, he had chosen to be called Schneider which translated as 'tailor', or really 'cutter'. A twisted sense of humour. Even the bastard's name had been taunting them.

Then she realised she had just been staring into space. To save her life she couldn't have said what she had just read even though she had been looking at it for ten minutes. She couldn't concentrate on it; on anything really. Her mind kept going back to that night in York's house. The tender way he had cleaned her wounds. The nurses and doctors had been kind and so efficient. They had saved her life and brought her through the months of rehabilitation. But none of them had looked at her like that; touched her like that. At the thought of his touch, her stomach fluttered.

Her mind cut to their conversation when she'd slapped him. If she thought about it for more than a minute, she could still feel the warm touch of his lips on hers and the tip of his tongue along the edge of her teeth. She could smell his aftershave and feel his hand on her back as he tried to pull her closer to him. But then his face when he spat out his words about Max filled her mind. It had hurt so much. She felt on the verge of tears again and worried that she was having another breakdown.

She knew she was a cynic. She had seen so much of the evil side of life; so many horrors. She thought of the mother who killed her children because they were an inconvenience to a new lover. The man who beat his wife's face to a pulp because his dinner was presented to him colder than he liked. The fanatic who was prepared to kill men, women and children and himself in the name of his god. So now she was confused that she was seriously contemplating ringing this man. To start what? She didn't know and that was the scariest feeling of all. To have things outside her control was an uncomfortable experience she tried to avoid at all costs in all aspects of her life. She suspected no one would ever control York and he would always be full of surprises.

She looked up. The office was half empty. It was lunchtime. She walked over and closed the door and then sat back down and lifted the phone.

* * *

He had been busy all morning since returning from Carrickfergus. Just as well really. Every time he had a free moment his mind would go to her. Her face would come into his thoughts unbidden at just the most inopportune moment. It was crazy. He was crazy for even contemplating seeing her again. She obviously didn't trust him. She was a workaholic, a cynic who had seen the worst sides of life, a control freak. Not his sort of woman at all. But then he had to ask himself – what was his sort of woman? He had had plenty of girlfriends and counted many women among his friends. He enjoyed their company and they seemed to enjoy his, but he realised he had never really had a grown-up relationship with a woman. At nearly forty years of age, he had never come close to committing to any woman. He was not into self-analysis but if he had been, he would say the break-up of his parents' marriage and the abandonment of his family had left a heavy mark on the young Sebastian.

And she didn't trust him. That was obvious. She had jumped to the wrong conclusion about his sister. Well, he had to give her some leeway on that. He guessed it did look a bit suspect, a semi-naked girl appearing from the bedroom searching for her jeans and expecting him to know where they were. If it wasn't so serious, it could be quite funny, like one of those old farces where everyone got the wrong end of the stick about everyone else, but it all came good in the end. He didn't think he was going to get the traditional happy finale in his story. He wasn't going to see her again unless perhaps in court if Lucy had to give evidence or something. He had more or less convinced himself to forget her and move on to the next attractive blonde who came his way, when she rang.

He was at his desk, going over notes for a lecture when the phone interrupted him. He wasn't expecting to hear her voice and almost spluttered his reply.

'Dr York?'

'Yes? I mean, of course, it's me. What can I do for you?'

There was a pause. Had they been cut off? Then she spoke again.

'I was ringing to see if you still wanted to meet up.' There was a hesitant note to her voice as if she was expecting to be turned down.

For one instant he was totally stunned. He had never expected to hear from her again. Hang on, Seb, don't sound too eager.

'Of course. I'd love to.'

Pause. Instead of waiting for her to speak again, he jumped in.

'What about tonight? I'm free. Are you?'

'Yes. I should be finished by six.'

She sounded relieved.

'Would you like to have dinner?'

'No. I think just a drink would be better.'

'OK. What about Albert Mooney's?'

Why did he suggest there? As soon as the words were out of his mouth he regretted them. She wouldn't want to be reminded of her last experience there. How crass could he be?

'Or wherever you like.'

'Would you mind coming to Carrick? It would let me have time to have a shower and change before we meet up. Can you drive?'

'No problem. I've got the all-clear. Have wheels, will travel. That's me.'

He was blabbering and he knew it. It wouldn't have mattered where she had suggested, he would have gone anywhere, driven anywhere to see her.

'Shall I pick you up at your apartment?'

'No.'

The response came instantly. She obviously wasn't ready for that yet. Don't push it, Seb, he thought to himself.

'We could meet in the car park outside the library. That gives us a choice of places to go for coffee or a drink.'

'Fine. Eight o'clock suit?'

'Eight would be fine.'

'Great. See you then.'

She rang off.

He was left looking at the phone in his hand, not sure if he had just imagined their conversation or it had really happened. What had he started?

Chapter 50

The full moon shone down brightly from a clear starry sky, its beam spreading across the dark waters like a searchlight. The scurrying clouds and gentle buffeting of the car as she drove along the main road skirting the side of the lough showed her the weather reports were accurate. The red light on top of the power station flashed out its warning. It had been cold when she was leaving headquarters but the wind was picking up now. Gawn had heard the weather forecast on the car radio. A storm was on its way heading up from the south. Heavy rain and strong winds were expected later in the evening.

She had left the office as soon as most of the others were gone. Maxwell was still at his desk and she thought he had looked surprised that she was going home. Normally she would be the last to leave. The search was continuing for Schneider but there had been no further sightings. It was now concentrated on County Fermanagh nearly one hundred miles away, so they just had to leave it to the locals and wait, which was always one of the hardest parts of any investigation – the waiting. One part of her just wanted to hear that they'd got him; another would have loved to make the arrest herself. She remembered his taunt that he hoped she would soon be face to face with her killer. At the time it had just seemed like clumsy use of language. Now the thought of it chilled her. She had told Maxwell to phone her if there was any news.

She had driven home feeling a sense of expectancy. It could just be her meeting with York, but she sensed their manhunt was coming to a climax. She expected news that he had been arrested. She had showered, changed into jeans, a check shirt and a navy puffa jacket against the cold. She looked at her watch. She was ready early. She decided, on the spur of the moment, to have a quick walk along the path by the side of the marina before meeting York. She wanted to gather her thoughts.

She was surprised to realise she was feeling nervous. It reminded her of the time she had gone to the cinema with Andy Mitchell. She'd had such a crush on him and been so delighted when he had asked her out. Her first real date. She hadn't told her parents of course, just made up some excuse about going out with girls from school. Her stomach had felt like this that night, sort of fluttery and slightly queasy. She had so wanted it to be wonderful. Instead, all he seemed interested in was getting his hand up her jumper. Would this meeting with York be similarly disappointing?

She had moved on from being that naive schoolgirl and had no illusions left about men but somehow York had managed to get under her skin. She realised that she wanted it to be different with him; for him to be different.

She still wasn't convinced that getting involved with him was a good idea. Did she trust him? She hoped some fresh air would clear her head; give her a chance to think. No one was about. She could see lots of lights in windows. Most people didn't seem to bother with curtains so from time to time she caught a glimpse of the lives of some of the other residents.

She hadn't gone very far – not as far as the gateway to the boats – when she suddenly changed her mind. She was just approaching the front of a local bar which sat right alongside the marina, a popular spot with the sailing crowd. The wind was picking up and she could feel a few spots of rain beginning to hit her face. Without warning, she swung around and collided with a dark figure who was right behind her. She hadn't realised anyone was there, so close, but an apology died on her lips as she recognised who it was. Schneider. He was wearing a black hoodie pulled down over his face, but his eyes were shining with an intense light. His mouth was half open and his teeth were bared like a feral animal.

The shock of seeing him made her hesitate and that was enough to give him an advantage. He grabbed at her arm, but her instincts drove her to push him away and start running. She hadn't seen a knife and her only hope was that he didn't have it at the ready to stab her or slit her throat. She could feel him behind her; almost feel his breath on the back of her neck. He was quick and strong and she knew she wouldn't be able to outrun him on the slippery pathway. She swung round again to face him ready to lash out and kick him, but he stopped dead before he reached her and stood just looking at her and then down at his hand. He raised his hand then. He didn't need to say a word. She recognised the taser he was clutching and now pointing at her.

She had been tasered once and once was enough. It had been when she was visiting New England as part of a group from the Met and reviewing the local cops' training methods for new recruits. They required all trainees to go through the experience of tasering so that they would know what effect the weapon had before they decided to use it on duty. They had invited her to take part and, not wanting to let the Met down or shirk the personal challenge, she had agreed. Only ten seconds, they had assured her, not the thirty recommended when arresting a perp. Two burly cops had bookended her ready to catch her when she fell. She had seen it done before, but the experience was not as she'd expected. The pain was intense. Her body instantly went rigid. She lost all control of her limbs and bodily functions. If the two guys hadn't caught her, she would have slammed face first straight down into the ground. They had eased her down. The recovery had been quite quick. She had never lost consciousness, only the ability to do anything; to control her own actions. Her greatest indignity was that she had wet herself, but no one commented. Apparently, that, and worsc, was what happened to everyone.

Now she was faced with a choice. If she yelled out or tried to turn and run, he would taser her. She was sure. He didn't need to tell her that. His look said it all and she thought he would enjoy doing it, seeing her helpless before him, at the mercy of his knife. She sure he would have a knife. If she cooperated with him, went with him, she could buy herself some time. Maybe there would be the chance to get away or to attract someone's attention. Her mind processed all these calculations in a microsecond. There was really no choice to be made.

'What do you want?' Her voice was shrill as it faded away on the wind, but it didn't disguise her fear. That was clear to hear.

'You, of course.' He leered at her. 'Give me your phone.'

He held out his hand, eyeing her warily and making sure to keep the taser out of her reach. She handed the mobile over. He flung it into the air and her eyes followed it as it landed with barely a splash and disappeared under the waves.

'Move.'

He grabbed her by the arm and dug the taser into the small of her back and then started marching her along the walkway until they were almost back to her building. Just as they were approaching it, a young couple came out of the door. Instantly, before Gawn could react or make a sound, Schneider had spun her round. His fingers snaked through her hair pulling her head down hard, threatening to pull her hair out at the roots. He brought her face right up to his. She could smell his sweat and realised he was enjoying his power over her, already aroused by her helplessness and the prospect of what he was going to do to her. The taser was pushed roughly into her stomach.

'Don't make a sound,' he hissed into her ear.

He kissed her violently. She expected to feel his tongue forcing its way into her mouth and had decided she would bite him hard but instead he was the one doing the biting. He bit her lip and then her cheek, bringing tears of stinging pain to her eyes. Then he smothered her mouth and face in slobbery licks like a dog licking up its dinner. Her stomach lurched and she thought she was going to be sick. The couple, if they had glanced in their direction, would only have seen two people kissing passionately locked in a close embrace. But they hadn't even glanced. They were too preoccupied with each other in their own little world.

Once they had moved off, Schneider released his hold on Gawn's hair. She used her free hand to wipe his saliva off her face as best she could. She wanted to obliterate any sign of his mouth on hers. She hoped he could see her disgust. And he did. He laughed at her but for one second he allowed his hand holding the taser to drop down to his side. This was her chance. Maybe her last chance. She brought her knee up hard into his groin and heard and felt the expulsion of air as she connected with his balls but not as firmly as she would have liked. She turned and started to run but slipped. He had straightened up again before she could barely start running. She was grabbed from behind, spun around and then… only blackness.

Chapter 51

York had arrived early. He sat in his car for a while. He checked his hair in the car mirror, running his fingers through it, not once but half a dozen times. He hadn't been so nervous about meeting a woman since he was a spotty teenager taking one of the local girls to the cinema on the bus, hoping for a quick grope in the back row to brag about to his classmates the next day. To his shame he couldn't even remember the girl's name.

To pass the time he played the kids' game of counting cars passing – red ones. He got to twenty. Then, when it turned eight o'clock, the time they had arranged to meet, he got out and sat on the low wall fronting the main highway – within sight of the subway where he'd been mugged in one direction and her apartment in the other. He should be able to spot her coming from quite a distance away. He watched the lights of the stream of cars come into view and then speed past him as they headed onwards on their journey. He probably looked suspicious sitting there. But there was no sign of her. It was a cold and windy evening and getting windier. It was threatening to rain. He could feel spots hitting his face. There were no walkers in sight. Only those with cars were venturing out. He was getting wet and he pulled his collar up closer to try to keep warm.

When 8.15 came, he began to be seriously concerned. He knew Gawn had a reputation for always being on time.

Surely, she would have let him know if she'd been held up at work. He wouldn't allow himself to think she might be standing him up. He didn't believe she was the kind of woman who would agree to meet him and then just not turn up. She wouldn't be so cowardly. If she didn't want to see him, she would tell him to his face. Perhaps she was in a meeting or had switched her phone off for some reason. But he couldn't settle. He wanted to hear her voice, to be sure she was alright, but her mobile just kept ringing out. He began pacing backwards and forwards in front of the library like a caged bear. Eventually, he could wait no longer. He would phone her office, ask to speak to her and, if she wasn't there, ask to speak to that sergeant of hers, the one who trailed after her like a puppy. He had seemed like a decent guy. He could explain that they had arranged to meet for a drink this evening and Gawn hadn't shown up. Perhaps there was a simple explanation.

As he dialled, he could feel a sense of panic rising. His hand holding his mobile felt clammy. It took minutes, which felt like hours, as he explained who he wanted to speak to, first to an operator, then some office junior before finally he heard Maxwell's voice on the line.

'Paul Maxwell.'

'Sergeant Maxwell, this is Sebastian York.'

'Yes, Dr York. Good evening. How can I help you?' His voice sounded tired and a little surprised. 'Have you remembered something else about your attacker?'

'No. That's not why I'm ringing. I was trying to get in touch with' – he was just about to say 'Gawn' when he realised he'd better not – 'your Chief Inspector. We'd arranged to meet for a drink this evening to discuss my attack.'

His excuse sounded flimsy. Why would she want to discuss the case with a witness over a drink? Maxwell would be suspicious; he wouldn't believe him. And he was and he didn't.

232

'Look, sir, the Chief Inspector left here nearly two hours ago. She didn't say where she was going but I expect it was home. She never mentioned meeting anyone and as far as I know there's no update on your attack. It's not our case.'

'But she's not answering her phone.' He sounded plaintive.

'Perhaps she's just not answering it to you, sir.'

Was it possible she had changed her mind? Had she had second thoughts about meeting him? Was he simply being stood up? He couldn't just give up without being sure.

'If she's not answering me, would you mind ringing her, Sergeant, and making sure she's alright?'

It was a bold request, and he wouldn't have been surprised if Maxwell had told him to get lost, in politically correct police speak, of course. But he didn't. Gawn had been acting strangely recently. Maxwell had realised something was going on between her and York, just hadn't known exactly what. He was worried about her too. Schneider still hadn't been found. He was out there somewhere, and she was his target.

'OK. Hold on a minute, doctor. I'll try her number.'

Maxwell took his mobile and selected the speed dial number for his boss. She would answer him. She always did. It started ringing. Any second he expected to hear her voice, probably sounding annoyed at being interrupted. But it just kept ringing out. Some of York's anxiety transferred to him.

'She's not answering me either but I'm sure she's probably just left her phone sitting somewhere and hasn't heard it ringing. I'll try again later.'

He made his voice sound calmer and more confident than he felt.

'Couldn't you send a local policeman to check on her at home?'

York was getting desperate now. He couldn't have explained exactly why but he felt Gawn was in danger. Maxwell sat back in his chair. He could just imagine the boss's reaction if a constable arrived at her door. He wouldn't want to be that constable and he didn't want to be the one who sent him. She would be livid. What was York playing at?

'Look, Dr York, I'm sure the inspector is fine. I'll try her again later.'

Maxwell wanted to get the other man off the line as quickly as possible so he could try her again. It was then that Seb decided he better come clean. If everything was alright and Gawn was furious with him for telling Maxwell about them, he could cope with that. What he wouldn't be able to cope with was something happening to her.

'Sergeant, I'm not some kind of stalker. Your inspector, Gawn, and I are…' Are what? He wasn't exactly sure what they were. Should he say, in a relationship? Was that true? 'Dating.' That sounded possible – just.

Maxwell wasn't sure he believed him. He didn't really know anything about Gawn's private life. She could be in a relationship for all he knew although he didn't think she was. Certainly, she would have to have a very understanding partner with the hours she put in at work. But dating a suspect? Dating York? She didn't even seem to like York. She had suspected him of being the killer, for goodness' sake. He hesitated.

'Please. I'm worried about her.'

There was an interminable silence on the line. Maxwell didn't speak. York was getting frantic. It was the tone of York's voice more than the words he spoke that convinced Maxwell to help him.

'OK, Dr York. I'll get someone out to check.'

'Thank you. Can you let me know what they find?'

He was sure, under normal circumstances, Maxwell wouldn't agree to any such thing, so he was surprised but relieved when the sergeant said yes.

Chapter 52

It was dark with only slivers of silver moonlight falling across the wall above her head. At first, she found it hard to focus her eyes. Her cheek was throbbing and then she remembered Schneider's fist coming towards her. Gawn didn't know how long she had been unconscious. Was it minutes or hours? Where had he taken her? She was aware of the room swaying slightly from side to side. She tried shaking her head to clear it, thinking the unsteadiness was all in her mind. Then she heard the familiar jingle jangle of the rigging and realised she must be on a boat. She was lying on her back on a hard narrow bed. Schneider must have removed her jacket, but the rest of her clothes were intact, thank God. She tried to move her hand to feel around her but realised her hands and feet were bound. She felt the zip ties digging into her skin when she tried to move. There was tape across her mouth. Her mouth felt dry and she suddenly gagged at the realisation of her predicament. She swallowed the bile back down. Mustn't choke. She reached up to her face and ripped the tape off her mouth taking a deep breath. The sound seemed so loud in the quietness.

Slowly, carefully, she managed to wriggle herself up into a sitting position and leant her head back against the cold wall. The pain in her cheek was gnawing away at her and she thought her eye might be closing. She must look a sight. As if that mattered. If Schneider got his way, she would be dead soon anyway. And God knows what horrors he had planned for her before that. She thought of the crime scene photographs she had casually glanced over without sparing a thought for the terror those young women must have gone through in the minutes before their death. If anyone had asked her then, she would have said a detective shouldn't get emotionally involved or they couldn't do their job well. What crap. She hadn't wanted to be emotionally involved with anyone. She didn't want to feel the pain of others – the rape survivors, the bereaved parents, the victims living with the scars inflicted by their attackers. Keep professionally detached, that was her mantra.

Well, there was no keeping detached now, was there? Would anyone spare a thought or shed a tear when she turned up in one of those photographs; when it was her mutilated body and glassy staring eyes they were casually perusing over a cup of coffee? Would Maxwell miss her for a week or two and then celebrate his promotion with Kerri and his children and get on with his life? Would York remember her after more than a month and regret they had never got together or simply move on to his next conquest?

She had never considered herself a deep thinker. She was not given to introspection. But now, sitting here, trussed up and facing the prospect of inevitable death at the hands of a maniac and God knows what before the final cut, she allowed herself the luxury of a little self-pity. What did she regret about her life? She regretted she had only had a few short months with Max to get to know her. Any mother would be proud to have that beautiful soul as a daughter. But she had never thought of herself as a mother; she didn't deserve that title. She never thought she had any maternal instincts until she got the news that day that Max was dead. Then it was too late.

She regretted that she'd never known what it was like to be really loved and to give love unconditionally. She'd had a few relationships. They didn't last long. She could never commit to anyone. She had made love – no, she corrected herself – she'd had sex, for that was what it was. There had been plenty of opportunities for that with her horny colleagues thousands of miles from home, facing the prospect of imminent death. But she had never known real love and she regretted that now.

The wind seemed to be strengthening, moaning mournfully in the rigging like the banshees of Irish myth and the boat was moving in response to the choppy waves. Now that her eyes had adjusted to it, there was enough light coming through the windows to make out shapes in the darkness. Moonlight reflected off metal on the wall opposite her. She could see a water tap and a saucepan sitting out on the surface. She could make out a row of bottles on a shelf above them. If she could get herself free from these ties the bottles could be useful weapons. But first she had to get her hands and feet free. And she had to do it before Schneider came back from wherever he had gone. She had no idea how long she had left before that would be. He could be back any minute.

Keep calm, she told herself. You've been trained for this. But doing it in a life and death situation when it was your life in the balance was something different. She focused on her hands. Please, God, let this work. It had worked in the training scenario with SWAT, but this was different. She could feel herself beginning to shake. It might be just the cold, but she thought it was more likely it was shock setting in.

Carefully she moved her hands until she had positioned the tie lock directly in front of her. Then she caught the end of the tie between her teeth. The surface was already digging into her skin. It was so counterintuitive to do what she was going to do. She had to make herself do it. She pulled the tie even tighter until the pain in her wrists was intense. She could imagine it was cutting into her skin and could feel a trickle over the back of her hand. Was that her imagination or her own blood? She wriggled forward on the bed and stood up. Her head swam and she felt woozy. She had to let precious seconds pass until her head had cleared and the circulation had begun to return to her legs.

As soon as the dizziness passed, she pulled her hands tightly into her stomach and bent slightly forward. Then, lifting her hands directly over her head and, with as much force as she could gather, she brought them down violently while pulling her arms apart. It didn't work. The ties only dug deeper into her flesh and she had to stop herself crying out in pain in case Schneider was on the deck above and heard. Try again. Concentrate. Every ounce of force she could muster. She felt a trickle of sweat run down her forehead into her eyes. This is it. Do it. This time. Do it. And she did it. And it worked. Just like at the training session. The ties broke at their weakest point and her hands were free.

She rubbed her wrists to get her circulation going again. She fumbled around, half hopping, half tiptoeing in tiny steps until she found a drawer under what was obviously the cooker. She hoped it was a cutlery drawer and it was. She pulled it open, fearful of making any noise. There was a collection of knives, forks and spoons all together in a heap. They felt light in her hands. Cheap lightweight cutlery, probably plastic, when what she needed was a good sharp knife to cut through the ties and to defend herself against the German. She ran the blades along her fingers. None seemed very sharp but she chose the one that seemed the best and began to hacksaw her way through the tie around her ankles. It seemed to take forever to work her way through it until it too snapped apart. For the first time then she glanced up and saw a sheet of white outside the porthole. Almost instantly she recognised it for what it was. It was her building. The bastard had been right here under her nose, watching her. With a flash of understanding she realised he had been the mystery workman Logan had never been able to find. Even as she was rubbing her legs she was listening for sounds of Schneider's return. She was alert to every creak as the boat seemed to bob and sway with growing intensity.

And then she heard it. A footstep, then another. Directly above her head. She thought of rushing towards the steps and door to the deck but was afraid of tripping in the dark and didn't know what might be facing her when she opened the hatch. Better to let him come down to her, use the element of surprise, hit him with a bottle and hopefully stun him to give her time to escape. She grabbed the heaviest one of the bottles she could feel in the gloom. She searched around and found the tape she had discarded, pressing it back onto her mouth so he wouldn't realise anything had changed. She forced herself to lie back down on the bed turning on her side with her back to the door. It meant she wouldn't be able to see him coming and could only listen intently to know exactly where he was, but it also meant he couldn't see her hands and feet were untied. She clutched the neck of the bottle, pressing it tightly into her side, hiding it from view.

Minutes passed which seemed like hours; nothing happened. Perhaps she'd been mistaken. Perhaps he wasn't back yet. Maybe she still had time to escape. Then she heard the engine starting up. He was going to take them out to sea. Panic rose in her chest and her stomach lurched. She couldn't let him get them out into the channel. There she would be at his mercy, no chance of escape. She felt the boat moving in the water and glimpsed the harbour lights as they passed through the opening at the harbour wall. Soon they would be out in the lough. Soon they would be out in the channel and heading who knows where. Although, she was certain what destination Schneider had planned for her.

Before she could move, she heard the door open and a stream of light beamed down into the cabin. The cool night air flooded in. It felt good. She took a couple of deep breaths. Her breathing sounded loud to her ears and she was worried he would suspect there was something different, that she was conscious.

Then he was beside her. She could sense him there even though she had her eyes tight closed now and could see nothing. She forced herself not to tense her body. She could feel his breath on her skin. He was bending over her, his mouth close to her ear. His saliva dripped onto her face and she couldn't help reacting. She wriggled away but that only seemed to amuse him.

'Liebling Gawn.'

His voice was eager, throaty as he stroked her cheek. His hands were rough and she thought of the manicured fingers she had noticed the first time they had met. He was enjoying this. She felt his hand gripping her leg just above her ankle. She must not tense her body. He would know she was alert. Then she felt liquid drip over her hair and face and the overwhelming aroma of flowery perfume filled her nostrils. She even recognised the brand. It was one she had used herself sometimes.

'Only the best for you, mein Schatz.'

His hand began to move slowly upwards from her calf. She visualised a tarantula moving slowly up her leg, its deadly venom ready to strike. She found herself holding her breath. Still his hand moved, slowly, so tantalisingly slowly, to increase his excitement until it reached her knee, then her pelvis and then it slid across her body forcing her legs apart, fingers probing, grasping, hand kneading her flesh remorselessly. There was no tenderness. There would be no mercy, she knew.

He groaned and then she heard him grunt. Like an animal but that was an insult to animals, she thought. This was her chance. He would be concentrating so hard on his own pleasure; she could catch him off-guard. She swung round and struck him with the bottle on his head using all her strength. She didn't care if it killed him, she just wanted to stop him; to get away. He slumped down with a groan and fell back onto the floor. She had to leap over his prone body to get to the ladder. Her foot was on the second step and her head almost in line with the deck, almost out in the night air when she felt his hand around her ankle again, hauling her roughly backwards. He was cursing her, the guttural noises loud in her ears. She clung on to the top rail of the steps and kicked back with her free foot. It connected with something. She didn't know what but she heard his stream of curses in German grow in intensity and felt his hand loosen on her ankle. That was her chance. Her last chance. She made it to the top of the ladder, landing on her hands and knees out on the deck and reached round to slam the door closed behind her.

Frantically she scanned the deck for something she could use to defend herself. She saw a screwdriver lying on the seat beside the helm. She grabbed it and jammed it through the two handles of the cabin door to stop him following her out. She heard him shouting, banging on the door. It rattled as he tried to force it open.

Only then, when she was able to stand still for a second and allow her thumping heart to calm a little did she look up. She was immediately aware of what seemed like a huge grey shape looming out of the darkness like some monster in a horror movie. Her mind took a second to recognise it was one of the large dredgers she had seen in the lough and they were directly in its path. Then she heard the door rattle behind her again as Schneider tried once more to get out. It was moving more this time. It wouldn't hold much longer. One more strong push and he would be free, the hinges ripped off. She had to make an instant decision. She threw off her shoes and hurled herself into the black waters of Belfast Lough. She couldn't stop herself from screaming as she fell through the air. The shock of the coldness of the water took her breath away. Then a cold blackness enveloped her. She seemed to be going down for a long time before she finally resurfaced gasping for breath.

She watched as the dredger moved almost alongside the cabin cruiser. Perhaps they were going to miss each other. Then she saw Schneider, his face bloodied where she had struck him with the bottle. He was half standing, half kneeling when the two vessels collided side-on, the cabin cruiser scraping along the side of the larger boat. The jolt catapulted him across the deck. She heard the thud as his head hit the edge of the railing and watched as he was flung into the water. With the detachment of a cinemagoer viewing the latest action movie, she watched Schneider disappear under the surface without a sound. It was surreal. She began to swim towards the boat. It took all her strength to reach it and grasp hold of a protruding arm. It was slippery and her hands were cold, so cold. Somewhere she was aware of voices, but her mind was numb and she could feel her grip loosening but could do nothing about it. She was cold, so cold and so tired. She needed to close her eyes for a minute, just a minute. Then she felt herself slipping back down into the waiting arms of the lough.

Chapter 53

To pass the time until he heard back from Maxwell, York had decided to take a walk along the harbour wall beside the castle. He could see Gawn's building from here but there was no sign of activity, no flashing blue lights; nothing happening. He wondered if Maxwell had lied to him. Maybe he had only said he would send someone to check on her in order to get rid of him. He needed to be doing something, couldn't just stand still and wait. The wind was picking up and the heavy rain couldn't be far behind. He had the path to himself. No one else was venturing out on such a night. In the dark, he could see the lights of the towns on the County Down coastline twinkling like a row of Christmas decorations strung along the side of the lough. He could make out the shape of one of the large cruise ships, its hundreds of cabin windows ablaze, moving silently through the darkness leaving the city behind.

The noise of a boat engine starting up behind him caught his attention. Funny time of night to be setting out. He wouldn't fancy it himself for he had heard the weather forecast earlier and knew a storm was on its way. He watched, with little interest, as a sleek cabin cruiser edged its way out carefully from its mooring just in front of Gawn's building and chugged out through the harbour entrance to the lough and the open sea. A man was standing out on the deck and, for just a second, he was caught in the lights of the pilot boat heading back into harbour after guiding the cruise ship out into the channel. The man was startled by the light and stood frozen for a moment, holding his hand up to shield his eyes until the pilot boat passed him and he was shrouded in the darkness of the night again with only the moonlight for illumination. It had been only a second but in that instant he had recognised Schneider from the picture Gawn had shown him. His blood froze in his veins. If Schneider was here, where was Gawn? Had he already killed her?

His ringtone cut through the night as his phone rang in his pocket. He cursed the silly tune he had chosen, its chirpy Mexican beat so incongruous tonight.

'Dr York?'

It was Maxwell. He could hear noises in the background and realised the policeman was on the move as he talked.

'We've checked the apartment. She's not there. And she's still not answering her phone.'

'I've just seen Schneider.'

'Where?'

'He's on a boat. He just left Carrick harbour.'

'How long ago?'

He felt like shouting at Maxwell. Hadn't the man heard him? Understood what he was saying? 'Only just now. A minute. That's all. He's just outside the harbour.'

York was running along the harbour pathway even as he spoke, making his way to its end where he would be able to see the lough lying spread out in front of him and watch Schneider and maybe Gawn, if she was still alive, sailing away.

'I'll get the coastguard on to it and the Harbour Police. They should be able to intercept him before he gets out of the lough. I'm almost there. Wait for me.'

Then York heard it. A scream, a splash. There was the sound of scraping and he could make out the shape of a larger boat. They had collided. He dropped his phone and ran. He got to the end of the harbour wall as the pilot boat had just reached the stone steps. They had obviously realised something was wrong too. They were manoeuvring their vessel to turn around, go back out. Seb was waiting for no one. He ran to the edge of the path where the steps joined it and, racing down them, yelled at the top of his voice, 'I'm coming with you.'

He was afraid his words would be lost on the wind, but they heard him. They were turned round now, facing towards the harbour opening, ready to move out, the boat parallel with the harbour wall. There was no time for a debate. They realised he was going to jump onboard.

'OK. Jump!'

He didn't need to be told twice. He didn't think about the jump, about the boat bobbing up and down, about the chance of being crushed between the boat and the sea wall. He thought only of Gawn and the danger she was in.

One of the crew handed him a lifejacket and he hastily put it on. He stood at the door of the wheelhouse and scanned the sea. He could make out the shape of the cabin cruiser listing in the water as they moved closer to it. The larger grey vessel was still moving, the crew on deck leaning over the side checking for damage, looking for bodies in the water. The pilot reduced the engine, moving so slowly but Seb realised they were being careful not to hit anyone in the water. She must be nearby. It had only taken a minute to reach the site but there was no sign nor sound of either Gawn or Schneider.

'Gawn! Gawn!'

He yelled as he had never yelled before. The wind caught his words and carried them away. There was no answering shout from the waters. A fast Harbour Police launch arrived alongside them with a powerful beam. It played over the surface of the water. For what seemed like hours, there was nothing. Only blackness. Only the white lines of spume as the waves gathered force. The pilot boat was rocking more noticeably now, and York had to hold on tightly to keep his balance. He realised his face was wet – a mixture of rain and tears.

Then a shout. One of the harbour policemen had spotted something in the water. He pointed past the cruiser in the direction of the lights of Belfast. York could just make out a shape, nothing more. It seemed to be rising and falling with the waves, making no attempt to move by itself. The police launch headed in that direction. York watched, his stomach churning from fear as well as sea sickness. He saw them drag a limp body out of the water and heard a shout.

'It's a man. He's not breathing.'

They hauled the heavy figure onboard and swung the boat around heading at top speed to the shore. York could make out blue flashing lights on the harbour ramp awaiting them.

'There!'

One of the pilot crew was pointing now but at first York could see nothing. Then he could just make out another body in the water, this time clinging to one of the dinghy davits at the back of the cabin cruiser which was listing dangerously in the dark waters.

'It's a woman.'

They began to manoeuvre their way carefully over but before they reached the spot he watched in horror as Gawn lost her grip and slid under the surface of the lough. Without thinking of any danger, York dived into the water. The coldness hit him like a brick wall and sucked all the breath out of him. He struck out for the back of the boat. He had been a strong swimmer in his youth but he had never had to swim at night in these conditions with someone's life depending on him. He could feel the water dragging at him as his clothes became more water-logged. A larger wave broke over his head and he gulped some water. He was getting tired already and so cold. He had reached the boat but at first there was no sign of Gawn. Then her body floated to the surface almost beside him. Dear God, don't let her be dead. He reached out and his fingertips connected with her arm. He grabbed hold. Nothing was going to make him release that grip. He eased her head out of the water keeping her face clear of the splashing waves. He held her there until the pilot came alongside him and strong hands pulled her up out of the sea. He didn't relinquish his hold until she was safely on board. Then he too was hauled unceremoniously up and deposited in a heap on the deck. One of the crew was working with Gawn checking for a pulse, while another steered the boat back into the harbour.

He had never really understood the expression 'to wait with bated breath' until that moment. It was as if every iota of his being, every nerve ending and all his senses were stilled, held in suspension. He could barely breathe. And then she coughed and water spouted from her mouth. She struggled to breathe but at least she was alive. That was all that mattered. He knelt beside her, displacing the crewman, and cradled her in his arms, stroking her face until they reached the shore. Her eyes were only half open. He wasn't sure how much she could hear or if she understood what he was saying to her. He couldn't remember afterwards exactly what he had said to her. He knew that his tears had mixed with the salt water on her face as he had begged her not to die but she lay with closed eyes in his arms and he was unsure if she had heard him.

Maxwell was there with a whole army of police, paramedics and a gathering crowd of onlookers when they reached the shore. If he was surprised to see a very wet York, he didn't say anything. The paramedics took over, carrying Gawn to a waiting ambulance. They tried to get him into another one, but he shrugged them off. They wouldn't let him in the ambulance with her but they couldn't stop him standing outside, waiting for news.

The police sergeant had ignored him at first. He was busy giving orders, allocating officers to control the growing crowd and cordon off the area. Someone had given Seb a space blanket like the ones he had seen marathon runners draping over their shoulders. It helped him to begin to feel some heat in his body again although his teeth were still chattering. He perched on a low wall waiting for news.

'They tell me we've you to thank for saving the boss.'

Maxwell approached him. He was smiling. Surely that was a good sign?

'Is she going to be alright? No one will tell me anything.'

He was sure that Maxwell would know.

'They say no lasting harm done. She swallowed a bit of water and she wouldn't have lasted too much longer at that temperature, but she'll be OK. She's made of tough stuff, our Gawn.'

Maxwell smiled at him again.

'Well done, Dr York. Thank you.'

Not as tough as you think, York was thinking to himself.

'They wanted to keep her in hospital overnight with her being knocked unconscious by Schneider, but she wasn't having it so they compromised and agreed she could go home if someone stayed with her all night and checked on her.' He smiled before adding, 'She's asking for you.'

He motioned in the direction of a car beside the ambulances.

'She's waiting for you.'

York walked across, aware of the space blanket around his shoulders billowing in the wind. It was the longest walk of his life. He wasn't sure what he would find. He opened the back door of the car and looked inside. Gawn was hunched up in the far corner, covered in a space blanket like his own, only her bare feet protruding. She looked so much smaller and so fragile. He slipped in beside her. He glanced across at her but she didn't move her head, didn't look at him. He didn't speak. Neither did she but she slid her hand from under the blanket across the car seat and sought out his. Their fingers intertwined and her grip tightened. The driver started the engine and they set off. It was a short journey.

They had still not exchanged a word. The policeman in front got out and opened the back door for the Chief Inspector.

'Here you are, ma'am.'

She didn't acknowledge him but started to slide out of the seat all the time clinging on to York's hand as if her life depended on it. He had no choice but to follow her.

'It's OK, Constable. I'll see the Chief Inspector gets safely home.'

He allowed her to lead him into the building, into the lift and within seconds they were standing in front of her door. She punched in the code, opened the door and walked inside drawing him after her. Only then did she react.

Chapter 54

As soon as the door shut with a heavy clunk behind them, Gawn collapsed against him. She was like a balloon that had been popped and had lost all its air in an instant. She had been holding so much in until she was out of public view; until she could contain it no longer. She clung to him. Huge sobs shook her violently. He had never heard anyone cry like this before. Her whole body was shaking. He felt so helpless. He just held her tightly and hushed her.

'Ssssh. It's alright. You're alright.'

They were wet. Their clothes were clinging to them. Seb was aware of the central heating in the apartment. Steam was beginning to rise off them. He was about to make a joke about always knowing Gawn was hot stuff but stopped himself just in time. He needed to get her out of her wet clothes. The water had been freezing. He had been so cold. She had been in the water longer. She must be even colder. Her fingers had been like icicles clinging on to his hand in the car. They needed to get out of their wet clothes and into a hot shower as quickly as possible. He just wasn't sure how he could achieve this or how she would react if he tried to undress her.

He pulled her closer to him. She didn't resist but snuggled into him. He liked the feeling that gave him. He could feel her heart pounding against his chest. Her body shivered and he enclosed her even more tightly. Slowly he felt her begin to relax and her sobs subside. Then, placing his hands on her shoulders, he gently moved her back until he could see her face. Her eyes were lowered; her long lashes wet from her tears. He brushed her hair back from her face revealing the livid mark of a scar on her right temple just at her hairline. He reached out and was about to touch it when she pulled back but he held her firmly with one hand while carefully tracing the line of the scar with his finger.

'Let me. Please.'

Their eyes met then, and he could see the depth of her anguish. Her beautiful green eyes were even more beautiful as they shimmered with tears. Gently, so gently, he kissed the scar. She closed her eyes and he watched as one silent tear trickled slowly down her cheek. He kissed her eyelids. She winced as his mouth brushed against the livid red mark from Schneider's punch which was already turning to an ugly bruise. He noted the bite marks on her cheek and lip. With the lightest of touches he placed his lips against hers. Just for a second.

Then he scooped her up in his arms as he had seen countless film heroes do and she responded, snuggling her head even deeper into his shoulder. He was aware of the burning pain in his shoulder and arm from Schneider's attack. He carried her into the bathroom and set her down on the side of the bathtub. He gently wiped her face with a towel taking special care with her cheek, all the time talking to her. His voice was gentle, soothing as he comforted her. The same voice he used with his little nephew and niece when they were scared or upset.

How could he undress her; get her out of her saturated clothes? There was only one way he could think of. Seb took her hand and led her into the shower, thankful there was room enough for them both. She followed him, unresisting. The two stood, still dressed, facing each other, not quite touching. He reached out and turned the water on full. It gushed out, the hot water bringing some instant heat to their bodies. It felt so good. Seb looked up and allowed the water to flow over his face. When he could put it off no longer, he reached out and tentatively began undoing the top button of Gawn's shirt. He fumbled as his still cold fingers worked at the tiny buttons. How often had he fantasized about undressing her? Never could he have imagined it like this.

Her eyes didn't leave his face. Slowly he undid the rest of the buttons and helped her remove the waterlogged garment. Her pale pink bra did little to hide the ugly ragged scar which ran down her body like a sinuous snake cast on her skin. He traced the line of the scar with his finger barely touching her skin until he reached her waistband. Then he unbuttoned her jeans. By now the material was clinging to her legs and he had to help her step out of them. She looked so small and fragile as she stood before him clad only in bra and pants, her nipples standing proud through the lacy fabric.

Seb turned the water off and led her out of the shower. He placed an oversized bath towel around her shoulders. Then after a moment's hesitation he reached round and undid her bra allowing it to fall to the floor. He couldn't help himself. He sighed at a glimpse of her full rounded breasts. He hooked his fingers in the band of her pants and hesitated before gently pulling them down. No sudden movements. He expected at any second, she would stop him, slap him again. He could still feel the sensation of her slap across his face when he had tried to kiss her – a lifetime ago. She was naked under the towel and her body was shaking. He was afraid she was going into shock. He wrapped the towel even more tightly around her, swaddling her like a baby.

He was about to move away to fetch a blanket when she reached out and stopped him. She began to undo his shirt, slowly. Now it was her hands shaking as she undid the buttons. Their eyes were locked together. He waited mesmerised, holding his breath, barely believing this was happening. Just as her hand moved to undo his belt buckle, he reached out and gently took her wrist to stop her. The sound of his own voice surprised him. He didn't recognise it, as if someone else was speaking the words.

'Are you sure?'

He waited for her answer, holding his breath.

'Please.'

It was all she said. One word. Her eyes, when he looked into them, were pleading with him. She pulled his face down closer to hers and kissed him. Hard. He savoured the sensation of her lips on his and imagined he could taste her blood from her injured lip. His tongue flicked instinctively deep into her mouth and he slowly withdrew it, watching her pupils dilate as he savoured her taste. And then he froze. God knows what Schneider had done to her; what she had been through in the last few hours. He wanted to make love to her, but he didn't want her waking in the morning hating him for taking advantage of her when she was so vulnerable.

He picked her up and carried her over to the bed. Gently he placed the covers over her.

'Try to get some sleep.' He tucked her in and she complied, turning onto her side and squirming down under the bed clothes. She pulled her knees up into an almost foetal position. She never questioned him. Like a small child, her eyes looked trustingly at him. He watched her until her eyelids slowly closed and her breathing slowed.

Seb discarded his own wet clothes. He needed something to wear and looking around his eyes fell on the one item of clothing in the room which might fit him. He lay down on top of the bedclothes beside her. He listened to her now regular breathing and knew she had fallen asleep. All night he kept watch, gently holding her when she cried out and stroking her face as he had seen his sister do to comfort her baby. Eventually, before dawn, he too fell asleep.

* * *

Gawn was first to wake in the morning. She was aware of someone spooning beside her, his arm heavy over her body holding her to himself; the feather-like touch of his breath on her spine as he exhaled. For a second she thought it was Schneider, and then she remembered.

She slipped out of his hold and looked back at him. He lay, legs drawn up mirroring her sleeping position. The pink dressing gown he was wearing, the present from her great-aunt, brought a smile to her face. She could see the ugly bruises on his leg from Schneider's attack. Wrapping a sheet around herself, she moved across to close the curtains. She heard Seb stirring behind her and looked round. He lay with a silly grin across his face and his hair tousled from sleep making him look younger and more boyish. He sat up in the bed, resting back on his elbows. He was watching her face and his voice, when he spoke, was soft and coaxing.

'Come back to bed, darling. It's still early. You need to rest.'

Gawn hesitated, but only for a second. 'I can't. I need to get to work.'

It sounded so cold and business-like, as if her work had mattered last night when she was unconscious and drowning and he had jumped into the sea to save her. She stopped just as she reached the door and turned. She hesitated for a moment considering what she was going to say, questioning in her mind what it meant that he had called her 'darling' and then asked, 'Did we…?' She left the question unfinished.

He shook his head and the look on his face let her know this time she could believe him.

She had barely stepped into the shower and turned the water on when she sensed him behind her. She felt his hands sit lightly on her shoulders. Her body involuntarily pulsed with expectation as he kissed her neck tenderly, his lips soft and warm on her skin. He nuzzled her ear lobe and then his hands reached around her body. She lent her head back against his shoulder and moaned as he began to gently caress her breasts. Suddenly she wheeled round and faced him reaching out and placing her hands, palms flat, firmly on his chest. She thought she could feel his heart beating.

'Seb, I can't. Not now. Not yet. Not like this. I need to process what happened with Schneider. I need to know that whatever happens between us is for the right reason.'

'He didn't...' Now it was his turn to ask an unfinished question, not wanting to even think of what she might have endured.

'Rape me? No. He didn't. He didn't get the chance to, thank God. But I can't just pretend nothing happened. I need time.'

She saw his look of disappointment. She owed him her life. But she didn't want him to think she only felt gratitude. This wasn't how she wanted it to happen. When they made love, she wanted it to be special for both of them.

She was surprised to see tears in his eyes. His voice was low and hesitant as he spoke – no longer the super confident man she had disliked so much at first.

'When I thought I'd lost you last night, Gawn, nothing else mattered. However long you need, I'll wait.' Then he took her hands in his and kissed them slowly never taking his eyes from hers before he turned around and walked away.

He quickly towelled himself dry and retrieved his boxers from the floor where he had discarded them. They were still damp so he lifted the fluffy dressing gown that reminded him of one his mother's and put it back on. Their relationship was fragile, he knew. He knew how he felt about her, but she obviously wasn't sure how she felt about him. He feared that faced with the demands of real life again, she would revert to her old self and he would be sent on his way, dismissed from her life.

While she dressed, he made breakfast. Sorting through drawers to find a spoon, he had instead found a black box. His curiosity got the better of him. He opened it and was stunned to see a medal lying on red silk. He read the citation, then quickly closed the box. When she was ready to talk to him about it, he would listen. He realised there was so much more to learn about her, but he wanted to be around to learn it. He wouldn't rush her. He would give her all the time she needed. She was worth waiting for.

He had ground some coffee beans and was just filling the cafetière with water when she appeared from the bedroom. She was dressed in dark trousers and a pale lemon top and carried her matching jacket over her arm. She still looked pale, but make-up covered the bruise and bite on her cheek, not quite concealing them totally but reducing the pallor of her complexion. She had put on some lipstick to hide Schneider's bite mark on her lip. Her hair was swept up and she looked every inch the Chief Inspector he had first met – was it only days ago? It felt like a lifetime.

'I don't think I have time for anything, Seb.' She sounded genuinely regretful.

'Don't you at least have a to-go cup?'

She walked over to him but stayed just far enough back that they were not actually touching.

'Afraid not. I'll get coffee in the office.'

She stepped closer to kiss him lightly on the cheek, but he grabbed her and held her tightly, turning the intended simple peck into a long slow kiss which left her breathless. Then he let her go and she stepped back. He laughed and she noticed the laughter creases by the sides of his eyes again.

'That should keep you going till you get your coffee fix to raise your blood pressure, darling.'

It sounded strange to hear him calling her darling. She liked the sound of it.

'Will I see you tonight?' she asked tentatively, afraid of what the answer might be.

'Do you want to?'

His eyes twinkled, she noticed, as he asked.

'I'm afraid I couldn't admit to anything on the grounds it might incriminate me, but, if you want to, you could wear that dressing gown again. It definitely does something for you.'

And she smiled and he smiled and now they both knew he wanted to and so did she. She turned to leave but his words followed her to the door.

'Oh, Chief Inspector, don't forget to bring your handcuffs home with you tonight. I'm sure we can find some uses for them.'

She came to a standstill with her back turned to him. For a split second he froze, a look of horror passing over his face. His bloody stupid sense of humour again. They hadn't spoken of her ordeal with Schneider. She hadn't told him what she had gone through, and he'd asked no questions, but it stood to reason she had been tied up when he held her prisoner on the boat. What a bloody fool he was. How insensitive could he be? He wanted to take the words back, unmake the moment in time but then she turned and looked at him and a smile spread slowly across her face. They both burst out laughing and he knew then everything was going to be just fine.

Chapter 55

As soon as she opened the door, silence fell. Every eye was turned on her as she began to walk across the open space to her inner office. Everyone, except her sergeant, had assumed they wouldn't see her today or maybe for many days. A few of them had been at the harbour last night and had witnessed her being carried barely conscious to the ambulance. All the others had heard the details – or at least as much as anyone knew yet.

Maxwell walked her into her office, having told everyone to get back to work.

'That was quite a scare you gave us all last night, boss. For a few minutes there I thought you were going to suffer the same fate as Schneider when I saw them carrying you to the ambulance.'

He explained that the German had died without regaining consciousness on the way to hospital. Perhaps that was better for everyone – no jurisdictional nightmares to unscramble, no long trial and media frenzy at a serial killer in their midst, no hours of giving evidence and having every grubby detail of the case and her ordeal gone over by some clever barrister trying to catch her out and paint Schneider as a victim.

Then he filled her in on what had been discovered so far. The German authorities had already searched Schneider's apartment and found trophies of not only the murders he had committed in Europe but three in the States as well. Ferguson and his team had been going over the boat and the car Schneider had been using. They had found photographs of Gawn and film from a camera hidden at her apartment.

'Shit. He was filming me all the time?' she said incredulously.

Maxwell explained they had also found a journal the German had kept. In it he detailed how he had recognised Weil as soon as he had stabbed him and, believing the coincidence was a sign he was to take Gawn as his perfect victim, had phoned his boss with some fake story about a lead on the Schwarzer Adler group in Ireland so they would contact him when Weil's identity was discovered. It had been so easy for him to ingratiate himself into their investigation just as they had once thought York was trying to do. A series of coincidences. That's all it was but it had nearly cost Gawn her life.

'I told you he was a nutter, ma'am. And I told you we would get him.'

Gawn didn't point out to him that they hadn't really got him at all. He had nearly got away. If it hadn't been for Seb... She left the thought there.

Maxwell was trying to make light of it all. He wasn't probing her for what had happened or being overly solicitous. She was grateful for that. She felt a bit fragile and suddenly realised she hadn't taken any tablets that morning or last night. For a second she was afraid she didn't have them with her but then realised they should still be in her bag. Maybe she would take one later, or maybe not. The future without medication didn't seem quite so daunting this morning.

'Thank you, Paul.'

'What for?'

'For believing Seb – Dr York – and doing what he asked you to do. If it wasn't for you and him, I wouldn't be here today.'

'I have to admit I was a bit surprised when York told me you were dating.'

'Is that what he said?' She raised her eyebrows and smiled.

'Wasn't it true?'

'It's such an old-fashioned word. I don't think many people talk about "dating" anymore. I guess I wouldn't have said we were dating exactly but I guess I would say it now.'

They were interrupted by a tentative knock on the door. It was Erin McKeown. The look on her face betrayed her distress as she hovered half in and half out of the room.

'I'm so sorry, ma'am. I should have realised there was something wrong about Schneider. I should have read the report more closely and maybe I would have picked up on the chocolate connection sooner and saved you all the...' She trailed off, unable to put into words what she imagined Gawn had endured and how guilty she felt about it all.

Gawn stood up and walked around her desk and across the room until she was facing the young policewoman. She wanted to reassure her. McKeown had a bright future ahead of her, Gawn was sure, and she didn't want this experience with Schneider to dent her confidence.

'If only I'd made the connection with the chocolate bars sooner.'

'You made it. That's what's important and you did it before any of the rest of us. Don't beat yourself up. You're a good detective, Erin.'

She walked the girl out the door, her arm around her shoulder, encouragingly. At that, her phone rang and she moved back into her office to answer it. It was Chief Superintendent Reid's office. He wanted to speak to her. She couldn't put it off and didn't really want to. Best to get back to some sort of normal. What exactly that would be, both professionally and personally, she wasn't sure.

* * *

The debriefing was gruelling. It seemed to go on forever. Reid had been sympathetic, but he was also thorough and went over every detail of the case. And then over them again. Better to get it all sorted while everything was clear in everyone's mind. Professional Standards would be questioning her later because Schneider had died. There would be a post-mortem and Gawn's part in his death would be scrutinised. There would be an internal investigation about the conduct of the case too.

Reid's questions had been probing. He wanted to make sure they hadn't missed anything along the way which might have led them to Schneider sooner. She had to go over every step of the investigation. Of course, she left out some details like her dinner with York and taking the comb from his house. He didn't need to know that. And about McKeown and the chocolate wrappers too. The girl had done good work and didn't deserve to be blamed because she hadn't noticed how the wrappers linked

Schneider to the park. They could have been left by anyone. As they'd never been tested for DNA it wasn't even certain that they had been left by Schneider. It could be just a coincidence.

Eventually Reid seemed satisfied and delighted that the PSNI would get the credit for identifying a serial killer who had eluded the police in five different countries. It would be quite a coup for them and would look well on everyone's record. Gawn made sure to mention the hard work of all the team but especially her sergeant and McKeown. With any luck they should both see the benefit of it sooner rather than later. It wouldn't hurt her own career prospects either although she was surprised to realise that that didn't really seem to be so important now.

When Reid eventually dismissed her, his parting words were to take a few weeks off. She wasn't sure whether this was a sign of his concern for her health or because of the internal investigation. She didn't mind whichever it was. She wanted to take time off and she had something in mind to do in that time now.

When she got back to the office, most of the team were already gone.

'Everything go OK, boss?' Maxwell asked.

'Fine.' She managed a smile.

'We're all heading to the Boat Club for a few celebratory drinks. Like to join us?'

She smiled again, a broader smile this time, pleased to have been invited. She had known they sometimes got together after work, but no one had ever invited her to join them before.

'Yes, why don't you, ma'am?' McKeown added.

For just one second, she almost wished she hadn't arranged to go straight home, but only for a second. York would be there waiting for her, she was sure. There would be other nights to get together with the team.

'I've already got plans for this evening. But thanks for asking. Some other time.' She took money from her pocket and handed Maxwell a wad of notes. 'Buy a couple of rounds on me.'

'Thanks, boss. Will do.'

She walked into her office and gathered her papers into her bag, put on her coat and walked to the door. She had just opened it and was about to switch off the lights, when she suddenly seemed to remember something. She turned back, went to her desk drawer and took something out of it. Making sure her back was to the general office so she couldn't be seen, she put it into her handbag. Maxwell wondered why she was smiling as she walked out past him.

'Goodnight, ma'am.'

'Goodnight, Paul.'

And she smiled to herself and patted the set of handcuffs in her handbag and headed for home. Seb would soon learn he wasn't the only one with a sense of humour.

If you enjoyed this book, please let others know by leaving a quick review on Amazon. Also, if you spot anything untoward in the paperback, get in touch. We strive for the best quality and appreciate reader feedback.

editor@thebookfolks.com

MORE IN THIS SERIES

All available free with Kindle Unlimited and in paperback!

MURDER SKY HIGH (Book 2)

When a plane passenger fails to reach his destination alive, Belfast police detective Gawn Girvin is tasked with understanding how he died. But determining who killed him begs the bigger question of why, and answering this leads the police to a dangerous encounter with a deadly foe.

A FORCE TO BE RECKONED WITH (Book 3)

Investigating a cold case about a missing person, DCI Gawn Girvin stumbles upon another unsolved crime. A murder. But that is just the start of her problems. The clues point to powerful people who will stop at nothing to protect themselves, and some look like they're dangerously close to home.

KILLING THE VIBE (Book 4)

After a man's body is found with strange markings on his back, DCI Girvin and her team try to establish his identity. Convinced they are dealing with a personally motivated crime, the trail leads them to a group of people involved in a pop band during their youth. Will the killer face the music or get off scot-free?

Available free with Kindle Unlimited and in paperback!

THAT MUCH SHE KNEW (Book 5)

A woman is found murdered. The same night, the office pathologist Jenny Norris goes missing. Worried that her colleague might be implicated, DCI Gawn Girvin in secret investigates the connection between the women. But Jenny has left few clues to go on, and before long Girvin's solo tactics risk muddling the murder investigation and putting her in danger.

MURDER ON THE TABLE (Book 6)

A charity dinner event should be a light-hearted affair, but two people dying as the result of one is certainly likely to put a damper on proceedings. DCI Gawn Girvin is actually an attendee, and ready at the scene to help establish if murder was on the table. But the bigger question is why, and if Gawn can catch a wily killer.

Available free with Kindle Unlimited and in paperback!

OTHER TITLES OF INTEREST

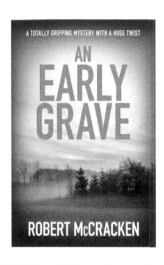

AN EARLY GRAVE by Robert McCracken

A tough young Detective Inspector encounters a reclusive man who claims he holds the secret to a murder case. But he also has a dangerous agenda. Will DI Tara Grogan take the bait?

Available free with Kindle Unlimited and in paperback!

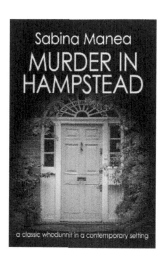

MURDER IN HAMPSTEAD by Sabina Manea

When ex-lawyer, now interior designer, Lucia Steer accepts a job renovating a large London house, she has no idea she'll discover the owner dead. Lucia is determined to unlock the secret of this closed room mystery, no matter the trouble she'll inevitably land in.

Available free with Kindle Unlimited and in paperback!

NO REFUGE by Nicola Clifford

Reporter Stacey Logan has little to worry about other than
the town flower festival when a man is shot dead. When
she believes the police have got the wrong man, she does
some snooping of her own. But will her desire for a scoop
lead her to a place where there is no refuge?

Available free with Kindle Unlimited and in paperback!

www.thebookfolks.com

Printed in Great Britain
by Amazon

20524791R00161